D0251637

# OTHER BOOKS BY GEMMA HALLIDAY

*Hollywood Headlines Mysteries:*
Hollywood Scandals
Hollywood Secrets
Hollywood Confessions

*High Heels Mysteries:*
Spying in High Heels
Killer in High Heels
Undercover in High Heels
Alibi in High Heels
Mayhem in High Heels
Christmas in High Heels (short story)
Sweetheart in High Heels (short story)


Viva Las Vegas
Haunted (novella)
Watching You (short story)
Confessions of a Bombshell Bandit (short story)

# WOOD SECRETS

---

a Hollywood Headlines mystery

## GEMMA HALLIDAY

For my littlest writing buddy, Tommy.
And for The Wiggles, Tommy's buddies, without whom this
book would never have been written.

## ACKNOWLEDGEMENTS

A great big heartfelt thank you to the Romance Divas for their ability to listen to me whine without judging me and celebrate without hating me.

Thanks to my wonderful family for their tireless support, fantastic plot ideas, and many bottles of wine.

And a huge thank you to Leah Hultenschmidt, a wonderful friend, and a fantastic editor, whose knowledge of the English language never cease to amaze me. Thanks for making my words so much gooder. And thanks to Sandy Johnston for being the coolest proofreader ever.

# Chapter One

"Come on, baby, just an inch to the left…" I shifted, feeling my feet go numb. "That's it," I coaxed. "Right there, that's the spot… yes!"

My finger hit the shutter, and I popped off five shots in rapid succession before my subject ducked back behind the curtain of magnolia trees shading his property. I lifted myself up onto my elbows, checking the digital window to see my handiwork. Hot. I'd caught Trace Brody shirtless, a beer in hand. I was too far away, even with my telephoto lens, to make out the label on the bottle, but I knew he always drank beer when the temp rose above 90. He was too manly for those fruity wines, not pretentious enough to drink the trendy martinis his other Malibu neighbors enjoyed.

I'd been watching Trace for weeks now, ever since his publicist had finally confirmed rumors that the hot young actor was engaged to American's sweetheart, Jamie Lee Lancaster. Think Angelina and Brad… without the tattoos and horde of kids. You'd be close. Then imagine if they suddenly announced they were going to have a blowout wedding on a cliff above the Malibu coastline. The press about peed their collective pants. My boss, Felix Dunn, editor in chief of the *L.A. Informer*, included. He'd pulled me from Britney watch and immediately put me to work documenting Trace's every move between now and the big day.

Not that I minded. I'm much rather spend my days laid out on the hillside above Trace's multi-million dollar spread in Richie-Rich-ville than chasing Britt on her latest Starbucks run. At least here I got the shirtless view.

I stretched out again on the grass, ignoring the way it tickled the exposed skin at my midriff between my too-low jeans and my too-high T-shirt. (The curse of being a nearly six-foot-tall woman - nothing was ever long enough). I wiped a bead of sweat from my upper lip and put the lens to my eye again, slowly sweeping the tree line for another glimpse of my subject.

"Come on, Trace. Play nice."

Miraculously, he walked right into my line of vision. I could swear sometimes he actually heard me.

"That's my boy. Now turn this way, give me a smile, honey."

I watched him set his beer down on a table. He reached both arms up to the sky, stretching, letting out a catlike yawn.

"Tired? Being a movie star must be such tough work, huh?" I clicked off a couple shots.

Trace moved his head side-to-side, working out the kinks in his neck. I lost him for a moment as he crossed the patio toward his Olympic-sized swimming pool, complete with faux rock waterfall and hot tub painted to look like a bubbling lagoon. But my lens caught up with him again as he approached the diving board.

"Fancy a little swim?" I asked the deserted hillside.

As if in answer, Trace dipped a toe into the water. Apparently satisfied with the temperature, he shrugged and walked out onto the diving board.

I hit the shutter, taking three quick shots. He bounced a little, staring down into the crystal clear blue water. But he didn't jump. Instead his hands strayed to the waistband of his trunks and, in one swift movement, they fell round his ankles.

I froze. My eyes glued to the lens, a small bead of sweat trickling down between my breasts. I think I might have even forgotten to breath. The only part of me that seemed to still be working was my trigger finger, clicking off shots like mad. Felix would have a heart attack when he saw these.

Then give me a raise.

Trace kicked his shorts away, then walked his gloriously naked self out to the edge of the diving board.

"Good God, you're beautiful," I whispered. Not that I expected anything less. He was, after all, a movie star. But this was one man who needed no airbrushing. How he managed to avoid that white-butt-tanned-torso thing, I had no idea. Lord knows I would have known by now if he were a nude sunbather. But he was a smooth, warm, honey color from his perfectly hardened six-pack abs to his perfectly hardened… other parts.

"Jamie Lee must be one happy women, huh, Trace?"

He ignored me. Of course. Somewhere in the back of my mind I knew it was weird to talk to him out loud. Almost worse than talking to myself. But I couldn't help it. He had no idea I existed, but he'd been my constant companion for the past six weeks. At a safe distance, of course. If I ever actually came face to face with the movie star, I'd probably wet my pants. With a telephoto lens and a football field between us, I was cool as a cucumber at a day spa. In person? Well, let's just say I've never been one of those people-persons. I liked people fine, but my gift has never been an ability to carry on clever conversations with the opposite sex while looking suave and sophisticated. My conversations with guys usually included lots of blushing and really smart comments that came to me only after the cute guy had moved on to the sophisticated brunette at the next table.

So, some people talked to their plants, I talked to movie stars who didn't know I existed.

Naked ones, currently.

I watched as he reached above his head, bounced once on the diving board, then cut cleanly into the pristine, blue water with hardly a splash.

Sweat slid down my spine, and I could almost feel the sweet, cool water washing over my own skin. I shivered, goose bumps breaking out on my arms as I popped off a few more shots of Trace resurfacing.

"Baby, that was amazing," I told him, suddenly feeling like I needed a cigarette.

I watched as he pulled himself from the water, shimmering droplets clinging to his gym-sculpted body, and wrapped a towel around his waist before picking up his beer again and heading inside.

I sat up and peeled the lens from my eye. The distance between my secluded hillside and his fancy pool was immediately apparent, and I let out a long breath as his French doors shut behind him.

I'm not sure how long I watched his closed doors, reliving my glimpse of Trace au-natural, before my phone rang from my pocket. Shifting in the grass, I slipped it out.

"Cameron Dakota," I answered.

"Cam," came my boss's voice. "Where are you?"

"Malibu. Why?"

"We got a tip that Jamie Lee's trying on wedding dresses in Beverly Hills," he said, his British accent giving his words a lilting rhythm. "How fast can you get there?"

I bit the inside of my cheek. "If I get caught speeding, will the paper cover the ticket?"

I could hear Felix's wallet squeaking in the silence in the other end. Finally he relented. "Yes."

"Give me twenty minutes."

Felix rattled off the address of the boutique where Jamie Lee had been spotted. Then he added, "If she settles on a dress today, I want to be the first to run with a photo, got it?"

"Aye, aye, chief."

"And Cam?"

"Yeah?"

"You get any good pics of Trace today?"

I pulled up my view screen again, checking out the series of nude shots that even a tabloid like the *Informer* would have to censor parts of. I couldn't help a grin.

"Did I ever."

What can I say? Being the paparazzi's a dirty job, but someone's got to do it.

# Chapter Two

Three hours later I pulled my Jeep up to the offices of the *L.A. Informer.* The paper was housed in an old building that once served as an apartment complex for up-and-coming starlets of Hollywood's golden era. And it had seen little improvement since the fab forties. The same dull beige paint covered the exterior, now peeling after years of exposure to the California sun. The same faded awning hovered over the entrance, and the same rusted, metal fire escape tilted haphazardly off to the side. In all, it looked just about as rundown as some of its former inhabitants now did. Only the starlets had all had facelifts.

But the rent was cheap, the location prime, and the parking plentiful. In L.A. there wasn't much more you could ask for, really.

I jumped in the elevator and rode to the second floor where the *Informer* kept its offices, then wound through cubicles of people busily typing up their columns for the next day's edition, their faces all tinted blue from the garish glow of their computer screens. I slipped into the last cube in the back, my personal haven.

While the cubes around me were filled with posters, colored pen holders, tchotchkes, and, in the case of our office manager, troll dolls and beanie babies, I prefer to keep mine as clean and streamlined as possible. Just the bare minimum of office supplies graced the top of my desk, while the fabric-covered half-walls were covered in sleek, simple, black and white photos. Mostly landscapes. Mostly filled with trees. None of them featuring celebrities preening for the camera.

I hooked my camera up to my computer, and a couple clicks later a series of shots of the vivacious Miss Jamie Lee Lancaster popped up on my flat screen.

A New York native, Jamie Lee had first hit Hollywood's radar three years ago when she'd appeared in an independent film that had garnered a record number of nominations, including one for the unknown actress. She'd lost to a film veteran playing a nun that night, but she'd captured the hearts (and money-making eyes) of Hollywood. The following summer she'd starred in a romantic comedy that ended up being the season's sleeper hit, and the following year she'd taken the role of her career opposite Trace in the mega-action Memorial Day opener *Die Tough*. She'd made millions and caught the attention of Hollywood's most eligible bachelor – a status she was making short work of changing.

I scrolled through the photos I'd taken of her that afternoon. Jamie in a strapless white gown. In a spaghetti-strap ivory gown. In a snow white, puff-sleeved thing that billowed around her ankles like a chiffon cake. Fifteen dresses in all. As you can guess, she did not, in fact, settle on one today. Instead, I'd watched as she whined about the imperfections of each one, tossing aside the pricey gowns as carelessly as if they were bargain bin T-shirts in her haste to try on the next. With the wedding a mere three weeks away, you'd think she'd be a little more decisive. But in Jamie Lee's world, dressmakers worked miracles with last-minute alterations. This decision could make or break her next film contract, and as long as photographers like myself were hounding her, we weren't likely to see the final version of her nuptial masterpiece until the blessed day itself.

I picked out a few of the clearest shots I'd been able to get through the glass front windows of Bebe's Bridal Salon and transferred them to my photo editing program. Then I did a little fancy enhancing – whitening up the whites, cropping out the homeless guy hanging around outside, erasing the few flyaway strands of hair around Jamie Lee's ears – and sent them off to Felix through the *Informer*'s secure network.

Next I checked my daily to-do list from Felix. And groaned. It was twenty photos long.

My boss was wasn't what you'd call a big spender. In fact, I was the only on-staff photographer the *Informer* currently employed, Felix preferring to buy the occasional shot from freelancers than fork out another whole salary. Unfortunately, that left yours truly with the job of cropping, editing, and formatting every picture that came through our offices. I glanced down at my watch. Twenty minutes to five. What were the chances Felix would pay for overtime?

"Hey, Cam?"

I looked to my right to find a pair of bloodshot eyes staring at me over the top of my cubicle. They were set in a jowly face surrounded by a mess of gray hair that looked at least a month past a decent haircut. Max Beacon, the *Informer*'s only original employee. Original, as in he'd been here since the wheel was the invention de jour. I wasn't sure of Max's exact age, but rumor had it his liver was at least a hundred and three, having been subjected to daily toxic infusions of Jim Beam since before any of us were a glimmer in our parents' eyes.

Max wrote the *Informer*'s obits and had his own remembrance ready to go, detailing how he'd died of cirrhosis of the liver, and tacked to the fabric walls of his cubicle right above a poster of a furry kitten clinging to a branch with a defiant, "Hang in there, baby." To say he was a character was an understatement. Hard not to have a soft spot for a guy like that.

"Hey, Max. What's up?" I asked.

"Need a photo to run with a story."

"Dead guy?"

Max nodded. "Gal, actually. Jennifer 'Tootsie' Wilson. Forties screen siren."

"Great name." Though it was probably fake. Chances were she'd been born Gertrude Burnbaum or some other hideous combination. Most celebs of the time had recreated themselves with fake names the second they'd hit the West Coast, a practice that hadn't entirely died out as P. Diddy and Lady Gaga could tell you.

"How'd she die?" I asked.

"She was murdered back in '45. I'm doing a piece on the anniversary of her death."

"Murdered, huh? Very film noir."

"Think you could find me a picture of her?"

I looked down at my mile long to-do list. "Um… well…"

"Thanks, kid. I really appreciate it."

"Sure." I pulled up a Hollywood archive site on my computer. "So, who killed her?" I asked, typing the year into the site's search engine. "Jealous husband? Lover?"

Max shrugged, his shoulders kissing his jowls. "Don't know. The police never solved it."

I did a low whistle. "That'll sell copy."

"Let's hope. Felix keeps threatening to cut me back to weekly. He says the only reason people in Hollywood read the tabloids is to see if they've been mentioned. My guys? They're not reading much anymore."

"Ouch. Sorry."

He shrugged again. "I've survived worse."

"I'll email a pic of your murdered starlet as soon as I find her," I promised.

Max nodded, then ducked back out of view, lumbering off to his own cube.

I typed Tootsie's name into the search field, coming up with a half dozen shots of the actress in question. I clicked the first one, a black and white deal, enlarging it to full screen. She was a slim woman, her sleek forties 'do curling under at her shoulders in a flattering wave. She was posing on a divan, a gauzy curtain flowing behind her. Exactly the type of scene that screamed old Hollywood glamour. She had smooth, pale skin and dark lips I could only assume were swathed in the popular blood red lipstick of the time. A strand of pearls was carelessly hung around her neck, her blonde hair pinned and tucked to perfection. I could easily see her playing opposite Cary Grant or Clark Gable without missing a beat. And her eyes sparkled with a quiet confidence that said she knew it, too.

Compared to Jamie Lee, she practically oozed sophistication.

I typed my username and password into the site and paid my usage fee. In return, I was shuttled to a page with a non-watermarked, high-res version of the photo. I quickly downloaded it and did a little cropping to get in close on her face, then sent the photo off to Max.

That task done, I dug into Felix's to-do's. An hour later, I finally had them whittled down to an impressive spread for tomorrow's paper. I did one last email check before leaving, scanning for any time-sensitive tips on celebrity happenings that night. One party in the hills, attended by all the usual suspects. Nothing really newsworthy there. A rumor that Courtney Cox was sporting a baby bump, which I filed away to check up on later. If it were true, I'd catch her at the farmer's market that Sunday. And one reported sighting of Joan Rivers' latest nose.

Though, honestly, how you could tell one version from the next, I wasn't all that sure. But I made a note to do the plastic surgeon rounds soon anyway. Those post-op, bandaged-like-a-mummy shots always sold well.

I was just doing my due diligence as an *Informer* employee by updating my Twitter followers with the latest on the Wedding Watch, when I felt a hand on my shoulder and looked up to find a purpled-haired woman in a pink, skull-printed baby tee hovering over my desk.

"She pick a dress yet?" she asked, squinting at my tweet on the screen.

Tina Bender was the *Informer's* gossip columnist extraordinaire and reigning goddess of dishing dirt on everyone who was anyone in this town. Trace and Jamie Lee included. Tina and I had bonded immediately when I'd come on board two years ago. Not that we had much in common looks-wise, but I'd immediately admired her brash, tell-it-like-it-is style. Most days I wished I had half the guts Tina did.

"Nope. The dress is still up in the air. But you'll be the first to know."

"Damn. I'm short today and was hoping to pad my column."

I cocked an eyebrow at her. "How about a top shelf actor caught swimming in the nude?"

Tine punched me in the shoulder. "Get out! Seriously? Who?"

"Trace Brody."

"Dude." She leaned in close. "You saw Trace's wee willy winkie?"

I nodded. Not able to wipe the stupid smirk off my face as I recalled his picture-perfect body cutting through his picture-perfect swimming pool. True art, I tell ya.

"So dish."

"What do you want to know?"

"Quarter roll or Kaiser roll?"

I choked back a laugh. "Um, definitely Kaiser."

"Jamie Lee is so lucky."

No kidding. I glanced at my desk clock. "I'll tell you all about it over dinner? Chinese?"

Tina bit her lip. "Oh, I wish I could. But I've actually already got plans tonight."

I tossed an eyebrow. "Hot lead?"

She shook her head. "Nope, tickets to the gun show with Cal."

I grinned. "Gun show? Is that what you kids are calling it these days?"

Cal was the built bodyguard Tina had recently started seeing. And when I say "seeing," I mean they spent every waking moment together, fawning over each other like a couple of teenagers. Most of the time it straddled that fine line between incredibly romantic and downright nauseating. But Cal was the first guy I'd ever seen Tina get serious about, so I cut her a little slack.

"No," she clarified. "I mean an actual gun show. Cal wants me to start carrying. He's going to help me pick out something."

"You ever shot a gun before?"

She shrugged. "There's a first time for everything. I'm just hoping they have one in pink."

I grinned. "Good luck," I said. "I'll email you the Brody pics."

"Awesome! And, hey do me a favor…" Tina looked over both shoulders for eavesdroppers before continuing. "If any leads come in overnight, forward them to me, huh? Allie's been scooping me lately and making me look bad."

Allie Quick was the newest edition to the *Informer*'s staff and had somehow landed herself in the position of Tina's arch nemesis. Which, I guess looking at the two side by side would be inevitable. Allie was blonde, bubbly, and had the body of a *Playboy* bunny – basically the embodiment of everything Tina wasn't. Personally, I had no beef with New Girl, but, then again, I wasn't competing for page space with her either.

"Will do," I promised as Tina sauntered off with a wave.

Which, I supposed, left me eating Chinese for one.

Again.

\* \* \*

After picking up a carton of broccoli bean curd at the vegetarian place around the corner, I pointed my Jeep toward home. Which for me was a studio loft above a surf shop in Venice. While we were at least a block from the beach, my third-floor studio was high enough above the trendy shops and tourist attractions to afford me a prime view of the ocean at a bargain price. Okay, well from the bedroom, I had a view of a corner of the ocean if I stood on tiptoe and craned my neck around the head shop across the alleyway. But, if I climbed onto the roof, the view was priceless.

Which was what I did as soon as I got home.

I dropped my camera bag inside the door, extracting my Nikon and taking it with me into the kitchen. I stuck a fork in my back pocket for the bean curd and dug in the fridge for a bottle of chardonnay. Forgoing a glass, I kicked off my shoes and padded barefoot out onto the fire escape. Carefully juggling my takeout and my wine, I climbed up the short flight to the roof, plopping myself into a folding chair near the AC vent.

I dug into my dinner, then took a long sip of chardonnay, the cool liquid a perfect contrast to the spicy tofu as it warmed my insides. I leaned my head back on the chair, watching the sun paint pink, purple, and golden hues along the ocean's surface. I inhaled deeply, catching just the faintest whiff of saltwater over the eau de car exhaust from the PCH.

I'll admit, I hadn't always been a fan of the California lifestyle. When I'd first moved here from Montana ten years ago, the city had thrown me into total culture shock. I was used to our family ranch, horses, skies so clear they looked like artists' paintings, air so clean it smelled like fresh rain all the time. And quiet. Something that you could never find in L.A. It drove me nuts those first few weeks and made me so homesick I'd cried myself to sleep every night.

Of course, I was only sixteen then, dreams of gracing glossy magazine covers anchoring me in the city even as my heart broke for the quiet hills of home.

I'd been discovered by Hal Levine of the Levine Modeling Agency when, after a nervous breakdown over a *Cosmo* shoot, his therapist had suggested a nice, quite vacation at a Montana dude ranch. Hal had reluctantly agreed and spent the next three weeks getting saddle sores and mosquito bites. I'd taken a summer job at the ranch caring for the horses, who, after being ridden all day by overweight tourists, I had much more sympathy for than the saddle-sore city slickers. Hal had picked me out right away and handed me his card. At first, I'd chucked it. I mean, how many times have we all heard the stories of the "agent" luring the teenager into the city, only to see her face weeks later on the ten o'clock news? Besides, I was not what you'd call a girly girl. While the California girls had played with Barbie and taken ballet lessons, I'd been making mud pies in a pair of hand-me-down overalls. Being a supermodel was the last thing I'd envisioned for myself.

But, after a full week of Hal promising he'd make me famous (and after I'd googled him extensively to make sure he was a real agent and not some serial killer), I finally agreed to let him fly me out to L.A. for a test shoot.

Twelve years later, I was still here. Though my modeling days were a distant memory.

And that was the way I liked them.

I polished off my takeout and traded the carton for my camera, putting the lens to my eye as I began my nightly ritual of roving the neighborhood.

To the right, I had a view through the living room window of a woman with a baby on her hip and two kids slurping spaghetti at a scarred dining room table. The Lopolattos. Not that I'd ever met them, but I peeked in on their lives at least once a day from this vantage point. I noticed the older of the two kids had recently gotten her ears pierced. Little gold stars. Cute. I popped off a shot as they caught the last rays of sunlight coming though the curtained windows. Mama Lopolatto looked tired today. Maybe the baby was keeping her up at night? The biggest commitment I had was to a house plant; I couldn't imagine the responsibility of taking care of three little human beings. Poor mom.

I zoomed in, capturing the weary look on her face, a sharp contrast to the fresh chubby cheeks of the baby on her hip.

Many native tribes felt that having your photo taken would somehow steal your soul. Personally, I've always seen the truth in that statement. Maybe it's not an actual act of larceny, per se, but a photo can break through those barriers we put up and freeze a moment in time where your soul does, in fact, reveal itself for all to see. It's always amazing to me how the camera lens can see what the naked eye passes by dozens of times a day without noticing.

I turned my camera left, checking in on my neighbors to the south. A Russian couple occupied the top floor of the condo building. He was in some sort of international banking, and she was the twenty-years younger trophy wife. In fact, I'm not totally sure he hadn't bought her and had her shipped in special order.

They were having sushi tonight, the wife's favorite. Not that the husband ate much. He usually spent the bulk of his evening meal on his cell, shouting at whoever was on the other end. The wife silently ate her sushi, staring out the other windows.

I zoomed in on her face and clicked the shutter on my Nikon. The look on her face was wistful defined. I wondered what she was thinking. Was she homesick? Lonely? Daydreaming about some young Russian stud she left back home?

She glanced at her husband, and I shot a series of photos as her expression turned from wistful to downright sad. Then her face disappeared from my view as she ducked her head to take another bite of sushi.

Maybe someday I'd meet her. Walk over and introduce myself as her neighbor. She looked like she could use a friend.

I moved on to the beach below me, snapping shots of the few straggling tourists catching the last of the sun's rays.

As the sky turned a dusky blue, I called it a night, turning in early in anticipation of a busy day on Wedding Watch tomorrow.

# Chapter Three

My alarm went off at six sharp, the Beatles' *Revolution* keeping me company as I grabbed a cup of black coffee and suited up for my morning run. I made a clean circuit down to the beach, along the Venice boardwalk (largely empty at this time of day), then back around to my apartment just as the sun was starting to warn of another scorching summer day.

I quickly showered, dressed in a pair of jeans, black tank top, and flip flops and hopped in my Jeep to get a jump on the happy couple's plans.

Which ended up being plentiful. I trailed Jamie Lee through her final visits to the caterer (the star of the high-intensity cooking show *Hades' Oven*), the florist (the star of TLC's *Flower Boss*), and her wedding planner (the star of Bravo's *Wedding Wars*). All three were top notch, all charged more than my yearly salary, and all were, as I found out, un-bribable for a sneak peek at their wares. Which sucked, but at least I caught a couple good pics of the bride-to-be licking frosting off her fingers as she exited the bakery.

While Jamie Lee dragged me all over town, Trace spent most of the day doing post production on his latest action piece, Held for Ransom, due out just in time for Christmas from Sunset Studios, a fortress so impenetrable as to be one of the only places on earth immune to my telephoto lens. But, as soon as Jamie Lee drove back home (speeding and talking on her cell phone, the naughty little fashionista), I parked outside the front gates of the studios and waited for Trace to make his appearance. I ate a granola bar, listened to the radio, and read the first three chapters of a mystery novel on my e-reader. It wasn't until after dark that I finally got a glimpse of Action Hero, driving his big, black SUV off the lot.

I set my e-book aside and pulled my Jeep into step behind him. Unfortunately, I wasn't the only one. Waiting along with me were four other cars carrying other hungry paparazzi. No big surprise there.

I joined the camera-toting crowd and immediately recognized a car carrying the guys from *Entertainment Daily* – our rival paper. Or, as we *Informer* staff affectionately referred to it, ED. (And, yes, we totally meant that kind of ED. You have no idea how many times I've seen them pull out their cameras, only to shoot blanks – or unusable close-ups of elbows, knees, and latte cups.)

Mike and Eddie were *ED*'s photographers. They were twins, sporting matching pregnant-looking bellies and scruffy beards, usually tinted orange with cheese doodle stains. They drove a beat-up Impala, smelled like day-old gym socks, and had, to the best of my knowledge, at least four restraining orders filed against the two of them. All from celebs they'd stalked. (Not that I hadn't stalked said celebrities myself, but Mike and Eddie had yet to learn the fine art of subtlety.)

As we turned down Sunset, Mike made kissy faces at me from the passenger-side window of their car, passing me on the right. I choked down a gag reflex, stomping down on the gas pedal and pulling ahead of them at the next light. Eddie revved his engine, causing a cloud of black smoke to explode from his tailpipe, and pulled up even to me, narrowly missing a beamer double parked in front of a tanning salon.

My competitive side came out in full force as we chased each other through Hollywood, one eye on the competition and one eye on the back of Trace's car, half a block ahead. Which finally stopped four blocks later, pulling to the curb at the Boom Boom Room, where Trace got out and handed his keys to the valet.

A move that caused a groan of disgust to bubble up in my throat. I had to ditch my own car fast if I wanted to get a shot of him going in, and the valet expense was not an option Felix would let me indulge in.

I made a hard left, illegally crossing three lanes of traffic, and shot into a gas station, pulling up beside the bathrooms where a homeless guy was taking a leak. Outside. On the door.

Welcome to Hollywood.

I ignored him, instead grabbing my camera and locking the doors behind me as I dodged a taxi and two Porsches crossing the street.

Miraculously, Trace was still outside the club by the time I reached the door. He was loitering, saying hello to his pals, posing for the camera, all while trying to look natural like he wasn't posing. It was a skill all young Hollywood perfected their first month in the spotlight, and Trace was a master.

Just beyond the bounds of the velvet rope stood a dozen paparazzi who had gotten there before me, cameras all flashing at the same time, popping off shot after shot, some even daring to come precariously close to the actor's perfectly chiseled face.

To Trace's credit, he neither preened annoyingly a la the Kardashians, nor got pseudo-Russell Crow pissed. If a guy could be alpha manly and graceful all at the same time, Trace was it.

I vied for position among the other photo hounds, my camera to my eye. Unfortunately, it appeared as if everyone else's editors gave them larger expense accounts than mine, though, as all the good spots had already been taken by those who valeted. Meaning I was stuck at the back of the pack of ravenous wolves all shouting, "Trace, over here! Look over here!"

Which, of course, he was veteran enough to know to ignore. Instead he made sure his "good" side was to the crowd, his nonchalant air betraying nothing of the awareness that he was being watched by dozens of eyes, popping off dozens of shots that would likely be seen by star gazers in dozens of countries by morning.

I caught a couple shots of his elbow, but with the jostling and my craptastic position it was hard to see anything of substance.

"Finally caught up with us, huh, Cammy?" Mike said, blocking my view with his Shamu-esque figure.

"Shove it, Mikey." I know, lame. But, as I said, I'm not the best at coming up with clever repartee on the spot. Besides, even if I had it would have been lost on Mike. Mike had the I.Q of a donut. Instead, I held my breath, ignoring his deodorant-defying stench as I jockeyed for position beside him.

"I'll shove it to you all night long, baby," he replied, giving me another kissy face.

Ew.

"In your wet dreams." I stood on tip-toe, just grabbing a shot of the top of Trace's head as he shook hands with the bouncer.

"Trace!" Eddie shouted, shoving a red haired guy with a camera around his neck out of his way. "Trace, you sample any of Jamie Lee's goods before the honeymoon, man?"

"Real classy, Eddie," I muttered.

But if he heard it, Trace was gentleman enough to ignore the comment altogether. Instead, he turned and gave the crowd one more I'm-not-posing-I'm-just-naturally-perfect smile, then slipped past the velvet rope into the club.

A collective groan went up from the crowd assembled outside. Myself included. A shot of Trace's elbow was hardly the kind of stuff Felix put on the front page.

"And that's all she wrote," Mikey said, dropping his camera to his side.

"Hey, Cammy girl," Eddie said. "Sorry you didn't get a clear shot." He snickered. Clearly not sorry at all.

"Better luck next time," Mikey said, his features echoing his twin's mocking grin.

"Say, if you want, we could let you stand in front of us when he comes out," Eddie offered. Then followed it with a loud, "Not!" He giggled like a twelve-year-old at his joke.

"Real mature," I mumbled.

Only I hated to admit that unless the twins took off, they had a point. No way was I going to be able to get a clear shot of Trace. The front of the club was packed with paparazzi that had all somehow managed to convince *their* editors that valet was a necessary expense. Either that or they were chancing the parking tickets in the red zones. Not something I could do unless I wanted to see my Jeep towed. I already had seven outstanding fines. Occupational hazard.

It was clear if I wanted to get any shot of Trace worth printing in tomorrow's edition, I needed a new angle.

I left the gruesome twosome arguing over whether they thought Jamie Lee liked it on top or on bottom (seriously, what were they, fifteen?), and decided to case the rest of the building. If I was lucky, there was a window or balcony that lead to the VIP area. Any place I could get a glimpse of Trace inside.

I rounded the corner of the building, coming into an alleyway housing a pair of green Dumpsters, a mound of empty Bicardi boxes, and one emaciated cat. I ignored the hissing from the cat, pressing around to the back of the club. The building jutted up against a chain-link fence and parking lot beyond. No windows. No balconies.

Shit.

At the rear of the building stood one metal door with a rectangular window atop it, the glass painted out black so that no one uncool enough to be denied entry could spy on the ultra-cool happenings inside the club. It was also pretty good paparazzi repellent, I decided staring up at it. I squinted, trained my lens on it. Couldn't see a damned thing.

Okay, I had three options. One - I could go back around to the front and pray for an opening between the blob brothers big enough to fit my Nikon and get a semi-decent shot of Trace. Two - I could concede defeat and call it a night, hoping for a better photo op tomorrow. Or three - I could set up camp here on the off chance that Trace decided to sneak out the back way. I did an einie meenie miney moe. But really, it was no contest. Going back out front meant enduring inane chatter from Mike and Eddie for possibly hours on end. Not my first choice. And going home meant a lecture from Felix in the morning. Again, not high on my list. So, while the alleyway wasn't the prettiest of places that I've spent an evening, waiting for the back door to open finally won out. What can I say? I'm a girl who believes in long shots.

After surveying the alley for a good place to hunker down, I settled on a wooden staircase snaking up the side of the building next door. It was dark, out of the way, and afforded me a place to sit down. Perfect.

I climbed up to the second-floor balcony, hiding in the shadows behind a billboard advertising the latest season of *Heroes* on DVD, and found myself a clean(ish) corner with a clear shot of the back door and sat down on the wooden planks to wait.

And wait.

And wait.

I waited so long my foot fell asleep. I counted the number of stairs on this side of the building fifteen times. I ran through the names of all fifty states, all forty-four presidents, and all seven dwarves. I made a mental grocery list, composed a thank-you letter to my grandmother for the fifteen-dollar birthday check she sent last month, and made up one dirty limerick involving Mike, Eddie, a goat and a bag of ho-hos.

Two hours later, the only action I'd seen was a delivery truck pulling into the alley by the dumpsters. I was about to give up and call my night a bust, when the back door of the club finally opened.

I rocked forward on my toes, put my camera to my eye, and held my breath as the door pushed open...

...to reveal a waitress in a tiny cocktail dress lighting a joint beneath the billboard.

Swell.

I leaned back again. Clearly, my gamble wasn't paying off tonight. I waited until Smoky was done, crushing the butt beneath her two-inch heels and disappearing back into the club, before standing up and stamping some feeling back into my right foot. I was just working out the pins and needles before descending the stairs, when I heard the back door swing open again. I was about to chalk it up to another smoke break, when a familiar head of golden blond hair emerged.

Trace.

My breath caught in my throat, and I did a mental "in your face" to the *Entertainment Daily* boys. I silently lifted my camera lens to my eye. I popped off three shots of Trace walking into the alleyway and stretching his arms above his head. He leaned against the side of the building, his usually perfect posture slouching. He tilted his head back against the stuccoed wall and closed his eyes.

Despite my journalist instincts telling me that a full body shot was what readers wanted to see, I zoomed in close on his face. I could see faint lines surrounding his eyes – evidence of fatigue that was usually carefully airbrushed away. His jaw was slack in the dark, his features blissfully unaware of being watched. A rarity. For a brief moment, he wasn't a movie star, just some guy trying to get a moment's peace in the whirlwind life of his own creation.

His long lashes made dark shadows on his cheeks, giving him a boyish look that made me wonder what Trace had been like before he became "the Trace Brody." Rumor had it he'd grown up in a small town in the Midwest somewhere. I wondered if he didn't secretly miss small-town life once in a while.

A sound down the alleyway broke into his respite, and his eyes popped open, his posture suddenly stiffening into a pose again.

I followed his gaze to the delivery truck parked at the mouth of the alleyway. Two guys emerged, both in nondescript gray coveralls. They were both about average height, one with jet black hair slicked back from his forehead, the other wearing a crew cut. Crew Cut was beefier looking, like he'd spent a fair amount of time either in a boxing ring. Or prison gym, if the litany of tattoos on his arms were any indication. The other guy reminded me a of ferret, all slim and slinky in a way that would make me wary of touching him.

Ferret stuck his hands in his pockets, coming around the front of the truck and looking over both shoulders as if scanning the alleyway for other inhabitants. The cat stuck his head out from behind the Dumpster, but luckily, I had this invisible thing down to a science. Ferret looked convinced they were alone.

At first I wasn't sure the two guys even saw Trace leaning back in the shadows. But as they passed the back door to the club it became clear they weren't here on a beer run. The movie star was their real target.

I could see the actor's "on" face sliding effortlessly into place, more of a reflex than a conscious effort at this point. I put my lens to my eye, popping off shots as the delivery men approached, envisioning the caption for tomorrows pics as: *Trace signs autographs in alley – what a guy!*

Only, as I watched the two guys approach him, I had to rethink that caption. The skinny guy pulled his hand out of his pocket, but it didn't emerge with a Sharpie for Trace to sign his John Hancock with.

It emerged with a gun.

I sucked in a breath, my body freezing in place. I willed myself to remain silent and inconspicuous on my perch as the guy pointed the gun straight at Trace.

Holy shit. What was going on here?

Was I witnessing a mugging? Instinctively I looked left, then right for help. Only the emaciated cat stared back at me.

So I did the only other thing I could think of. I kept shooting, keeping the telephoto lens to my eye and popping off shot after shot in the dark.

It took Trace a second longer than me to see the gun, but when he did, his reaction was much the same as mine. I saw his eyes go wide, his shoulders lock up, his gaze shoot from side to side instinctively looking for an escape route.

But the two guys had any chance of escape blocked off, coming at him from both angles, their truck blocking the alleyway.

They advanced on him, the skinny guy moving in gun-first. Trace put both hands up in a surrender motion, backing up until he was square against the wall again. He said something to them, his lips moving rapidly.

After years of watching people through a telephoto lens, I was beginning to learn the fine art of lip reading. I squinted my eyes and tried to follow along. I'm pretty sure Trace said, "My chicken is under the bus."

Okay, so I hadn't perfected my skill yet.

But whatever Trace really said, it didn't seem to appease the guys any. The big guy moved in closer, saying something. Which, even though it looked a lot like, "Your mother ate the washing machine," I'm pretty sure it wasn't. Trace shook his head side to side in the negative to whatever Crew Cut had asked. Only that didn't seem to be the answer they were looking for as Ferret waved his gun in Trace's direction in response.

Trace threw his hands up higher, a frown creasing his forehead as he let out a rapid stream of words, again shaking his head. Ferret stepped forward, shoving the gun into Trace's ribs. Painfully, if the wince between the actor's eyebrows was any indication. He held his hands up higher, his gaze pinging between the two men in what, even at this distance, was so clearly marked with fear that I could almost smell it.

Crew Cut leaned forward once more. All I could see was the back of his head, but I could tell that whatever he was saying wasn't pleasant as the color drained from Trace's face. Again, he shook his head, protesting, but whatever he was saying, the two men weren't buying it. The big guy grabbed Trace by the arm and shoved him toward the delivery truck. Considering guy number two still had a gun on him, Trace didn't have much choice but to stumble along.

The skinny guy went back to the driver's side and hopped in. The second guy walked around back of the truck with Trace in tow and lifted the rolling door, shoving Trace inside. He jumped up himself, then pulled the door after him.

The truck roared to life. Before I could react, it was backing out of the alley and out onto Sunset.

I got off three quick shots of the truck's license plates, then quickly jogged back down the stairs. Well, I *intended* to jog back down. My foot was still asleep so it was more like an ungraceful stumble, missing the bottom two stairs altogether as I clung to the railing.

Ignoring the pins and needles shooting up my right leg, I raced through the alley, emerging onto Sunset just as the tail end of the delivery truck made a right at the corner. I bolted across the street, blocking out the curious looks from Eddie and Mike in my peripheral vision, and jumped in my Jeep. My fingers fumbled just a second with the keys as I turned over the engine and peeled out of the gas station's parking lot, jumping the curb and taking a right at the intersection.

I scanned the three lanes of traffic, searching for the telltale height of the delivery truck over the roofs of luxury sedans and eco-friendly Priuses. A block later, I spotted it – two lanes over on the right. Quickly navigating though the Hollywood cruisers, I pulled two car lengths behind the truck, keeping an eye on the back doors. Was Trace still in there? Was he okay? Who the hell were these guys? Kidnappers out for ransom? They certainly hadn't looked like your average celebrity stalkers. Last year I knew that Trace had gotten a restraining order against some woman who kept breaking into his house and digging strands of his hair from his shower drain. She'd claimed she was weaving them into a necklace. Which was super weird and kinda icky, but nowhere in the ballpark of two guys with a gun.

I followed as the truck passed by the trendy clubs, then farther down the street past the strip of clubs that had seen trendy five years ago, and finally into the neighborhood of dive bars that played host to the majority of the city's pharmaceutical trade. I got cut off buy an aging El Camino and fell a few cars behind the delivery truck as we passed a twenty-four-hour pawn shop, but managed to cut over into the left and pass him, pulling up again directly behind the truck at the next intersection. Which, unfortunately, is where the truck made a sharp right onto a side street. I moved to do the same, but a seven-foot-tall guy in a spandex miniskirt and platform heels jumped into the street in front of my Jeep.

I slammed on the brakes, my front bumper kissing the transvestite's legs.

"Watch it, chick! I'm walking here!" he/she shouted.

I raised my hand in a silent apology, willing him/her to get the hell out of the way as I watched the truck make another sharp right a few feet ahead of me.

I finally navigated around the shemale, and gunned the engine. I pulled the steering wheel to the right, accelerating so fast I swear I almost took the turn on two wheels as I followed the truck's path.

Only as I turned the corner, the street in front of me was empty. I drove another three blocks, glancing down each side street I passed for any glimpse of the truck, but came up empty.

Shit. I'd lost Trace.

## Chapter Four

I pulled over to the side of the road, illegally idling in a red zone, while I scanned the empty street. Granted, this was L.A. so no street was *totally* empty. But at the moment I only had eyes for one white delivery truck. Of which there was no sign whatsoever.

I leaned my head back on my seat, trying to figure out what to do. Call the police came to mind, but just as quickly I dismissed it. The cops and the paparazzi have a tentative relationship as it is. Most of what we do rides that fine line of legality and certainly falls on the shady side of morality. We weren't exactly on one anothers' Christmas card lists, if you get my drift.

Instead, I grabbed my camera and scrolled through the photos I'd just taken. Unfortunately, the only ones I managed to get of the two kidnappers were either too dark or at the wrong angle to clearly make out their features. Fortunately, however, I did manage a couple clear shots of their license plates as the van pulled into the alley.

I pulled out my cell and hit number one on my speed dial. I heard the phone ring on Tina's end five times before a perky voice finally picked up. "*L.A. Informer,* may I help you?"

If there was one thing I knew about Tina it was that she didn't do perky. Clearly someone else was answering her phone.

I took a stab in the dark.

"Allie?"

"Uh... who's asking?" the new girl hedged.

"Cameron. Where's Tina?"

"Oh, hey, Cam," she said, relief mixing with the perk in her voice. "Tina cut out early again today. Some self-defense class she's taking with Cal."

"And you're answering her phone why?"

"Uh, well, you know. Just in case anything important came in."

"Uh huh." No wonder she'd been scooping Tina. I made a mental note to give my friend the heads-up. Forwarding her calls to her cell might be a wise idea in the future.

"So, what's up?" Allie asked. I thought I heard her pop a wad of gum between her teeth and pictured her twirling a lock of blonde hair to go with the audio.

I hesitated. I wasn't quite sure I wanted to share the bizarre turn of events my evening had taken with the new kid. She'd yet to prove herself trustworthy in my book. However, if it was between her and the cops, there was a clear winner.

"I have a favor to ask."

"Shoot."

"I need you to run a license plate number for me."

"Like from a car?"

Again I had those second thoughts. Rumor had it Felix had hired Allie more for her double-D chest than her investigative savvy. And she wasn't exactly disproving that idea with her genius at current. "Yeah. From a car."

"Okay. Sure thing. Just gimme a sec." I heard the phone click over to the *Informer*'s Muzak system as Allie disappeared. Then a moment later her voice popped back on the line again. "'K, I'm at my own desk now. What's the number?"

I looked down at my camera screen and rattled off the number to Allie.

"Checking now…" she said, and I heard her keyboard clacking in the background to confirm.

If there was one thing our editor-in-chief didn't skimp on, it was computer databases. The *Informer*'s staff had access to all sorts of websites that tracked phone numbers, credit info, criminal history, and DMV stats – just to name a few. I doubted even the FBI had the kind of resources our tabloid had. Then again, our most-wanted list had a lot more high rollers on it than the FBI's did.

I'd learned early on in my *Informer* career to enjoy the fruits of his data sharing capabilities and not to ask too many questions about where our info came from and if these channels were 100% legal.

"Got it," Allie finally said a beat later. "Plates belong on a white, Ford utility vehicle, 2007 model."

That sounded consistent with the truck I'd seen spiriting Trace away.

"Owner?" I asked.

"Registered to a Buckner Boogenheim of Pacific Storage."
She paused. "Seriously? Boogenheim? What kind of name is
that?"

I ignored the commentary. "Got an address?"

"Um… 715 Halliburton, L.A."

I plugged the address into the GPS unit on my dash (one
splurge I'd cajoled Felix into letting me indulge in), and waited
an excruciating sixty seconds while it calculated a route from my
current position. While it couldn't have been more than five
minutes tops since I'd lost sight of the delivery van, every
second that went by felt like an eternity as I imagined reading
about the actor's demise in the morning paper.

And, unless I caught up to that truck, that paper would not
be the *Informer*.

Finally the route calculated, and my GPS lit up with a
highlighted map to Pacific Storage.

"Thanks, Allie," I shouted into the phone.

"So what's the story? Where'd you get the plate number?
Is this Boogie guy someone I should know, or-"

But I didn't let her finish, hanging up midsentence instead.
I gunned the engine, pulling back into traffic, and followed the
highlighted route on my dash out of Hollywood and south into
L.A. proper.

At this time of night, the traffic was sparse past the club
district, making for a manageable drive. Though the entire way I
had my eyes peeled for any sign of the truck. My only hope was
that they were headed to the same place I was.

Fifteen minutes later, I pulled up in front of a darkened
building with a faded blue sign that bore a cartoon picture of a
surfing dog next to the name "Pacific Storage." Behind it were
lines of storage units, squat little buildings in neat rows with
locked rolling doors every four feet. A chain-link fence
surrounded the entire complex, dotted with floodlights along the
perimeter. I passed by once, then doubled back and parked my
Jeep across the street. I cut the engine and, sticking to the
shadows, jogged to the main entrance.

I peeked through the links in the fence for any sign of the
delivery van. I'll admit I wasn't exactly sure what I'd do if I did
see it. These guys were armed. I was not. And "hero" was

neither something I'd ever been accused of nor aspired to be. But I'd been the only other person in that alley. The only other person who even knew Trace wasn't still shaking his perfectly sculpted ass on the dance floor of the Boom Boom Room. It was a responsibility that spurred me on despite my lack of plan.

Well, that and the promise of a hell of a story if I really was the sole witness to an A-lister's kidnapping.

But mostly that altruistic responsibility thing.

I jogged around to the side of the complex, doing an over the shoulder for any passersby and a quick scan for security cameras. None that I could see on this side of the complex. Probably any on site were pointed at the storage lockers themselves. At least, I hoped.

I grabbed onto two of the diamond-shaped links in the fence with my fingers, stuck the toe of my right sneaker in another, and quickly hoisted myself up. Awkwardly, I navigated over the top, just slightly grazing my midriff on the top links, before dropping with a thud onto the pavement on the other side.

I paused, listening for any sound, any signal that my presence had been detected. All I got back was the distant hum of traffic on the nearby 101.

So far so good.

Keeping close to the buildings, I quietly made my way through the complex, straining to catch any signs of people. Specifically ones yelling a muffled cry for help from the back of a delivery truck. However, all I heard was my own footsteps, padding along the outskirts of the buildings.

At the back of the complex the rows of warehouses gave way to a large parking lot. In the first row of slots sat a line of trucks. All white. All unmarked. All exactly like the one that had taken Trace earlier.

Bingo.

Doing another over-the-shoulder for good measure, I sprinted toward them, trying to keep to the shadows. I ducked down as I reached the first one, staying well out of the line of floodlights on the off chance I was not here alone. I circled the truck, then gingerly stood on tip-toe, peaking in the passenger side window. All dark. I could make out a couple seats in the front, a few blankets and bungee cords for securing cargo in the back. No guys with guns. And no captive movie star.

I moved on to the second truck. The interior was almost an exact duplicate of the first, only this one sported an ashtray overflowing with cigarette butts and gum wrappers. I moved on.

The third and fourth trucks were just as empty. I was just about to give in to the fact that I was on a wild goose chase when I tip-toed up to number five and hit pay dirt. As soon as I touched the hood, I knew I had the right one; heat radiated from the engine. A sure sign that it had recently been driven. I ducked down low, suddenly feeling my heartbeat kick up a notch as I slunk around back and checked the license plate number.

A perfect match.

I lifted my head just high enough to peer over the window frame into the truck. Same two seats, same blankets and bungees in the back. Only these weren't piled neatly in the corner. They were strewn haphazardly across the floor. Indication of a struggle? I tried not to picture Trace fighting off his crew-cut captor. Because, as cut as Trace was, he was all lean, tight angles. His body was made to show well on camera. Strong, sure, but no match for the beefy-looking guy. Especially since his buddy had a gun.

I wasn't sure whether I was disappointed or relieved that, as I circled the truck, it became apparent it was empty. At least there wasn't a dead movie star's body in the back. On the other hand, that didn't lead me any closer to finding out where said movie star was now.

I glanced around the complex. If the engine was still warm, they must have just been here. Either they'd transferred Trace into another waiting car, or they were still here, hiding somewhere.

I scanned the empty lot. Clearly nowhere to hide. I turned back toward the rows of storage lockers. Unfortunately, they looked like an awesome place to hide. I jogged across the empty lot, backtracking the way I'd come, and poked my head around the end of the first row of lockers.

Just as a hand clamped down on my shoulder.

"Sonofa-" I jumped a full foot in the air, my voice rising two octaves into Minnie Mouse range. I spun around, heart hammering in my chest, to find...

Allie.

"Sorry. I didn't mean to scare you." She popped a pink bubble between her lips.

"Jesus, Allie!" I leaned against the building for support, my legs buckling with relief. "You almost gave me a heart attack. What the hell are you doing here?"

"Nothin'. I just thought you might need backup."

I shot her a look.

She shrugged. "Okay, that and there might be some sort of story here," she conceded. While anyone else would have had the decency to at least look a little sheepish, she just twirled a lock of bleached hair around her index finger and popped her bubble gum. Watermelon scented, I noticed.

"If I'd needed backup, I would have said so."

"Oh. My bad. Sorry."

Though neither of us believed she meant it.

"So, why are we here?" Allie asked. "What's the story with this place?" She scrunched up her nose, looking around at the lack of anything obviously celebrity related.

As reluctant as I was to drag New Girl into anything, especially considering my promise to keep Tina in the know, the cat was half out of the bag here already. And, considering I wasn't really sure what the story was myself, I figured I didn't have much to lose. So I quickly filled Allie in on the weird scene I'd witnessed in the alleyway and Trace's subsequent abduction.

"This reeks of publicity stunt to me," Allie said when I'd finished. She scrunched up her pert little nose. "Isn't his latest flick about some sort of kidnapping?"

I paused. She was right. I'd forgotten all about that. And, I hated to admit, she had a point. Stranger things had happened in the name of marketing in this town. "But I think he plays the kidnapper in that movie. Not the kidnapee," I pointed out.

Allie shrugged. "Still. This seems a little staged, doncha think? I mean, how would the kidnappers even know Trace was going to go outside at that particular moment?"

Again, the new girl had a good point. "I don't know," I conceded. "Maybe they didn't. Maybe they were just following him like I was."

"Did you see a truck following him?"

I thought back to my vigil outside the Sunset Studios that evening and the subsequent ride to the Boom Boom Room. I hadn't noticed any delivery van. Then again, I hadn't particularly been looking for it either. It would have been easy for them to blend in with the other half dozen cars following in Trace's wake. And I had been a little preoccupied with racing Mike and Eddie to the club to notice exactly which other cars had followed our same route.

"Not really," I admitted. "But whatever their motive is, their truck is still warm. They could still be here."

She contemplated this for a beat. "Okay, tell ya what? You take the rows on the left," she said, indicating the two lines of units beside me, "and I'll take the ones on the right. Meet in the middle?"

I nodded. "Fine."

Allie turned, walking purposefully toward the rows on the right. I could tell by the usual swing in her step that she only halfway believed there might be dangerous criminals lurking in the shadows. Me? I'd seen the gun. Granted, Allie's theory of a publicity stunt was creating a niggle of doubt in my mind. But I'd also seen the very real fear in Trace's eyes. And, despite the logic behind her theory, the fear was what stuck with me as I turned to scan the first row.

I slid toward it with m back against the wall. I did a silent "one, two, three" count, then quickly spun around the corner, *Charlie's Angels* style.

Nothing.

I did a quick survey of the other two rows, with the same negative outcome, before meeting up with Allie in the middle of the complex.

"Well?" I asked.

She shook her head, her blonde shag whipping at her cheeks. "Nada. If anyone was here, they're gone now."

Which was pretty much the same thing I'd concluded. Wherever the guys in the truck had transferred Trace to, he wasn't here now. I was at a total dead end.

Maybe this was all a publicity stunt, and maybe it wasn't. But unless I wanted to be responsible for Trace's body ending up on the morning news, I was left with no other alternative. I pulled out my cell and dialed the police.

\* \* \*

Twenty minutes later Allie and I had hopped back over the chain-link fence (Allie needing a boost on both sides), and we were sitting on the curb, watching the red and blue glow of lights from a pair of black and white cruisers parked in the drive. A couple of guys in navy blue uniforms circled the perimeter of the complex with flashlights, while another stood in front of us, the creases in his shiny blue pants staring me in the face as he took copious notes in a little booklet that looked suspiciously like the ones those parking tickets came from.

"You actually got a look at these so-called kidnappers?"

I nodded. Though I noted his use of the word "so-called".

"Can you describe them, please?"

I cleared my throat. Talking to law enforcement always made me a little nervous. Probably because we were usually talking about the large parking fines I'd incurred.

"Well, the first guy was slim and had black hair. The other guy was heavier. Not fat though. More muscular. Short hair, possibly a former inmate."

The cop raised one eyebrow that was in desperate need of waxing. "Former inmate?"

I nodded again. "He had a lot of tattoos"

The cop grinned, giving me a placating smile. "Honey, lots of guys have tattoos. Don't mean they're felons."

I tried to ignore the "honey" part. "It was more than that. The way he carried himself, maybe. His back was really straight and strong."

"So a guy with short hair, tattoos and good posture?"

I wasn't explaining this very well, was I?

"Look, I got a really good look at him. Maybe you should put me with a sketch artist?"

The cop gave me a 'yeah right' look, then consulted his notebook again.

"And you say these two characters kidnapped Trace Brody? As in, the movie star, Trace Brody?"

I nodded.

"Right in front of you?"

"Look, I know what I saw. These guys had a gun on Trace."

"And what did Trace do?"

"Nothing. What could he do?"

"Call for help?" the cop offered.

I clamped my mouth shut. Okay, maybe he could have done that. "They had a gun," I repeated.

"Look, honey-"

"My name is *not* 'honey.'"

But instead of taking me seriously, again I got the placating smile. "Look, chances are this was just some sort of publicity stunt. Doesn't Trace have a new movie coming out about a kidnapping?"

I could feel Allie doing a silent "I told you so" beside me.

"Yes, but-" I started.

Only Placating Cop didn't let me finish. "And aren't you one of them people that prints celebrity stories?"

"Well, sort of, yes, but-"

"Kind of a coincidence him getting 'kidnapped'," he said, doing air quotes with his fingers, "right in front of you, isn't it?"

I clamped my mouth shut, crossing my arms over my chest. "I know what I saw. Trace was scared."

"He's an actor. Isn't it possible he was *acting* scared?"

I had to admit, the more he pressed the issue the more that niggling doubt was growing into a full fledged tickle.

On the other hand, I knew Trace. I know, I know. I didn't know him personally. I mean, I'd never actually *spoken* to him. But I'd been watching him for weeks. I knew his habits, his style, his personality. And pulling such an elaborate publicity stunt didn't fit. Trace was a straight shooter. And, as much as I enjoyed watching him strut his stuff on and off the big screen, the truth was, he wasn't *that* good of an actor. Trace had been scared. Deadly scared. And I was the only one who knew it.

One of the other uniforms approached, and our cop stepped away to consult with him. They did a lot of whispering and gesturing first toward me, then the complex. Then back at me again with their eyebrows drawn down in concerned lines. I squinted at the pair, trying to read their lips. The second uniformed guy was either saying, "We didn't find anything," or, "We love fly fishing." Either way, not helpful.

The first cop finally sauntered back over to us. "Thank you for the report," he said. Then flipped his little notebook shut and shoved it back into his pocket with an air of finality. I had a bad feeling that about all he'd written down was my name, the paper I worked for, and a "watch this one" note to self.

"So that's it?" I asked, hearing desperation creep into my voice.

He shrugged. "We'll look into it," he said.

Though neither of us believed that for a second.

# Chapter Five

After making Allie swear on the life of her Siamese cat, Mr. Fluffykins (gag), that she would not print anything about Trace's kidnapping until I gave the go-ahead, I headed for home. I took a long, hot shower, ate the remains of some leftover Indian food in the back of my fridge, and watched the late news for any mention of Trace's disappearance. The forty-something, Hispanic newscaster prattled on about a shooting in La Puente, earthquake retrofitting of an overpass downtown, and a high-speed chase on the 405. Not a word about Trace.

I flipped off the set and crawled into bed, falling into an uneasy sleep as my subconscious conjured up all kinds of horrible scenarios of where Trace might be spending his night.

\* \* \*

The next morning I was up before dawn for my usual run. After putting a good five miles on my Nikes, I did the quick shower thing, letting my hair air-dry as I threw on a pair of jeans, sneakers, and a T-shirt with a picture of Kermit the Frog on it that read, "Think Green."

Twenty minutes later I was at the *Informer* offices, and this morning I was on mission. Maybe the cops didn't believe that Trace was in any real danger, but I didn't buy that his abduction was entirely a fake either.

And I was going to prove it.

I flipped on my computer and pulled up my address book. If Trace had been seen anywhere within a hundred mile radius of Hollywood this morning, I was sure there was someone in the paper's little black book who knew about it.

I picked up the phone and started at the top, dialing Bert Decker, Trace's agent. Unfortunately, I got a receptionist who said Mr. Decker was unavailable, but I could leave a message. I did. Even though I was pretty sure that as soon as I gave her the *Informer*'s name, it went right into the wastebasket. Tabloids weren't exactly at the top of every agent's list of movers and shakers. Go figure.

Undaunted, I dialed his publicist next, getting much the same response. Though this receptionist was a little icier – I think the words "bloodsucker" and "filthy vulture" might have been used - assuring me that my message was hitting the round file bin. Fabulous.

Not that I'd expected much help through the official channels, but I was leaving no stone unturned. The unofficial channels, however, I had higher hopes for.

I scrolled through the entries I had listed under "Trace's Peeps," and dialed the number for the Starbucks on Palm and Shoreline. Trace rarely went a morning without his caffeine latte fix. I listened to the phone ring four times, then asked for my favorite barista, Michelle. My favorite because, in addition to brewing a latte to rival any along the entire California coast, she also had a set of loose lips that had garnered me more than one awesome early morning shot of Trace with his vice of choice. Unfortunately, today she wasn't the well of information I'd hoped. Trace hadn't been in that morning. Not a good sign.

I hung up and hit the next guy on my list, the owner of the bookstore along the route of Trace's usual morning run. Only he hadn't seen the actor either. Neither had Trace's dry cleaner, his hair stylist, or the guy at the Ralph's where he bought his groceries. In short, Trace had been MIA all morning.

While a part of me felt slightly vindicated (Publicity stunt, my ass! No one misses their morning coffee for any amount of publicity.), the larger emotion slowly building in my gut was worry. It was beginning to look like Trace really was missing.

Again, that feeling of responsibility hit me. If I was the only one who believed he was missing, did that mean I was his only hope of rescue?

I stuck the capped end of a ballpoint pen in my mouth, chewing as I contemplated this thought.

I decided to change tactics, focusing instead on what I did know for sure: who the delivery truck that had spirited Trace away was registered to. Buckner Boogenheim, owner of Pacific Storage.

I set the pen down and turned to my computer again. I started by running the basic searches on this Buckner guy:

Google, Yahoo, Ask. Which gave me an overview of the public Mr. Boogenheim.

The guy owned a few businesses, including Pacific Storage, a car wash in Northridge, a deli downtown, and what appeared to be a failed chocolate factory in Nevada. Though I had to admit the few pictures I could find of him didn't really scream "dapper entrepreneur." More like "dapper mafia don." Or at least a great imitation of De Niro playing a mafia don. He was short, a full head shorter than the congressman he was pictured shaking hands with in the *L.A. Times.* He had a squat build, broad in the shoulders, broader in the belly, and was standing on a pair of legs that looked like thick tree stumps. His hair was thinning and beginning to show salt and pepper signs at the temples, though he still had enough to slick back from his forehead in a greasy kind of look. A scar cut through his left eyebrow. He may run with politicians now, but he'd lived a rough life at some point in the past. His tailored clothes spoke to the fact that, while the chocolate business might not have taken off, his other ventures appeared to be doing quite well. That and the fact that he'd contributed several zeroes to the congressman's campaign.

On the outside, a self-made business man.

Let's see what was on the inside…

I set aside the public search portals and rolled my sleeves up to dig in for the real dirt. For that, I turned to my editor's numerous "mostly legal" databases to ferret out the real Buckner Boogenheim. Hoping against hope that he had some long criminal history of kidnapping, I grabbed a cup of black coffee from the break room and settled in.

Unfortunately, two hours later, when I finally came up for more caffeine, I was no closer to finding a link between Boogenheim and a gun than I had been last night. The guy was clean. So clean he squeaked. Compared to my parking-violation history, he looked like a virtual saint.

Which, in itself, was enough to make me suspicious that he was up to something.

"Cam!"

I spun around in my chair at the sound of Felix's voice hailing me from his office.

I rubbed my eyes, retraining them to focus on 3-D objects again after staring at my screen so long, then grabbed my empty mug and crossed the newsroom.

"You rang?" I asked as I pushed through his door.

Felix's office was a glass walled cage situated centrally in the newsroom where he could keep an eye on all of his reporters. His desk faced the door and was, as usual, piled high with papers that were organized according to his own system of "set it wherever there's a free space" filing. Total chaos. Which perfectly matched his appearance.

Felix was a few years older than I was, probably in his late thirties to early forties if I had to guess. He stood about eye level with me, had a head of sandy blond hair that always looked in need of a good haircut, and blue eyes so piercing rumor had it he could pull a baby bump confession out of even the most tight-lipped OB/GYN to the stars with just a look. He was dressed this morning in his usual uniform of a white button-down shirt and khaki pants, both a day overdue for a good press at the dry cleaners. Despite his I-slept-in-my-car appearance, Tina told me that Felix was actually a millionaire several times over, thanks to some obscure British lordship he'd inherited a few years back. The word around the office was that he was even some distant cousin to the queen, though no one had had the resources (or guts) to try to prove or disprove that one yet.

"Where are we on the wedding watch?" Felix asked. "Jamie Lee settle on a dress yet?"

I shook my head in the negative. "I have a feeling she's going to jerk us around to the bitter end."

"Fabulous." He rolled his eyes. "What about Trace?"

I bit my lip, reluctant to reveal my night's adventure to him. Even ignoring the fact that I had bupkus to print, Felix had an even more tenuous relationship with the L.A.P.D. than I did. According to the gossip mill, he'd had the hots for some woman who had hauled off and married a member of their boys-in-blue club last year, leaving a less than stellar taste in Felix's mouth. So I decided glossing over a few minor details might be a good idea.

"Trace?" I asked, blinking innocently.

My boss shot me an annoyed look. "Yes, Trace. Where are we with him?"

"Trace will be wearing a tux to the wedding."

Felix looked up from the copy he was editing with a frown. "No one cares what Trace is wearing. Tell me what he's up to today."

"I'm… not 100% sure."

"Not sure? You've been his shadow the last six weeks. What do you mean you're not sure?" He narrowed his eyes at me. While Felix's exterior may be less than spit shined, his intellect was sharp as a tack. And he knew something was up.

I shifted to my right foot. "I haven't seen him today," I hedged.

"And why not?"

"I… kinda lost him last night."

"He's a movie star. How lost can he get? Just follow the line of paparazzi down Sunset."

"Yeah, see, here's the thing…" I shifted back to my left foot. "He's kinda… disappeared."

"Disappeared?'

"Yeah. In the sense that someone sorta helped him disappear."

If Felix's eyes got any narrower, they'd be closed. "What exactly do you mean by 'helped'?"

"Um. Technically speaking? I guess you'd sorta say he was kidnapped?"

"What!" Felix bellowed so loudly the glass walls shook and Tina, two cubicles over, jumped in her chair. "What the hell do you mean he was kidnapped? Why am I just now hearing about this?"

So much for glossing over. I did another shift from right to left, then reluctantly spilled my guts and told him everything about last night. He listened, his sandy brows pulling together into a tight line until they were almost touching.

When I finished he just had one thing to say.

"Publicity stunt."

I bit my lip. "That seems to be the consensus…" I trailed off.

He frowned at me. "But?"

"But I don't think so. I think this is for real. Felix, I think Trace may really be in danger."

"He was dramatically whisked away at gunpoint right in front of a member of the press. Love, even you can't be that naïve. This was clearly staged."

I ignored the way the naïve comment stung. I may have grown up ten miles past Nowhereville, but I was a fully integrated city mouse now. Very little snuck up on my naïveté these days. "Trace didn't see me in the alley. He didn't even know I was there. The scene was not for my benefit."

"You sure?"

"Yes." Honestly? No. I mean, I didn't *think* he saw me. Then again, when he'd first arrived he *had* lingered outside the Boom Boom Room for an awful long time. He'd made sure a large group of paparazzi had assembled to see him before going in. It wouldn't have been much of a gamble on his part to assume someone from his crowd of camera toting followers would be watching the alleyway, too.

But, I shoved my warring doubt aside, sticking to my guns.

"Trace is out there somewhere, Felix. In trouble. Alone."

He bit the inside of his cheek. "What do the police think?"

I repeated their phrase from last night. "They said they're looking into it."

"Case closed, then," he said.

"*Not* cased closed. I know what I saw. It was a genuine kidnapping!"

Felix thought on this for a beat. Then finally shook his head. "You know what? It doesn't matter whether it was genuine or a stunt. We can't run with a story like this either way without some sort of proof. We'd open ourselves up to a whole host of lawsuits. What matters is that I have a shot for tomorrow's paper, a color photo fabulous enough to tempt every happy housewife standing in line at the grocery to plunk down three-fifty to read more."

"But what about Trace?"

"What about him? If on the off chance you're right and he's in some sort of danger, the cops will be looking into it. Let them do their job. We bloody well pay enough in taxes for it," he mumbled. "You, on the other hand, go do *your* job. Photos.

Jamie Lee. Chop, chop." Felix looked up from his desk. Then made a shooing motions with his hands. "Now! Go!"

"Right, chief. On it," I mumbled. Mostly because I couldn't think of a wining retort on the spot. Instead, I slipped out the door, my proverbial tail between my legs even though I knew Felix was dead wrong about one thing. There was no way the cops were really looking into anything except maybe a box of jelly donuts. If Trace was in danger, I was it as far as the search-and-rescue party went. And if he wasn't... Well, just call me the laughing stock of the thirty-mile zone. Either way, Felix's orders had given me an idea. I knew there was one person who would know without a doubt if Trace were sitting at home sipping a beer or tied up in the back of some bad guy's trunk.

Jamie Lee Lancaster.

After a couple well-placed calls, I ascertained that Jamie Lee was "at the doctor's office" this afternoon. Which was thinly veiled code for getting a little pre-wedding work done. It looked like today was as good a time as any to hit the plastic surgery beat after all. Who knows, maybe I'd get lucky and get a pic of two of Jamie Lee post-op to appease Felix, too.

I grabbed my Nikon and turned to go.

Only I didn't get far.

I looked up at the entrance to my cubicle. And blinked. Twice.

Standing in front of me was a three-hundred-plus-pound woman filling the entire doorway and then some. While some women her size might have tried to minimize their appearance in slimming black or subdued navy blue, she clearly was not of the "less is more" school of thought. She wore a neon pink and green floral muumuu, complete with matching pink flamingo earrings that dangled all the way to her shoulders. Her hair was a flaming Lucille Ball red (most of it... conspicuous gray at the roots suggesting it was a home dye job), and her eyes were rimmed in bright green eyeshadow that was eerily reminiscent of that character on the *Drew Carey Show*.

"Uh... can I help you?" I asked. Trying my hardest not to stare. Though with her size she was kind of everywhere, giving me precious few other places to avert my eyes.

"Dorothy Rosenblatt." She stuck one pudgy hand my way.

I shook it, surprised at how strong her grip was. "Nice to meet you, Mrs. Rosenblatt."

"Max told me you were the picture lady?"

I nodded. Slowly, as I wasn't sure exactly where this was going. "I guess so."

"I'm working with Max on his piece about the dead movie star. Jennifer Wilson."

"Right," I said, pieces clicking into place. "Tootsie. Did you, uh… know her?" I hedged. With the fake hair, shapeless muumuu, and tri-layered makeup, it was kinda hard to place Mrs. Rosenblatt's age. I didn't quite see her in the octogenarian set yet, but then again, with the wonders of Dr. 90210, one never knew.

"Oh, no. She was way before my time."

"Oh. Right. Sorry."

"I did have a conversation with her last night. But that was the first time I've met her."

I blinked again.

"You got something in your eye?" Mrs. Rosenblatt leaned in, squinting at me.

"No, I'm fine, I just… did you say you had a conversation with her last night?" I peeked over the top of my partition, looking for someone to signal that we might need security soon. I was used to dealing with crazies – this was Hollywood after all – but generally they stuck to the streets and didn't make it into my actual office.

"That's right," the women nodded, her hair moving in one sprayed-on piece. "Oh, wait. Oh, dear. I'm sorry, I didn't really explained well. You must think I'm crazy!" Mrs. Rosenblatt let out a chuckle.

I echoed it with one that I hoped didn't betray the fact that was exactly what I was thinking.

"Sorry. You see, I'm a psychic. I talk to the dead through my spirit guide, Alfred."

I resisted the urge to blink at her again. Was this lady for real? I peaked around her frame, half expecting to find Tina smirking behind her at the practical joke.

"Max brought me in to see if I could get Alfred to talk to Tootsie," Mrs. Rosenblatt went on. "You know, to ask her who murdered her."

"And did you?" Despite the fact I wasn't totally buying what this woman was selling, I couldn't help asking.

She shook her head, her fleshy cheeks vibrating with aftershocks long after her head stopped moving. "Yes and no. Alfred got a dialogue going all right – in fact once he got Tootsie talking, it was hard to shut her up. You know how these actress types are," she said, giving me a conspiratorial nudge with her elbow. "Anyway, turns out, Tootsie didn't see him. Or her. The killer snuck up behind her. Awful, huh?"

I nodded in agreement "Awful." I paused. "So... how exactly can I be of help?" I asked. I was hardly the talking to the dead type.

"Max said you provided him with the picture of her for his article?"

"Right. From an archives database."

"You wouldn't happen to have the original, would you?"

I shook my head. "No. Actually, the archives are all digital. I just downloaded the image online."

"Oh." Her face fell.

"Um... why?"

"Well, there's usually a strong aura surrounding items like that. Photos capture the essence of a moment. A vibration that holds that emotion captive in time."

While I wasn't sure about vibrations, I could almost understand the whole essence thing.

"Anyway, the photo was taken just the week before she died. I thought maybe if I could get hold of it, I could gleam some clue from the vibrations."

I nodded. Again, I wasn't a total believer in the whole psychic phenomenon thing... but I could see it making an interesting story to our readers nonetheless. Besides, Max appeared to need all the help he could get. The last thing I wanted to see was the old timer cut to a weekly. Weekly columns were one small step from being replaced by diet pill advertisements.

"Let me see what I can find on the original," I said, pulling up the database once again on my computer.

Mrs. Rosenblatt leaned over my shoulder, her hot breath a mixture of tuna fish and Polident. I tried not to inhale too deeply.

A few clicks later, I found the photo in question again. After pulling up the licensing information, I saw the rights belonged to a Fred Arbuckle in Palm Springs. Quickly pulling up a people finder database, I plugged in the name and got a listing for a Frederick Arbuckle in the Shady Palms retirement village just outside of P.S. I wrote down the address and phone number on a post-it and handed it to the psychic.

"He owns the rights. If he doesn't have the original, he may at least be able to help you track it down."

Her face lit up like a Kewpie doll's, dimples popping out in each fleshy cheek. "Max was right. You are a gem, dear. Thanks a bunch!" And with that she waddled away toward Max's cube.

I watched her muumuu sway above a pair of cankles shoved into metallic silver Crocs. Shudder.

## Chapter Six

Once I'd done my intra-office good deed for the day, I rode the elevator down to the ground floor, hopped in my Jeep, and headed toward Beverly Hills.

The Beverly Hills Paparazzi Plastic Surgery Beat (or the BHPPSB, to those in the know) consisted of about five buildings situated along the Wilshire corridor in Beverly Hills. All were gleaming metal and glass, never daring to fade even the slightest in the blazing California sun, with elegant palms and vibrant annuals planted along the walkways. While plastic surgeons outnumbered pediatricians ten to one in Beverly Hills, only a handful were considered top dogs in the celebrity circles, making them big red dots on the paparazzi map.

Jamie Lee was scheduled to see one Dr. Hammond Bashamatari, whose offices were smack in the middle of the BHPPSB.

Dr. B was an Iranian-born surgeon with a reputation for never saying no, never disclosing names, and always going at least a cup size larger than conventional wisdom would dictate. He had been the subject of a TV reality show a couple of years back which had earned him world-wide fame, a waiting list six months long, and a mansion in the Hollywood Hills rumored to be worth more than the *Informer*'s entire operation. His office staff consisted of women between the ages of 22 and 29, all blonde, all buxom, all wearing the shortest skirts imaginable. I had a feeling he had a mold somewhere in the back where he just popped them out whenever he needed a new one.

And the best part about Dr. B's office was that he had a very gullible receptionist who, thinking she was speaking to Jamie Lee's driver (no idea where she got that idea… walking away whistling innocently…), informed me that Jamie Lee would be finished being handled by Dr. B's skillful hands by two.

I hit the end button on my cell and pulled a U-ey on Wilshire, doubling back to park in the back of Dr. B's building. Almost legally. Just my luck that every legitimate spot was taken. I glanced down at my watch. 1:49. Definitely not long enough to play the waiting game for a spot. I crossed my fingers and pulled into a tiny piece of unclaimed asphalt between the Dumpster and a Hummer, praying the Hummer didn't back out too suddenly. And that this particular garage's parking-enforcement officers were on their lunch break.

I grabbed my Nikon and headed for the lobby. Though, as soon as I swung through the glass doors, I realized I wasn't the only photographer in town hot on Jamie Lee's trail. Mike and Eddie were already sitting on an overstuffed sofa by the elevator, a pair of digital cameras and a bag of barbequed pork rinds shoved between them.

"Well, well, well. If it isn't Cammy-Can't-Catch-a-Break." Eddie gave me a grin displaying orange crumbs liberally scattered throughout his teeth.

I looked away, fighting off nausea. "She come out yet?" I asked, gesturing to the elevator doors.

Mike shook his head. "Not yet. Make yourself comfortable, doll." He patted the square inch of sofa left next to him. "Rind?" he asked, gesturing to the bag.

I passed – on both offers - setting up vigil in a chair opposite the twins. I slung a leg over the side of the chair, shifting sideways, ready to spring into action at the first sign of Jamie Lee's lustrous brunette locks.

"How long you two been waiting?" I asked.

"A couple hours," Eddie said, around a crunchy bite. "Long enough to get before pictures." He grinned.

"Seriously?" Crap. Before pics were priceless when doing the plastic surgery stories. I mean, it was one thing to point out that Lindsey Lohan's lips were expanding, but it was another to have a pic of fish lips next to a formerly paper-thin kisser. I tried to remember if I had any photos of Jamie Lee wrinkling her forehead pre-Botox stored on my computer.

"How'd your shots of Trace turn out last night?" Eddie asked.

"What?" I snapped my head around, suddenly wondering if I'd really been the only one to witness Trace's abduction.

"In front of the club. You didn't exactly have a prime position." Mike snorted. It reminded me of a pig we'd once had back in Montana.

We'd killed it and eaten it.

"Oh. Right. Out front. Yeah. Didn't see much." Though, around back, I'd gotten more than an eyeful.

Eddie did a big self-satisfied grin. "Better luck next time, eh, cupcake. You know what they say? The early bird gets the worm."

"They also say pork products are the leading cause of worm infestations among humans." I stared meaningfully at his bag of rinds.

Eddie gave me a blank stare that said he clearly didn't get it. Shocker.

"Hey, did either of you happen to catch a glimpse of a delivery truck pulling into the alleyway behind the club last night?" I asked.

Mike and Eddie looked at each other, then shrugged. "Might have. I dunno. Why?" Mike asked.

I shook my head. "No reason." Not that it would have made a difference. Mike and Eddie's word was hardly going to convince the cops – or Felix for that matter – that I was on the up and up. Besides, I was pretty sure that from my vantage point last night I'd been the only one to see Trace and what had transpired once the truck had moved into position.

"There!" Mike sprung up from his perch on the sofa, pork rind crumbs raining round his feet as the lights above the elevator indicated someone was coming down from the 6th floor – Dr. B's suite.

I twisted around in my seat, training my lens on the elevator doors.

The three of us held our breaths, the only sound in the hushed lobby the crunch of Eddie's last bite of rind.

Finally the numbers above the elevator doors counted down, and the "L" lit up. My index finger hovered over the shutter button, ready to pounce.

The doors slid open and a woman wearing a pair of huge black sunglasses, a raincoat clearly for show (the last time I remembered an actual downpour in L.A. had been sometime during the Clinton years), and a pair of designer boots came waltzing out of the elevators, flanked by two burly guys who would have given the NFL's finest a run for their money.

Jamie Lee.

I snapped off shots like crazy, hearing the brothers do the same behind me. Our collective flashes caused the starlet to duck her head and throw one hand up to shield her post-procedure face from inquiring minds.

"Whatcha have done, sweetheart?" Eddie called after her. "Nose? Thighs? Boobs?"

"Get lost, asshole!" Jamie Lee shot back as she quickened her pace toward the back doors.

I popped up from my chair and took off after her, the brothers a mere step behind me as we moved en masse toward the underground parking.

"Your lips look huge, baby! That the way Trace likes them? Huh?" Mike yelled.

I could swear I saw Jamie Lee blush, and I felt just the slightest bit sorry for her. Here she was expected to look absolutely perfect all the time, but when she made steps to do so, she was ridiculed almost as badly as if she'd never tried at all.

Though my sympathy didn't stop me from shouting out a few questions of my own.

"Have you seen Trace today? Have you heard from him?"

She shot me a funny look. We both knew that wasn't the average paparazzi line of inquiry. One didn't corner an A-lister like Jamie Lee just to ask them about another.

Again, she quickened her pace, pushing through the glass doors that led to the underground parking.

I bit my lip. In a few more strides she'd be at her Hummer with tinted windows, roaring out of the parking garage. I had to act fast.

"I heard that Trace called you this morning and told you the wedding was off. Is that true?"

Three heads whipped my direction – two in need of a shower and some Head & Shoulders and one salon-perfectly styled with an expression on her face that might have been read as utter shock had she not just had the emotion Botoxed out of her.

"Who told you that?" Jamie Lee demanded, suddenly now giving me her full attention.

"I... I can't divulge my sources," I answered. "But is it true?" I persisted.

"Of course not! It's total crap!"

Though I could already see Mike pulling out a notepad and writing said crap down. True or not, it was a great story.

"So Trace did not call you and break the engagement off today?"

"No! God, no. He's madly in love with me." She tossed her shiny hair over one shoulder as if to say, "Who wouldn't be?"

"Besides," she continued. "I haven't spoken to Trace all day."

Bingo.

"Really?" I asked. "When was the last time you talked to him?"

"Last night, if you must know. He was calling to invite me to some club. But I couldn't go because I was busy officiating a charity event," she said, emphasizing the word, "charity." I'll say one thing for her, even under pressure she wasn't one to let an opportunity for good press pass her by.

"Which charity?" Mike asked, his pen hovering over his notebook.

Jamie Lee bit her lip, leaving a little ridge in her lipstick. "Uh..."

I swallowed a smirk. One clearly close to her heart.

"Red Dress," she finally managed. "I think. Or Pink Ribbon. Some sort of colorful clothing one."

What a humanitarian.

"You haven't seen or spoken to Trace since last night before he went to the club?" I pressed.

Jamie Lee shook her head, her loose curls bouncing over her shoulder like an Herbal Essences commercial again. "No. Whatever rumor you may have heard is totally false." She looked pointedly at Mike and Eddie. "Totally false, you got that?"

The brothers grim grinned. Oh yeah, they got it. But what they actually printed, I couldn't wait to see.

Having said her piece, Jamie Lee let one of her linebackers for hire help her into the passenger seat of her Hummer while the other climbed into the driver's side and roared the engine to life. I popped off one more picture of Jamie Lee's silhouette through the window as she and her entourage pulled out of the parking garage, leaving the brothers and me in the dust.

"Nice work, Cam," Eddie said, as he and Mike rushed off to their Impala. "Thanks for the scoop!" He waved as he hopped into the rusted excuse for a car.

I waved back. While the brothers may have gotten a great story out of the encounter, I got something even more.

Confirmation that Trace Brody was officially missing.

*  *  *

When I trudged back to my own car it was to find a bright pink slip of paper stuck underneath my windshield wiper. Mental forehead smack. I peeled it off, and, sure enough, I'd racked up another parking ticket. I wondered just how many one had to accumulate before the cops actually showed up with a warrant in hand. Hopefully more than seven. Or was this eight?

I shoved the ticket into my glove box and, for lack of a better direction, I drove north up the PCH.

Half an hour later, I hit Trace's Malibu estate. If there was any clue as to where he'd gone, why he'd gone there, and who had forced him, this was the best place to begin looking.

Malibu was a good thirty-five miles from Los Angeles, giving stars who could afford it a nice buffer from the city. Depending on traffic, the drive could vary anywhere from half an hour (if you drove like I did) to well over an hour and forty minutes crawling up the PCH in bumper to bumper style. By three in the afternoon, the bumpers were just starting to come out, which meant my travel time today was closer to the latter.

Trace lived on a long, winding street, filled with lush, mature trees, palms every three feet, and a half dozen other palatial estates all discreetly tucked behind wrought iron gates and hundreds of security cameras.

I took a long look at the front gate to his place. No sense going that route. As far as I knew, hell hadn't frozen over, so his security team was not likely to welcome a member of the paparazzi through the front gates with open arms. Instead, I drove around the block, circling Trace's property to the back, where I was sure there had to be some sort of delivery entrance. Not that security wouldn't still be present there, but at least I had a shot.

I circled around the back and parked across the street from the house, under two shady palms that I hoped didn't shed on my Jeep.

I grabbed an Angels baseball cap from my backseat and shoved it onto my head, trying to decide my strategy. A wrought-iron fence spanned the property. Easy enough to jump, but I had a feeling cameras would be watching my every move, some guy in a little room with monitors waiting to "release the hounds" a la Mr. Burns the second my feet dropped onto private property. Beyond the fence lay the house itself, just barely visible some thirty yards away. To my right was the service entrance – a large gate giving way to a winding drive that meandered through the property up to the main house. A big black camera was pointed at the gate, a large talk box attached to the side of the iron fence.

Considering the type of security I was up against, there was no point in trying to be sneaky. Instead, I got out of my Jeep and rummaged through my trunk, looking for anything I could use as a convincing prop. Bike chain, down vest, spare sneakers, water bottle, and an emergency roadside kit. I looked at the roadside kit. It was a red metal box filled with things like a flashlight and screwdriver. I grabbed it and marched right up to the talk box, hitting the intercom button. A few seconds later a static-filled voice responded.

"May I help you?" some guy asked. He had an East Coast accent and kind of sounded like Sylvester Stallone's long lost brother.

I cleared my throat. "Yes. I'm here to fix the Koi pond," I said, holding my red box up for the security cameras to see. I hoped that through the grainy footage it looked like the sort of toolkit a Koi pond fixer would use.

I held my breath as the guy in the other end paused.

"I don't have you on the list," he finally responded.

I bit my lip. "It is Tuesday, right?" I asked, pulling my phone from my pocket and pretending to read the tiny screen.

"This place is definitely on my schedule. You do have a Koi pond, right?"

I knew he did. I'd seen it enough times through my Nikon. And, since Koi ponds generally spent ninety percent of their lives in some state of disrepair, this wasn't a total shot in the dark.

Again the guy on the other end paused.

"Yeah," he finally said. "Lemme check with maintenance first, though."

"No problem!" I lied, my voice going just a little too chipper.

I stood at the gate for what seemed like an eternity, sweat gathering beneath my cap as I prayed maintenance didn't force me to think up a plan B.

Finally, five minutes later, the talk box crackled to life again. "Okay, Julio says go ahead and come on up. Someone must have mixed up the schedules, but maintenance is the second building on the left."

I said a silent thank you to the gods of disorganized household staff as the heavy gates swung open. I quickly walked through before anyone could change their minds, then hightailed it up the winding drive.

In hindsight it would have been a lot easier on the legs to have driven into the estate, but for some reason I felt a quick getaway was much more feasible with my car on the outside. So I made the long hike up the hill on foot, past a couple of outbuildings (including the second on the left) and toward the main house. I figured I had at least fifteen minutes before Julio started to wonder where I was. Maybe twenty before he actually checked the Koi pond and realized I was missing.

I planned to make the most of it.

I jogged up to the main house, my makeshift tool kit jangling at my side, and peered in the windows of what appeared to be Trace's dining room. A sparkling chandelier topped a long cherry table big enough to fit the entire cast of *Desperate Housewives* and then some. Large modern art pieces hung on the bright white walls, and the floor gleamed as perfectly waxed white marble. I resisted the urge to shoot photos. While they would have made Felix drool, I knew the reflective glare off the windows would give me away for sure.

I tried the handle on the pair of French doors leading inside. It jiggled in my hand, but didn't turn. Locked. Disappointing, but no big surprise.

I tip-toed around the corner, looking for another way in.

I passed what looked like a game room, housing a foosball table, two pinball machines, and framed comic book covers on the walls, and a granite and stainless-steel kitchen that would have made a gourmet chef weep with jealousy. Next to the kitchen sat another pair of French doors. They were tall, flanked by thick, burgundy curtains, leading into a sunny sitting room. Doing a slow over the shoulder for Julio or any armed bodyguards, I gingerly tried the door handle. What do you know? It turned easily in my hand. I pushed the door open and crept inside.

I quietly shut the door behind me, sweeping the room for any signs of life.

I wasn't 100% sure what I was looking for here, but I knew if I got caught by a housekeeper or personal assistant, my mission ended there. Luckily, the room was still, an oversized sofa and chairs in deep rich woods my only companions. I silently took stock of the room, but it was as benign as they come. Tastefully decorated with the help of an overpriced designer but void of any real personal touches. Whatever secrets Trace's home may have held, they clearly weren't here.

I silently glided across the white carpet, making footprints in its freshly vacuumed tracks, and peeked through the doorway. A large, marble-tiled hall greeted me, the massive wood front door visible to the right, the locked dining room to the left. I took a small step out into the open area, which I'm sure had some very fancy French name, and cringed as my sneakers squeaked on the polished floor.

An ornate, iron staircase wound upward to my left while three doors stood directly across the hall from me – all closed. I walked across the floor, my footsteps echoing with each squeaky step. I tried the first, peeking my head in the door. A study. Furnished in more dark woods, a wall of tastefully displayed books, and an oriental rug in deep burgundy hues. Unoccupied. Perfect.

I was just about to push into the room and start rummaging through the drawers of that huge desk when a voice stopped me in my tracks.

"Who the hell are you?"

I froze. My heart suddenly leaping into my chest.

While I might have been able to bluff a member of Trace's household staff, I knew that voice. And I knew there was no chance of sweet talking my way out of this one.

I slowly turned around…

…to find myself face to face with Trace Brody.

**Chapter Seven**

I blinked, my brain trying to process what my eyes were telling me.

"What the hell are you doing here?" I blurted out.

Trace cocked his head to the side, a strand of hair slipping off his forehead in exactly the same way it had in his last movie, *You've Got Email*. Sexy.

"I could ask you the same thing," he replied.

I felt my cheeks redden. Right. I suppose I was the one trespassing.

"No, I meant... well... you're gone. I mean, clearly you're not gone because, duh, here you are. But you weren't here. Last night. At the club. Okay, well, if you were at the club then you weren't here, but you weren't at the club either. Or the storage place. Or at the Starbucks or dry cleaners or anywhere! Which isn't surprising, considering you were kidnapped!"

I stopped to take a breath, painfully aware that I wasn't making a whole lot of sense. As I may have mentioned, on a good day I'm not necessarily the most suave when it comes to talking to guys. But faced with a real live movie star, one I'd been basically stalking for the last six weeks, my tongue had suddenly turned to rubber, spewing out babble every which direction. I bit down on it. Hard. Willing myself to shut up as I took a deep, cleansing breath.

God, he was just as good looking in person. No. Scratch that. He was better. Airbrushing didn't do him justice. His tanned skin wasn't quite as picture perfect IRL, hinting at stubble along his jaw line. But instead of flawed, it made him look more real, like a true man's man. Faint laugh lines creased the corners of his eyes, speaking to the fact that, unlike his fiancée, he wasn't a devotee of Dr B's. His hair was a little mussed, but not the perfectly gelled into a fake bed-head look that was currently all the rage, but an actual I-just-came-out-of-the-wind muss that made him look rugged and vulnerable all at the same time. And he had a pair of sandy eyebrows that were perfectly plucked to still look masculine yet avoid the unibrow look. A pair that were, I noticed, currently furrowing into a look of concern as they studied my face.

"Who let you in here?" he asked, his gaze shifting behind me.

"Uh…"

"And who exactly are you?"

I cleared my throat, getting over my initial surprise at finding him here (and hotter than hell) instead of in some guy's trunk. "Cameron," I answered.

"Cameron what?"

"Dakota."

"Great. Nice to meet you. Now what the hell are you doing in my house?"

"Your Koi pond is broken."

"My Koi pond is outside. You are in my foyer."

Is that what they called it?

"Right. Well, I… uh… took a wrong turn."

Trace crossed his arms over his chest, a motion that showed off biceps to make his personal trainer proud. I wondered whether the move was deliberate preening or just a lucky break for me.

"I'm not quite buying that," he said. "Wanna try again or should I just call security?"

"Okay. You're right. I'm totally lying. The truth is I'm a…" I racked my brain for a better lie. But as Trace's clear blue eyes stared me down, I found the truth inconveniently falling from my lips instead. "I'm a photographer."

Trace's eyes narrowed. They did a slow sweep of my frame. So slow and lingering that I felt my cheeks heating again and shifted nervously under his gaze.

"I know you," he finally concluded.

I swallowed back a dry gulp. "You do?"

"Yeah. I've seen you following me around. You work for some tabloid, right?"

A teeny tiny part of me was flattered that he'd taken notice of me. It was kind of like the star football player in school admitting he actually *had* seen you in the back of science class all year.

I nodded. "The *Informer*."

"Riiiiiight." He shook his head, a small smile tugging at the corner of his mouth. It was the same sexy little half-smile that women the world over paid ten bucks a pop to watch larger than life on the big screen. And in person, it was twice as nice. Worth a twenty at least.

"Cameron Dakota at the *Informer*," he repeated.

Ohmigod, the star football player said my name.

"Hi. Nice to meet you." I stuck my hand out.

Only Trace didn't move to shake it, instead raising one eyebrow in a questioning motion.

"How the hell did a tabloid reporter get into my house? Security slacking out there?" he asked.

Only he didn't seem as pissed as I might have imagined at the idea. More... amused. His eyes were still crinkling in the corners, his mouth threatening to crack into a full-fledged smile any second. It was his boyish "romantic comedy" face, and, I had to admit, I was having a hard time not melting under it like his *Email* co-star.

I cleared my throat, trying to clear out my hormones' goofy teenage reaction to him as well. "How I got in isn't important."

"Maybe not to you."

Good point.

But he let it go. "Okay, let's move on then. Why are you here? From what I've seen in your paper, you get plenty of intimate enough shots with your telephoto lens."

I bit my lip. "You saw those, huh?"

"The pool montage in yesterday's paper? Yeah. I got that."

I felt my cheeks warming further.

"Are you blushing?"

"No!" I protested. Way too loudly and in way too high a voice to be anywhere near believable.

His smile cracked, showing off a row of perfectly white teeth. "A paparazzo that blushes. Cute."

The movie star called me cute. Jesus, if I didn't get out of here soon, I was gonna be a gonner.

I cleared my throat again. "Yeah, sorry about those shots. Just, you know, doing my job."

He shrugged, still grinning. "Just give me a little airbrushing next time, okay?"

Gemma Halliday | 62

Like he needed it.  But I nodded anyway.

"So, Cameron-"

"Cam," I said automatically.  "My friends call me Cam."

"Okay.  Cam."  He paused, as if contemplating the aftertaste of that name.  Apparently it worked for him as he continued, "Once again I have to ask - why are you here?"

I hesitated.  Okay, standing here seeing him in person – and clearly not kidnapped, shot, missing, or otherwise in any danger – I suddenly felt very silly.  A little relieved, yes, but mostly silly.  And embarrassed.  Reluctant to even admit that his act last night had fooled me.  That, apparently, everyone else in Hollywood could spot a publicity stunt from a mile away but Cameron Dakota fell hook, line and sinker.

On the other hand, unless I did some explaining, and fast, I was likely to be escorted out in handcuffs.  Trespassing was something the Malibu police didn't take lightly.  So I took a deep breath and spilled it.

"I saw you last night."

He shrugged.  "You and about a hundred other media vultures."

Ouch.  Did the cute guy just call me a vulture?

I shook my head.  "No, I mean after that.  In the alley."  I leaned in, whispering as if we were both in on a secret.  "I saw you get kidnapped."

"Kidnapped?"  He let out a blast of laughter.  "That's a new one."

My eyebrows drew together.  "In the alley behind the Boom Boom Room.  I fell for your publicity stunt, okay.  Ha ha, pull one over on the tabloids.  You got me good.  I totally believed you were kidnapped by those guys."

"What guys?"

"The guys who forced you into the back of the delivery truck.  At gunpoint?"

Trace laughed again, his voice echoing oddly off the marble tiles.  "Wow, I knew the tabloids were famous for making shit up, but this takes the cake."

"Wait," I said holding up a hand.  "What do you mean making shit up?  You're denying someone forced you into the back of a van last night?  That two guys abducted you at gunpoint outside the Boom Boom Room, kidnapping you and driving away?"

Trace spread his hands out in front of him. "Do I look kidnapped?"

No. He didn't.

But I knew what I saw.

I narrowed my eyes at him. He was a good actor, but he wasn't that good. Just beneath his air of levity I could swear another emotion was lurking. He was still doing that sexy half smirk, but the smile didn't reach his eyes now. His voice was light, but his arms were still crossed over his chest in a protective gesture. And he'd taken a step backward, as if the mere mention of the guys with guns had him on the retreat.

"Wait a minute… this wasn't a publicity stunt after all, was it?"

"I'm sorry, but I don't know what you're talking about."

"You're scared."

"You're crazy."

"That was real last night."

"I don't know what you mean."

"And I saw it all go down."

"I don't think so."

"I have photos."

"Tabloids doctor pictures all the time."

"Deny it all you want. I know what I saw."

"You must be mistaken."

I clenched my jaw, the rapid back and forth suddenly giving me a headache. "What happened after they transferred you at Pacific Storage?"

I saw Trace's leading-man face falter for a second and did a mental, "Ah ha!"

Only that was about all the victory I was going to get.

"I think maybe you should leave now," he said, his amused smile a thing of the past.

"I think you should tell me about what happened last night!"

He took a step forward, his expression hard, his eyes dark. It was his action-hero face, the one that he'd worn when he'd beaten the confession out of that guy in the subway bathroom in *Die Tough*.

"Time to go, tabloid girl."

He grabbed me by the arm and steered me toward the front door. I could have protested, but honestly I was lucky he hadn't called the cops and had me arrested for trespassing already. Instead, I let him lead me through the front foyer, and out the ornately carved door.

Apparently his security was not, indeed, slacking, as waiting for me right outside the door were two big bodyguards. They looked like former WWF guys and were both dressed all in black. The first one took over Trace's grip, clamping down on my arm as he led me down the pathway. The second fell into place beside him, should I try to make a run for it. I could have told him that was highly unlikely.

I snuck one look over my shoulder at Trace before he shut the door. Action Hero was slipping. And in its place was a part I'd never seen Trace play before.

The victim.

I could read the look of fear on his face as plain as day. Of me? Of what he'd find splayed across the *Informer*'s pages tomorrow? Or of two guys and a gun? I wasn't sure. But I knew one thing for certain; no way was I going to let this thing go without getting a straight story first.

Flanked by the two gargantuan goons, I made the walk of shame down the driveway and out the ornate front gate, now standing wide open in anticipation of my eviction. It wasn't until the iron doors had swung closed behind me (with a clear look of reproach from both big guys), that I remembered my car was around the back of the massive property.

Great.

I shoved my hat down low over my eyes and prepared to make the two-mile hike to the other side of the estate.

\* \* \*

"Something weird is going on," I said around a bite of Caesar salad.

Tina wiped a glob of mayo from the corner of her mouth and put her sub down. "I still think the most likely scenario is publicity stunt."

*Et tu*, Tina?

"Okay, assuming that you're right, that I've been totally played here, why would Trace deny it altogether now?"

She munched another big bite. "I dunno."

"And why put on the act for an empty alley? I'm pretty sure the skinny little cat behind the Dumpster wasn't on Twitter."

Tina swallowed loudly, washing her sub down with a swig of Diet Coke. "You got me. I have no idea."

The first thing I'd done when I'd gotten back to my Jeep was head straight back to the *Informer*. Okay, the first thing was drink an entire bottle of water. The hike around the property in the sweltering sun had had me sweating off at least five pounds. So, I guess the *second* thing I'd done was head toward the *Informer* for reinforcements. I'd snagged Tina out from under a story about Jennifer Aniston's latest bad breakup, and filled her in on everything that had happened since last night. She'd apologized profusely for not being around, said a few choice swear words when she heard Allie had been picking up her phone, then offered to get us an early dinner while we sat in the break room and figured out what to do next.

"I hate to say it, Cam, but I really don't see a story here. I mean, Trace is fine. Whatever happened or didn't happen last night, he's clearly not kidnapped now."

I nodded. She was right. There was no way I could print any of this without being a laughingstock. Or sued. Or both.

"Buckner Boogenheim," I said, ramming my fork into a crouton. "Know anything about him?"

Tina paused, searching her mental memory banks. "Name doesn't ring a bell. Should it?"

"He owns Pacific Storage, among other holdings. Prominent businessman. Too clean for his own good. It was his truck that took Trace."

Tina nodded. "I'll put out some feelers. See what I can dig up."

Tina was famous for her network of confidential informants all over town. If anyone could get the goods on Boogenheim, it was her.

"All right, I gotta go. I'm late to meet Cal," Tina said, shoving the last of her sandwich in her mouth and tossing the crumpled wrapper into the trash.

"What have you two kids got planned tonight?" I asked, feeling just the teeny tiniest bit jealous that Tina always had plans now that Cal was in her life.

"Shooting range."

I raised an eyebrow her way.

"Cal said if I'm going to carry, I need to know how to handle my weapon."

"I take it you did buy a gun the other day, then?"

"Yep." Tina grinned. "Pink with purple flames on it. I'm so badass now."

The look in her eyes scared me just the slightest – like she almost wanted some guy to mug her so she could show off her new toy. I pitied the guy who tried.

"Have fun! And good luck," I offered as she did a little wave and took off for the elevators.

I finished my salad in silence, trying not to feel too depressed that my evening's plans consisted of chardonnay for one while Tina was packing heat with a guy who was... well... packing heat, if you know what I mean.

"Hey, picture lady, what's shakin'?"

I looked up to find Mrs. Rosenblatt's rotund frame filling the doorway.

"Just finishing dinner," I said, gesturing to my salad.

Mrs. Rosenblatt scrunched up her nose. "Rabbit food." She reached into the refrigerator and pulled out a chicken. A whole one. She grabbed a leg and dug in, settling herself on a chair (that all but disappeared beneath her) beside me. "Now this is a meal."

I smiled. "For six," I mumbled.

"What was that?" she asked, chicken drippings dribbling down her chin.

"Nothing. You've, uh, got a little something right here," I said, gesturing to her chin.

She grabbed a napkin and dabbed in a dainty motion that did zilch.

"So you get a hold of that guy with Tootsie's photo?" I asked, trying not to stare as she inhaled her poultry.

Mrs. Rosenblatt nodded. "Yep. Fred says he'll be in town tomorrow visiting his grandkids. He'll stop by with it then. I'm hoping to get some really strong vibes off this sucker."

I nodded. "Good. I hope it works."

"Me too." She paused, a chicken breast hovering next to her mouth. "Speaking of vibes, I'm getting a few off of you. Everything all right?"

"Me? Yeah. Sure. Great." Sort of. Though I couldn't help asking, "What kind of vibes."

"Your aura's red."

Instinctively I glanced down, as if colorful smudges might be staining my t-shirt. "Red?"

"It means you're worried about something." She leaned one pudgy elbow on the table next to me. "What's on your mind, bubbie?"

I bit my lip. I was a hair's breadth from unburdening my troubles onto the woman when Allie walked in, her perky little ears tuned our way.

"Nothing," I mumbled instead.

"Nothing, what?" Allie asked. "Did I interrupt something?"

Clearly, she had. Clearly, she'd meant to. Clearly, she was nosing around for a story.

"Oy vey!" Mrs. Rosenblatt shouted out.

Allie and I both jumped.

"What?" I asked, expecting her to be choking on a chicken bone or something.

"Your aura, honey," she said, pointing at Allie. "It's streaked with lemon yellow!"

Allie looked down at her shirt in an exact replica of my first reaction, a look of panic on her face. "Is that bad?"

Mrs. Rosenblatt clucked her tongue. "Well, it ain't good, honey. Watch out. Mercury's in retrograde and with an aura like that… Oy. Let's just say, watch your back."

Allie's perfectly waxed eyebrows drew together in a look of concern. "Oh. Okay. Thanks for the warning," she mumbled as she backed out of the room.

Mrs. Rosenblatt turned and gave me a wink. "I hate eavesdroppers."

I snorted. She was an odd duck, but I had to admit there was something very likeable about her. I found myself hoping Max kept her around for a while.

That is if Felix kept Max.

Which reminded me… I had some photos to turn in if I wanted Felix to keep *me*.

I quickly finished up my salad and headed out to my cube, downloading the photos I'd taken of Jamie Lee leaving Dr. B's earlier onto my computer. After a couple of minutes scrolling through my archives, I found a perfect pic of Jamie Lee's wrinkled "before" forehead contemplating her choices on Mori Sushi's menu last month. I pasted it next to the incredibly smooth one of her leaving the good doctor's office today and dropped them both into proper formatting for print before sending them off to Tina's inbox to provide a snarky headline to accompany them.

Then I set to my daily ritual of going through shots on my camera, deleting the useless ones and filing the keepers in appropriate places on my hard drive for future use. I deleted half a dozen blurry shots as I'd jogged toward the club last night. Another handful of Eddie's elbow with the slightest glimpse of Trace's features behind.

Then I got to the ones in the ally.

Trace leaning against the brick building, moonlight and neon creating soft shadows on features. I moved that one to my personal file.

The next two were similar, the third showing Trace's expression as he heard the guys in the truck.

If I'd had any doubts before, this picture nixed them. The fear on Trace's face here was plain as day. Whatever I'd been witnessing, Trace had been genuinely freaked by these guys.

I squinted down at the picture. I would have given my right arm to know what they'd really said to him. Instead, I created a new file and archived the photos. Both guys had stood with their backs to me, so I never had the opportunity for a good shot of their faces. Though I had caught a profile image as one had ushered Trace into the van. Nothing particularly notable about him, but I decided to keep it anyway. One never knew.

By the time I was finished, I looked up to find most of the office empty, everyone else having called it a night already.

I shut my computer down, following their lead.

But, for some reason, when I hit Venice, I didn't make the left toward my place. Instead, my car jagged right. Onto the PCH. Up past the Santa Monica pier. Toward Malibu, where a big fat question mark was still dominating my thoughts.

It was fully dark by the time I arrived outside Trace's house for the second time that day. I parked again across the street from the back gate, staring up the hill at the scattered lights illuminating the windows of his estate. From what I knew of the layout from earlier, I could tell someone was in the kitchen. Another light blinked on in the room next door – maybe a living room? And three upstairs lights were brightly lit behind half-closed shutters. Bedrooms? Offices? Maybe a combo of both.

I watched a shadow cross in front of the middle window, the outline of a man's shape coming into view. Trace? Was I watching Trace in his bedroom?

I closed my eyes, trying to envision what Trace's bedroom might look like. It was clear from my earlier visit that he enjoyed the help of a decorator. No big surprise there. Even if he had time to do the place himself, I had a feeling Trace's style was more utilitarian bachelor than Hollywood chic.

I pictured navy blues for his room, maybe some dark chocolate browns. Deep, masculine colors. Lots of wood, maybe some shiny chrome to bring in a modern touch. Painted walls, no frou-frou wallpaper or faux finishes for this guy. I vaguely wondered what plans Jamie Lee had for the place once she got her hands on it. Rumor was she'd already sold her Hollywood Hills place in favor of moving into Trace's estate after the wedding.

I was just envisioning Jamie Lee's pink and frills attitude toward life clashing with Trace's masculine furniture when a noise jarred me from my thoughts.

It was loud, sharp, echoing through the still night. Like a car backfiring.

Or a gunshot.

My eyes shot open. The house looked exactly the same, standing like a silent sentinel upon the hill. In fact it looked so still and serene that I might have chalked it up to hearing things… *might* have. If the sound hadn't rung out again. Clearly a gunshot. And clearly coming from Trace's place.

My heart leapt into my throat, my hands fumbling in my bag for my cell phone. My fingers were shaking as they finally grasped around my cell and tried to dial 9-1-1. All the while my gaze pinging back and forth between my Motorola and Trace's back door. Three tries into it, I finally managed to hit the right buttons.

Only I never got to press send.

Just as my index finger hovered over the button, the passenger side door to my Jeep flew open and Trace launched himself inside.

# Chapter Eight

I stared, my mouth hanging open at what I'm sure was a very unattractive angle.

"Go!" Trace shouted, slamming the door shut behind him.

"Go...?" I looked from him to the house and back again, the word not quite computing.

But he didn't wait for me to catch up, instead reaching over and turning the key in the ignition himself. The engine roared to life. "Go! We need to get out of here. Now!"

As if to illustrate the seriousness of his words, two more gunshots ripped through the night, the second accompanied by a metallic thunk on my rear bumper.

"Go!" Trace yelled, again.

Believe me, this time I went.

"Holy shit! I think someone just shot at my car!" I slammed my foot down on the accelerator, causing the Jeep to lurch forward onto the street with a screech of rubber on asphalt. Behind us I could hear more shots being fired. Louder. Closer.

I willed myself not to pee my pants.

I fishtailed down the street, narrowly avoiding an ornate iron lamppost on the corner, racing downhill at a breakneck speed.

"Left!" Trace yelled, as we reached the intersection.

I complied, making the turn so fast my tires squealed.

"Ohmigod, ohmigod, ohmigod," I chanted, my heart beating so hard I feared it would crack a rib.

Trace ignored my babbling, instead barking, "Right! Go right!" as we neared the next street.

My fingers gripped the wheel so hard I feared someone might have to pry it out of my hands as I turned right. I gunned the engine, then took another left at the next light. We crossed two more streets before hitting a red light, where I quickly merged into the right lane and turned down the side street instead of idling.

We were deep in Malibu's residential area now, the streets lined on both sides with mature trees and two-story family homes set back from the street. Most were silent, a few lights upstairs lit, the occasional glow of a TV screen in the window. A sleepy community that seemed totally at odds with the frantic surge of adrenaline currently pumping through my veins.

I drove another three blocks in silence before daring to check the rearview mirror. Two Jags vied for space on the road behind me, but neither had a gun poking out the window. I made another right, scanning my rearview again before pulling over and idling at the curb under a pair of palm trees.

Trace spun around, his gaze whipping out my back window. "Why are we stopping?"

"I... I think we lost them," I managed, surprised at how calm my voice sounded when my insides were shaking worse than a Jell-O jiggler in the hands of a Ritalin addicted preschooler.

"How can you be sure?" Trace asked. His pupils were so wide that if I didn't know Trace better, I'd swear he was on something. Only I did know him. And I had a sinking feeling what he was on was a cocktail of adrenaline and pure, unadulterated fear.

I turned off the car and took a deep, cleansing breath that served to ramp my insides down from NASCAR to L.A. freeway. "Okay, Trace. Game's up. Tell me what's really going on."

His eyes pinged between me and the back of the car. "We have to go. They're right behind us. They'll be here any minute."

I looked in the rearview again. The road was empty. Just us.

"I'll go. But first I want some answers."

He paused, focusing on me for the first time. "What kind of answers?"

"Who was shooting at you?"

He swallowed, his Adam's apple bobbing up and down. "I don't know."

"Bullshit."

More bobbing. "Okay, I don't know their names."

"But you know who they are?"

He nodded. Slowly.

"The same guys from last night?"

A longer pause this time, but again he nodded.

I should have felt vindicated. Finally someone admitted that I'd actually seen what I knew I saw! But instead of doing the I-told-you-so dance, the fading adrenaline left a nauseous feeling in my belly too strong for any other emotion to creep in.

"What do they want?" I asked.

Trace sighed, licking his lips. Then he glanced behind us again. "Look, just drop me off in town, okay?"

"No, you look," I said, my voice rising. "I've had about enough of this. I just got shot at. With a gun! I don't like being kept in the dark, and I *really* don't like people shooting at me. I think I deserve an explanation, don't you?"

"You know what?" he said. "Never mind driving into town. I'll just get out here."

He made a move to open the passenger side door, but I was faster, my hand shooting out and grabbing his upper arm.

"Oh no you don't!"

He winced as my fingers clamped down on his bicep.

And that's when I noticed the bright red stain on the sleeve of his super chic hoodie.

"Whoa." I let go of his arm. "You're bleeding."

Trace looked down at his arm. And winced again. "I'm fine," he said. Though for a top-shelf actor, it wasn't very convincing at all.

"You've been shot!"

I put the car in gear.

"Wait," he said, his eyes going all wide and wild again. "Where are you going?"

"We need to get you to a hospital."

"No! No way."

"Trace, you've been shot," I pointed out for the second time.

"I'm fine."

"You're bleeding."

And, I realized, he really was. The red stain was rapidly spreading down his arm. I was no Clara Barton, but this didn't look good.

"I can't got to the hospital," Trace protested. "They have to report all gunshot wounds."

"And?"

"And they said no cops or I'm a dead man."

I cut the engine again.

"Okay, what the hell is going on here?" I asked.

Trace leaned his head back on the seat. Beneath the glow of the streetlights he really did look pale. And kind of like he was in pain, the line of his mouth pulled taught in a grimace. I was beginning to worry.

"Look, just…just drop me off somewhere. I'll be fine."

The last thing Trace looked right then was fine. I had visions of dropping him off on Sunset only to read about his body being found the next morning by a transvestite prostitute. He did not look well enough to be wandering the streets by himself. He looked like he needed a hospital. And a morphine drip. His eyes were closed, his face pale and pinched around the eyes. This was clearly his dramatic end-of-year Oscar film face, though I had a sinking feeling it was no act.

I leaned over the consol to get a better look at his injury. Growing up on a ranch, I'd seen my fair share of injured animals, and with the vet living a good twenty miles away, I'd learned at an early age how to administer basic first aid myself. I tried to imagine Trace as a wounded gelding instead of a movie star as I took stock of his injuries.

Okay, there was blood. A lot of it. I tried to ignore it – and the automatic rolling sensation in my stomach at the sight of it – as I examined the wound itself. I'd expected to find a nice round hole, but discovered a long cut instead. It looked like the bullet had only grazed his arm. No doubt about it, there was a chunk of skin missing. But it didn't look as though it had done any real structural damage. Kind of like a large scrape, I decided.

I looked from Trace's face to the wound.

Clearly he was on some someone's shit list. Clearly the mysterious "they" he was running from were serious. Crazed fans? Professional killers? I had no idea. And until I did, this was one story- I mean, *actor* - I wasn't letting out of my sight.

I turned my keys in the ignition.

Trace's eyes flickered to life. "We can't go to the hospital!"

"I know."

For the first time that night his features relaxed. Just a fraction. "Then where are we going?"'

"My place."

He opened his mouth as if to protest, but changed his mind mid-thought, instead closing his eyes again and leaning his head back on the seat. "Fine."

*　*　*

It was a long, dark drive down the PCH back to Venice from Malibu. At any other time the luminous moon casting white-golden streaks upon the ocean's surface just to our right would have been a peaceful, calming sight. Tonight, I hardly saw it, my eyes flicking every few seconds to the rearview to make sure our unknown attackers hadn't tracked us down.

Trace spent the entire ride with his eyes closed, resting his head on the seat beside me. By the time I pulled up to my building, it was closing in on midnight and I was having a hard time keeping my eyes open myself. Early risers did not make for good night owls.

I shut off the engine and silently led Trace up to my apartment, praying I hadn't left anything embarrassing sitting out in my haste to get to work that morning.

I did a quick scan as I unlocked the front door. No dirty clothes on the floor. No half-eaten food in the kitchen. No boxes of tampons visible in the bathroom. So far so good.

I settled Trace down on the futon sofa that also doubled as my bed and went to grab the first-aid kit from the bathroom.

"Nice place," Trace said, his gaze sweeping over the room. Which didn't take very long. My entire studio probably could have fit in his butler's pantry.

"You know, sarcasm doesn't suit you."

"I wasn't being sarcastic," he protested.

"Oh." I glanced around myself, wondering exactly which part of the bland renter's unit the interior-designer-hiring star found "nice."

"Well, in that case, thanks."

"You're welcome." He attempted a feeble smile my way.

I ducked my head, for some odd reason blushing again under his gaze. "Let's check out that arm, shall we?" I sat down on the sofa beside him.

By this time the bleeding had stopped, but his cut had dried to a crusty dark crimson color that still had my stomach churning.

"You'll need to take off your sweatshirt so I can clean it," I said.

Trace complied, slowly lifting the hoodie over his head. He winced just slightly as he tugged at the fabric stuck to his skin with dried blood, but finally managed to not only extricate himself from the sweatshirt, but also a blood stained T-shirt he'd been wearing beneath it.

I blinked. And had a mild out of body experience as I stared at his bare torso. Good God the man had some abs. And pecs. And delts. And they were niiiiice. Better, I'd venture to say, than they played on camera, even. I swallowed. Hard. Hoping I wasn't actually drooling.

"Is it that bad?" Trace asked, turning his arm over to look at his wound.

"What? Oh. Uh, no. No, it, um, looks okay." I struggled to find my voice, mentally slapping myself back to reality and my nurse's duties.

As I'd guessed in the car, the cut didn't look too deep - just enough to hurt like hell and bleed like a stuck pig. I carefully wiped around the area with a damp cloth, then sprayed Bactine on the wound.

"Sonofa-" Trace sucked in a breath through his teeth. "Jesus, that hurt."

"Big baby," I teased him. Though I could tell the anti-bacterial had jolted him wide awake now.

Time to find out just what the hell was going on here.

"So just what the hell is going on here?" I asked.

Trace squared his jaw. I could see trust warring with common sense behind his eyes. Not that I blamed him. Despite the fact that I'd just cleaned his boo-boo I was still, after all, a member of the paparazzi.

"Nothing," he said.

"Oh, don't give me that crap. 'Nothing' doesn't leave bullet wounds like this," I said, gesturing to his arm.

Trace shrugged. "It was just a misunderstanding. Nothing important."

"Right. Important enough to shoot you."

"It's nothing," he repeated.

I narrowed my eyes at him. Then sprayed him with the Bactine again.

He jumped. "Jesus! Okay, fine. I'll talk. Just...lay off, all right?"

I set the can down, trying not to smirk as I stuck a large Band-Aid on his cut. "So, what's really going on?" I asked.

Trace took a deep breath. I could still see the trust not quite taking hold behind his eyes, but he'd either decided to ignore it or he'd had the fight Bactined out of him, as he began to talk anyway.

"A couple of nights ago I attended the MTV movie awards. I was up for best onscreen kiss or something like that."

I remembered. It was a scene between him and Katie Briggs that had launched him onto the cover of *People*'s 50 Most Beautiful People issue. I'll admit, it had been a hell of a scene. The kind of kiss that made me suddenly aware of how long it had been since anyone had kissed me. I think my nephew had given me a peck on the cheek last Christmas when he'd opened the Xbox game I'd bought him. Did that count?

"Go on," I prodded.

"My agent always hires a limo to arrive at these events. So I get in the car with Bert, and halfway there we run into traffic."

Typical L.A. Nothing noteworthy here yet. "And?"

"And I got antsy. I started fidgeting in my seat. I hate these award shows. They're all rigged for max publicity, and the whole thing is just a big joke of a schmoozefest. Hollywood honoring Hollywood – aren't we all great? And everyone's always trying to get something out of you, ya know?"

No. I didn't. Usually I was the schmoozer not the schmoozee. But I nodded anyway.

"Well, like I said, I started kinda fidgeting, and that's when I felt something between the seats."

"What kind of something?"

"A flash drive."

I lifted an eyebrow. "Like one of those memory sticks that you plug into your computer?"

"Exactly. I didn't think much of it. Just figured it must have fallen out of the pocket of the person who'd used the car service before me."

"Logical," I agreed.

"Anyway, I didn't think anything of it at the time. Then, a couple days later, I'm at the Boom Boom Room, and these two guys shove me into the back of a van."

"I saw," I said, pointedly.

"Right. Well, they said if I didn't give them their flash drive back, they were gonna kill me."

"So why not just give it back?"

"Trust me, I would have. I didn't have it. Bert took it from me before we got out of the limo. He'd said he'd contact the car company and turn it in."

"But he didn't?"

"I guess not, because the two guys were still looking for it. After they shoved me in the van, I told them about giving it to my agent. They asked me a bunch of questions about him, and then they pulled over and shoved me out of the truck. They said if I told anyone about this they'd hunt me down and kill me." He paused, doing a self deprecating grin. "Not that they'd have to hunt far. It's not like I can keep a real low profile, ya know?"

I knew. "So what happened tonight?"

Trace shrugged again. "I'm sitting at home, minding my own business, watching *Survivor*, and these guys come bursting through my living room door."

"Past your security?"

Trace shot me a look. "In case you haven't noticed, my bodyguards aren't the brightest bulbs. They let *you* in."

Good point. I made a mental note to give him Cal's number later but motioned for him to go on. "Alright, so they slip past security, interrupt your reality show, then what?"

"They start yelling about the drive again. I told them I didn't have it, but they didn't believe me this time. Then they just started shooting. I dove for cover and luckily made it out the back door. But just barely," he said, looking down at his arm.

"What was on this flash drive?" I could only imagine if there were people who were willing to kill for it.

He shrugged. "No idea. Like I said, I gave it to my agent and forgot about it."

"Where is your agent now?"

"Vegas."

I raised an eyebrow.

"First thing I did when those guys cut me loose last night was call my agent. He said he was in Vegas booking a gig for another client, which is why he hadn't turned the damned thing into the car company yet. But he said he'd have a look at it, and we'd talk when he got back into town."

"Which would be?"

"Tomorrow morning. His flight gets in at ten and we're meeting at Nico's at noon."

I nodded. Nico's was a popular lunch place among the privileged and determined-to-be-seen crowd. Needless to say, my camera lens was a regular there. "Listen, does the name Buckner Boogenheim mean anything to you?" I asked.

Trace shook his head. "That's quite a mouthful. But, no, I don't know him. Should I?"

I shrugged. In reality, it hadn't been all that hard for me to break into Pacific Storage. Not hard to believe someone else might do the same thing to borrow a delivery van.

Trace leaned his head back on the cushions of my sofa, and I could tell the evening had taken its toll on him. I silently went to the linen closet (which also doubled as my clothes closet and the food pantry) and grabbed a couple spare pillows and blankets. By the time I got them back to the sofa, Trace was already asleep. I covered him lightly with a blanket, then hunkered down next to him, where, amazingly, I fell asleep sitting up as soon as I closed my eyes.

* * *

The first thing I noticed the next morning was the heavenly smell of freshly brewed coffee. If angels had alarm clocks in heaven, they'd be coffee scented.

Unfortunately, the second thing I noticed was that one should never fall asleep sitting up on a sofa. A sharp pain hit my neck as I twisted it to the right. I turned left. Ouch. More pain. I rubbed it as I got up, trying to work out the kinks.

"Morning," I heard from my kitchen/dining room.

I looked up to find Trace leaning against my Formica counter with a mug of coffee in hand.

"Morning." I did a little wave, suddenly hit with a bout of self-consciousness. Did I have bed-head? Morning breath? One of those whiteheads that magically appears overnight blooming on my forehead? I ducked my head, letting my potential bed-head hair cover my face just in case of the latter.

"Coffee?" he asked.

"Please. Black."

He complied, grabbing a mug from my cupboard (yes, singular) and delivering the cup the three paces across the room.

I noticed that he did *not* have a case of overnight acne, bed-head, or, as he moved closer and handed me the cup, morning breath. If anything, Trace looked even better in the morning than he had last night. Kind of soft and tussled. Like I'd expect him to look after a long night under the sheets.

I ducked my head even lower, sure that last thought had put a bright pink blush into my cheeks.

"Thanks for letting me stay here last night," he said, thankfully oblivious to my R-rated thoughts.

"Yeah. Sure. No problem."

"If it's not too much of an imposition, you think I could use your shower before I go?"

I cocked my head to the side. "And then what?"

"Then I thought I'd get dressed," he said, grinning as he looked down at his still bare torso.

The heater in my cheeks turned up a notch. Was it wrong that the thought of him putting clothes on kinda bummed me out?

I shook my head. "No, I mean, where are you going to go? Obviously your house isn't safe."

He opened his mouth to speak…then shut it with a click, clearly not having thought that far ahead in his plan.

Luckily for him, I had.

"I was thinking last night," I started. "It's probably a good idea if you lay low until you can get this drive thing from your agent."

He glanced down at his bandaged arm. "Yeah, probably," he agreed.

"And, you probably could use a little help with that."

He cocked an eyebrow. "I could, huh?"

I nodded with conviction. "Yes. I mean, how many reporters do you have following you around town on any given day?"

He shrugged. "Three?"

I raised my eyebrows. Apparently he didn't look in his rearview mirror very often. "Try half a dozen."

"Wow."

"You're not exactly inconspicuous. I could help you get around unnoticed. Otherwise, how long do you think it will take before the paparazzi is following your every move?"

He gave me a look.

Point taken. "Okay, the paparazzi *other* than me."

He crossed his arms over his chest. "And you could help me be more inconspicuous?"

"I can. I mean, who knows better than I do how the paparazzi thinks?"

He grinned. "Good point."

"Thank you. I thought so."

"And why exactly are you willing to put yourself out like this?"

I'd like to say it was out of the goodness of my heart. But, instead, I told the truth. "For the story."

"Ah." Trace put his mug down on the kitchen counter. "No thanks."

"Oh, come on. This is tabloid gold! The story of the century!"

"I'm pretty sure when they said 'no cops,' it went without saying that they meant no front-page stories either."

"Okay, I'll make you a deal then," I said, getting up and moving to stand right in front of him. "I won't print anything until it's over."

"Over?"

"We find the flash drive, what's on it, and the identity of these goons who are trying to shake you down."

His lips quivered into a grin. "'Goons'? 'Shake down'? Someone's been watching too much Law & Order."

I waved him off. "What, you'd rather let them track you down and shoot at you again? You think they're really gonna miss a second time?"

He winced, glancing down at the mega band-aid gracing his upper arm. I could tell I was wearing him down. I took a step closer.

"Face it, you need me."

He raised an eyebrow my way. But he didn't deny it. I took that as a good sign.

"What do you say? Do we have a deal?" I stuck my right hand out in front of me.

Trace looked at it. Then up at me. Back at the hand.

Finally, he grabbed it and shook. "Fine. Deal." He shook. I grinned.

He sighed. "Oh, boy. Why do I feel like I just made a deal with the devil?"

# Chapter Nine

I grabbed a quick shower, throwing on my usual uniform of jeans and T-shirt, then towel dried my hair and did a quick swipe of lip gloss, my only concession to the makeup industry. I emerged from the bathroom to find Trace on his cell.

"Last night? Yeah, I, um, got kinda busy. Sorry I didn't call, babe."

Babe. It had to be Jaime Lee. I fiddled with my shoelaces on my Nikes as I pretended not to listen.

"Cake? Um, sure, any flavor's good." Pause. "Well, it's not like cake can be bad, right?" Pause. "Well, he's the professional, maybe we should listen to his-" Pause. "Oh. You already fired him." Pause. "Sure. Whatever you want. Listen, babe, I'm going to be kinda… busy again today." Pause. "Oh, you know. Just stuff. Anyway, I'll call you later, 'k?"

She must have hung up because he pulled the phone away from his ear a second later, hitting the "end" button.

"I'm gonna grab a shower. Cool?" he asked.

I nodded, keeping my non-eavesdropping eyes glued to my shoes.

"Sure. Mi shower es su shower," I said.

Then spent the next ten minutes trying not to dwell on the fact that he was naked just feet away from me as I listened to water run down the drain. Note the use of the word, "tried." It doesn't entirely imply that I succeeded. In my defense, considering that I knew exactly how easy on the eyes his naked body was, I did as well as any redblooded American woman could. I flipped on the TV, letting the hens from *The View* drown out the sound of the shower, and hopefully my lustful thoughts along with it, while I rummaged in my closet for something Trace could wear.

If we were going to move around Hollywood unaccosted by Trace's adoring fans, the first thing we needed was a disguise. I dug through my piles of clothes for anything that might fit him. It was slim pickings. While I was only a few inches shorter than he was, clothes built for my slim frame had no chance against his personal trainer made bod. However, since his shirt was currently caked with blood, not to mention had a bullet hole through it, almost anything would be an improvement. I finally found a T-shirt I'd bought for my brother on the boardwalk last month that read, *I heart Santa Monica.* I coupled it with my Angels baseball cap and a pair of cheap gas-station-quality sunglasses. As soon as he emerged from the bathroom, I thrust the ensemble at him.

He looked down at it. "What's this?"

"Your disguise."

He raised an eyebrow. "Tourist garb?"

I shrugged. "It was the best I could do on short notice."

He grinned. But wisely threw the items on anyway.

Fifteen minutes later we pulled into the parking lot of the *Informer*'s offices. Despite the detour my life had taken into gunfire and wounded movie stars last night, I still had a job to do. If I was lucky, I could sneak in and download the day's list of photos, leaving Felix none the wiser. While I'm sure he was going to sing my praises in the highest key once I turned in the finished story, I had a feeling it was going to be harder than stale biscotti to keep my promise to Trace if Felix started grilling me.

And on the upside, tabloid office was probably the last place anyone would be looking for Trace. Two birds, one stone, perfect plan.

I parked in my usual spot by the entrance and scanned the lot. Felix's dented Dodge Neon was parked two cars over. Damn.

I could see Trace squirming in his seat.

"Trust me, you're safe here," I promised.

He nodded. Though he didn't look all that reassured. Not that I blamed him. A celebrity walking into the offices of a tabloid was like a mouse walking into a cat's mouth. While holding a bottle of cream.

Trace pulled the cap of his hat down low over his forehead as we rode the elevator to the second floor in silence. I could feel him sticking close to my back as we exited into the newsroom, busy with the hum of clacking keyboards and phone lines buzzing with the latest gossip.

We made our way to my desk – me ducking behind the partitions to keep out of Felix's eyeline and Trace ducking down to keep out of everyone's eyeline. Luckily for me, Felix was on a phone call, chatting into his Bluetooth with his back to my cubicle. Luckily for Trace, everyone else's eyes were glued to their computer screens, scanning the internet for anything verifiable or printable. (And often just the latter.)

I quickly logged into the system, and, sure enough, there was an email from Felix containing my photo backlog for the day. I forwarded the whole lot to my personal account, hoping I'd get the chance to deal with them later. I was just logging back out when I heard a high-pitched voice scream behind me.

"Oh. Meh. Gawd!" came Allie's perky alto. "Trace Brody?"

Trace shot me a look. It was the same one I imagined a wild bear would have when the ranger started posting "hunting season" signs.

Before I could attempt any kind of rescue mission, Allie swooped in, the scent of her peachy lotion enveloping us as she flapped her hands in front of her like an overexcited five-year-old.

"Ohmigod, Ohmigod. I totally love your work," Allie gushed, sidling up to us. Or, more accurately, sideling *past* me, all but running me over, and *up* to Trace. "Allie Quick," she said, sticking one hand out his way.

Like the pro he was, he shook it, despite his misgivings, his meet-and-greet public smile sliding into place seemingly effortlessly.

"Nice to meet you, Allie," he said. Even though I knew it was anything but.

"Wow, Trace Brody. Huh. I never would have thought your presence would grace our humble offices?" Allie said. I noticed it was phrased as more of a question, sending an inquiring look my way along with the not so subtle hint.

One I elected to ignore.

"Actually, we were just leaving," I said instead, ushering Trace toward the door.

"Where are you going?" Allie asked. I could see her mental reporter's notebook already out, notes being taken in sparkle pen, no doubt.

"We're going out."

"Where?"

"Someplace."

"Why?"

"We have stuff to do."

"What kind of stuff."

"Just stuff."

She paused, puckering her pink, glossy lips into a frown at clearly not winning our battle of twenty questions. She turned back to Trace.

"I'd love to do a quick interview with you," she gushed, standing directly in our path to the elevators.

"Look, Allie, we're kind of busy," I pointedly said before Trace had a chance to respond. I shot a look toward Felix's office. He was still on the phone, but I knew it was only a matter of time before his gaze wandered our direction.

"Busy with what?"

Damn, she was a persistent little bugger.

"Big important movie-star stuff. Now move."

"This 'stuff' wouldn't have anything to do with that whole fake abduction thing the other day, would it?"

Trace tensed beside me, and again I got that caged animal vibe from him.

"Look, we really have to go-" I started.

But I didn't get to finish as another voice piped up behind me.

"Holy moley, is that Trace Brody?"

I spun around to find Mrs. Rosenblatt's ample frame bearing down on us.

I closed my eyes and said a silent swear word. A really bad one.

"This disguise sucks," Trace whispered to me before once again pulling out his "on" smile as Mrs. Rosenblatt bore down on us.

"Wow, you ladies really do get the cream of the crop at this here paper." She turned to Trace. "Dorothy Rosenblatt," she said, sticking a pudgy hand out at him.

Reluctantly, he shook it.

"Nice to meet you," he said again on auto-pilot. I silently wondered if he ever got tired of uttering stupid pleasantries like that.

"I remember you from that suspense movie you did with Jamie Lee where she showed her tatas," Mrs. Rosenblatt went on. "One hell of a sexy movie. Tell me, were those fake? 'Cause I know you've gotten a handful of 'em since, huh? Huh?" She elbowed Trace in the ribs, giving him an exaggerated wink.

"Uh…" I think I saw the tips of Trace's ears go red.

"I also loved you in that Roman flick with all the togas," Mrs. Rosenblatt continued. "They use a body double for that or was that really your tushie? 'Cause that was the kind of hiney I'd love to sink my teeth into."

"Uh… thanks," he said. Though it sounded more like a question. Or maybe a plea for help.

I turned to politely extricate us from the situation (Felix was hanging up. Any second now he was going to see our growing band of misfits!), but Mrs. Rosenblatt was just that much faster than I was.

"Listen, Cam, I got a hold of that photo from Fred," she started. Then off my blank look added, "Of Jennifer Wilson? Tootsie?" She turned to Trace. "This murdered movie star from the forties."

Sensing a story, Allie perked up beside her. "Murdered? Really?"

Mrs. Rosenblatt nodded. "Yeah. I'm trying to find out who killed her for Max."

"Oh." Allie's perk deflated. "*Max*'s story."

"I got this photo of her taken the week before she died, and, boy howdy, did that sucker have some strong vibrations. Anyway, I could use your help checking some of this stuff out, Cam."

"Uh… sure. But listen, now's not a real good time…" I trailed off, glancing up at Felix's office again. He was sipping his coffee. Eyes roving the other half of the room.

Unfortunately, neither Allie *nor* Mrs. Rosenblatt seemed capable of taking a hint today.

"See, the vibrations were kinda jumbled," Mrs. Rosenblatt went on, "but I think Albert and I have narrowed down the field to a likely list of suspects in her murder."

"Albert?" Allie asked, cocking her head to the side.

"My spirit guide," Mrs. Rosenblatt explained.

Oh boy.

"Anyhoo, you being a pro at this kind of stuff, I thought maybe you could if I could help me investigate these characters and get some feeling about which one did her in."

"I'd love to, but we're kinda in a hurry-"

"Who are your suspects?" Allie asked, running right over me.

I shot her a look. Curiosity might have killed the cat, but I was looking at one blonde who didn't have nine lives.

Only too happy to oblige, Mrs. Rosenblatt started rattling off names. "The first guy on our list is Johnny Rupert. He was a bit actor at the time and apparently had a terrible crush on Tootsie. He worked on her last film with her. Unfortunately, he died in the eighties in a car wreck out on highway 15, but that don't mean he didn't off Tootsie first."

"Second character on our list is Becky Martin. She played supporting actress to Tootsie in that last film and, from what I gather, was extremely jealous of her. They were seen fighting the day before Tootsie died. Unfortunately, she dropped off the Hollywood radar shortly after Tootsie's death, and no one has seen her since."

"This is all fascinating," I said, "but we really have to go-"

"And the third on my list," Mrs. Rosenblatt went on, totally ignoring me, "is Tootsie's boyfriend. Ben Carlyle. He was a director in those days, and a good fifteen years Tootsie's senior. Rumor had it she was going to leave him, but she never got the chance."

She paused for breath.

"Is that all?"

Luckily her psychic abilities didn't extend to sarcasm detection.

"For now. Anyway, I was just about to go question the boyfriend."

"Wait – he's still alive?" I asked, doing some quick mental math. If he'd been fifteen years older than Tootsie in the forties, he'd have to be at least… "He's gotta be what, ninety?"

"Ninety-four," Mrs. Rosenblatt confirmed. "Lives at the MPTF retirement home in Woodland Hills."

The MPTF was the Motion Picture & Television Fund home, a community of little cottages nestled in the hills that housed the retired members of Hollywood society who hadn't quite ever made it into Trace Brody territory. While the big stars usually retired to their multi-million dollar mansions, the bit actors and extras often found their golden years leaving them with less than stellar bank accounts. Instead they played out their final roles at the MPTF home, staging readings of *Fiddler on the Roof* from their wheelchairs.

"So, what do you say? Wanna come help me interrogate Mr. Carlyle?"

While "interrogating" a ninety-four-year-old fell somewhere near kicking puppies on my moral radar, we still had a good two hours before the meeting with Trace's agent. Of all the places in Hollywood to hide him, a retirement home would be the last one someone would go looking for Trace.

I glanced up at Felix's office. He was setting down his coffee cup. Seconds away from spotting me.

"Okay," I quickly said. "As long as we leave *now*, I'm in."

"Me too!" Allie piped up behind me.

I refrained from pointing out that no one had actually asked her.

"Great! Just let me grab my purse and I'll meet you all downstairs," Mrs. Rosenblatt said, waddling off.

Allie shot me a smile so sweet it would give a Care Bear the runs, then flounced (there was no other way to describe the way her mini-skirt floated around her thigh-high boots) back to her cubicle to grab that sparkly pen and her notebook.

"Interesting people you work with," Trace mumbled to me as we watched her. Though I noticed his expression was more of genuine interest than disgust as Allie's pert little backside wiggled behind the partition. Figures he'd be an ass man. I woefully glanced at my own flat fanny as I turned and pulled Trace with me toward the elevator.

Only I never quite got there.

"Cam?" came Felix's bellowing voice.

Shit.

On instinct, I shoved Trace toward the nearest cube. Hard. So hard he kinda stumbled, catching his balance on the edge of the desk.

"Hide," I whispered out of the corner of my mouth.

"Where?" he shot back.

"I don't know, you're the actor. Improvise!"

Out of the corner of my eye I saw him dive under a desk as my boss purposefully crossed the newsroom toward me.

"Hey, chief, what's up?" I asked, in a voice that was, in hindsight, two octaves higher than warranted.

Luckily, if he noticed, Felix didn't comment on it. "Where are we on Wedding Watch today?" he asked, getting right to the point.

"Um. We're, great."

"You track down Trace?'

I nodded. "Yep. Totally got him." If he only knew...

"Good."

He stared expectantly at me.

"And?" he asked, motioning with his hands for me to go on.

"And what?"

"The whole kidnapping thing?"

"Oh. Right. Totally a fake. Publicity stunt, just like you said."

"I'll be the bigger man and refrain from telling you. 'I told you so.'"

"Gee. Thanks." I was so remembering this when I finally turned in my story.

"So what's our Jamie Lee up to today?"

"Jamie Lee?"

Felix crossed his arms over his chest. "The *bride*."

"Yeah, right. Of course. The bride." I made a "pft" sound, blowing air out through my lips as I smacked my forehead, ever so eloquently illustrating that of course I wouldn't forget the bride. "I was just going to catch up with her now," I lied.

"Fab. By the way, those pictures you took of Jamie Lee coming out of Dr. B's yesterday were perfect. Just what our readers want to see."

"Thanks."

"I expect three more like those by the end of the day," Felix informed me as he marched back to his office.

I waited for him to close the door and turn his back to us again before shooing Trace out from under the desk. I grabbed him by the arm (careful to avoid the bandaged one) and quickly steered him toward the elevator before anyone else noticed us on this less-than-stealth mission.

Once inside, I heaved a sigh of relief that ruffled my hair and sagged into the metal walls.

Trace on the other hand, looked slightly disturbed, a frown furrowing between his brows. "Why was she at the doctor's office?"

"What?"

"Jamie Lee. Your boss said that you took pictures of her at the doctor's office yesterday? Is she okay?"

"Oh. That. Yeah. Dr. B's a cosmetic doctor. She was just getting a little pre-wedding refresher."

"Refresher?" The frown deepened. "Like a facial?"

I grinned. "Well, from what I could tell it was a little Botox, a little collagen in the lips, and possibly a little thigh lipo."

Trace blinked at me. "You're kidding."

"Scout's honor." I held up two fingers.

"Wow. I had no idea." He paused. "Girls really do all that stuff?"

"Girls? No. Jamie Lee? Yes." I cocked my head at him. "Seriously, you thought she just naturally looked like she stepped out of a Photoshopped *Sports Illustrated* spread?"

He shrugged. "I guess I never really thought about it."

"Yeah, well, you don't get to look like Jamie Lee does by leaving it to Mother Nature."

He paused. "Do you get that kind of stuff done, too?"

"Me?" I snorted. "No way. Even if my salary afforded me the luxury, I'd probably be spending it on camera equipment before I injected it into my face."

"Huh," he said. Then gave me a long, assessing stare.

So long I felt my cheeks go red.

"You're staring."

"Sorry. Just trying to figure out which part of you Mother Nature's screwing with. Personally, I don't see it."

I bit my lip. Did the hot movie star just give me a compliment? While I was pretty sure he was being more nice than honest, my cheeks heated some more anyway, and I ducked my head, letting my long hair cover them.

# Chapter Ten

Twenty minutes later all four of us were piled into my Jeep – me, Allie and Trace squished together in the front, and Mrs. Rosenblatt taking up the entirety of my miniscule backseat. And then some. (We had to roll the windows down to let her arm-jowls hang out the sides.)

"Why do they make these cars so small? I swear cars keep shrinking. The Buick Park Avenue. Now that was a good size for a car."

It was a good size for a small country.

I noticed Trace, on the other hand, didn't complain in the least about his seating arrangement. Probably due to the fact that Allie's man-made tatas were shoved up against his person. In fact, I'd swear Trace was even smiling. Allie was definitely smiling. A big toothy thing complete with baby-doll eyes. If she got any cuter, fluffy kittens the world over were going to go on strike.

I averted my eyes, firmly gluing them to the road in front of me instead as I pulled up into the MPTF complex, passing row after row of bungalows that housed Hollywood's fading stars.

According to the mailboxes lining the street, Ben Carlyle lived in the third from the end, a one-bedroom, beige affair with turquoise trim and shutters. Under the front window hunkered a turquoise window box, a row of bright pink plastic geraniums "planted" in the dirt. A two-foot-tall garden gnome guarded the front door, next to a welcome mat that read, *If it's not Scottish, it's crap!*

The place didn't exactly scream cold-blooded murderer.

I followed Mrs. Rosenblatt as she led our merry band up the steps to the front porch and rang the bell. From inside I could hear the TV at top volume, canned laughter breaking up the sounds of a sitcom family.

We waited two beats in silence for a sign of non-televised life from within. Nothing. Mrs. Rosenblatt rang the bell again, adding a shave-and-a-haircut knock with her pudgy knuckles.

This time shuffling greeted us a beat later on the other side of the door. It opened a crack, the security chain still firmly in place.

"Whatcha want?" came a gravelly voice laced with an eighty-year cigarette habit. And, if the wafting from the interior was any indication, a liberal layer of boxed wine.

"We're looking for Ben Carlyle," Mrs. Rosenblatt responded.

"What fer?"

"You Ben Carlyle?" she asked, squinting through the door crack.

"Maybe."

"We wanted to ask you a few questions about Jennifer Wilson."

There was a pause. Then, "Tootsie?"

Mrs. Rosenblatt nodded. "That's right. Can we come in?"

He thought about this for a second. Then the door shut, the sounds of a chain rattling on the other side, before it popped open again, this time opening wide to reveal the bungalow's inhabitant in all his splendor.

Ben Carlyle didn't look a day over a hundred and ten. His ears were big and complemented by a large, hooked nose that covered half of his pointed face. His pale skin was wrinkled into a pretty good imitation of tissue paper, thinly covering a network of blue and purple veins that protruded like little mountain ranges down his neck. Two beady eyes were set behind a pair of smudged bifocals with thick, black frames. (At least Trace wouldn't have to worry about being recognized. I'd eat my Nikon if this guy could see past the end of his own elongated nose.) He was hunched at the middle, leaning on a walker with two tennis balls stuck on the back feet, and wore a plaid bathrobe over a white T-shirt and slacks that were hiked up to his armpits.

Again, the term "ruthless killer" didn't quite seem to fit.

"I guess you might as well come in," he said, gesturing to a small living room. A chintz sofa and La-Z-Boy chair in 1985 brown corduroy sat in front of a small television showing a rerun of *Mr. Belvedere*. Mr. Carlyle parked himself in the La-Z-Boy. Mrs. Rosenblatt sat on the sofa, Allie scrunching in beside her. Trace and I hung back, standing near the TV.

"Why you askin' about Tootsie? No one's asked about her in ages."

"I'm working with the *L.A. Informer*," Mrs. Rosenblatt explained. "We're doing a piece on the anniversary of her death and wanted to get some insight from people who knew her."

I nodded. Not a bad explanation. Close enough to the truth to intrigue her subject, if the way he cocked his head to the side, perking up his Dumbo ears was any indication. But not specific enough to scare him off from a choice quote or two. Mrs. Rosenblatt was catching on quickly.

"Is it true that you and Tootsie were dating at the time of her death?" Allie asked, pulling a notebook and pen (Pink. Sparkly. Writing in iridescent gel. I knew it.) from her purse.

Carlyle nodded. "That's right. We were engaged."

I raised an eyebrow. "Really?"

He frowned at me. "Yeah, *really*."

"That's not what I heard," I said.

"What did you hear then, girl?" he asked, his tone mocking as if I was too young to have heard anything of consequence. Granted, at his age he probably thought Regis Philbin was a young whipper-snapper.

"I heard that she was about to break things off when she was murdered," I said, quoting the info Mrs. Rosenblatt had dug up. At least, I hoped she had dug it up and heard it from her informants in the great beyond.

"Not true!" he shouted, his face going red, showing off a network of broken capillaries that confirmed my theory of his box-a-day merlot habit. "Categorically not true. Tootsie loved me. I was the sun she revolved around."

I raised an eyebrow. It was hard to imagine anything beyond a slight eau de denture cream revolving around the shriveled man.

"I never read anything about the two of you being engaged," Allie said, pen hovering. "When did you propose?"

He pursed his lips together. "Well, we were *going* to get engaged. I had the ring picked out and everything. I was going to propose on Valentine's Day but... well, you know what happened to her."

"She was shot, wasn't she?" Mrs. Rosenblatt said.

Carlyle nodded, his eyes staring at a spot on the wall just above the TV, as if lost in some far away thought. "Poor thing," he whispered.

"And the murder was never solved?" Mrs. Rosenblatt pressed.

He shook his head. "No. The police questioned everyone. Even me, if you can believe it. But, in the end, they didn't have anything solid on anybody. This was before all that CSI stuff and DNA, mind you."

"Did they have any suspects?" I asked.

He nodded. "Sure. Plenty of those. Tootsie was young, beautiful, successful. That combination always makes for plenty of enemies in Hollywood."

"Anyone in particular?"

"Johnny," he quickly shot out. Almost too quickly.

"That would be Johnny Rupert?" Allie clarified, jotting it down in her little notebook.

He nodded. "That's the guy. He made so many advances toward Tootsie that I lost count. The creep."

"I take it the advances were unwanted?" I asked.

"Of course they were!" he bellowed, his voice matching the TV volume. "She was with me. What would she want with a snake like Johnny?"

I tried to picture Carlyle as the catch he might have been in his heyday. If I tilted my head to the side, squinted until he was blurry and mentally Photoshopped out the bristly hairs growing from his ears, I could almost think of him as appealing.

Almost.

"Tell me about these advances," Allie pressed. "What specifically did he do?"

"Well, I dunno. What do men do when they're courting a girl? He brought her flowers, candy. Took her to the theater a couple o' times."

So far, not exactly homicidal behavior.

"Sounds like Tootsie didn't completely discourage these advances," I observed.

He shrugged. "Tootsie was a sweetheart. I told her she should flat out tell the guy to take a hike, but she didn't want to hurt his feelings. She said he was harmless." He paused. Then shook his head. "Poor Tootsie. She was a doll, but she didn't know much about men."

"You don't think he was so harmless?" I asked.

"Well he shot her, didn't he?"

"You think Johnny killed her?" Allie asked, jotting down notes so fast her pen was a pink blur.

"The guy was obsessed with her. When it became clear she was in love with me, he must have killed her in a jealous rage," he said.

It was clear he'd had a few years to formulate a theory. Personally, I thought it wasn't half bad. I made a mental note to track down more info about this Johnny character.

"What about Becky Martin?" Mrs. Rosenblatt jumped in. "She was in Tootsie's last picture, wasn't she?"

He grinned. "Sure, I remember her. She started out as Tootsie's assistant. Followed her around the studio lot like a little puppy, feeding on whatever castoffs Tootsie threw her way. She was a second-rate actress and an even worse singer. She'd learned to tap dance as a kid and thought that entitled her to a piece of the Hollywood pie."

"I take it you disagreed?" I asked.

He waved me off. "She was nothing. Girls like her were a dime a dozen. They arrived on the buses from the Midwest in droves in those days, all bright-eyed brunettes. Within a week, they were blondes with shorter skirts, stuffed bras and new names, ready to do anything to make it in this town. And I do mean *anything*. No character at all." He grinned. "Did you know that Becks was originally Rebecca Lubenschwartz." He chuckled at the thought. "I almost felt sorry for the kid when I heard that."

"If she was so second rate, how did she end up landing the role opposite Tootsie?"

He shrugged. "Like I said she started at the bottom, and Tootsie helped her out. At first she was a stand in, then she got a bit part here and there. I was against it, but Tootsie finally convinced me to give Becky a shot at a real role."

"And how did she do?" Mrs. Rosenblatt asked.

He shrugged. "She knew her lines. But you'd get more emotion from a trained monkey than you did Becks. She was more wooden than Pinocchio."

"I take it you weren't a fan," Allie said, her pen furiously taking notes. "Did Tootsie feel the same way?"

"Tootsie had a heart of gold. She'd help anyone in need."

I noticed he didn't actually answer the question. "I heard that Tootsie was seen arguing with Becky the day before her death. Any idea what they argued about?"

He shot me a look, his eyes magnified to three times their real size behind his glasses. "Girl, that was over sixty years ago. How'm I supposed to remember something like that?"

"Was she jealous of Tootsie?"

"Who wouldn't be? Tootsie was perfect." Carlyle shook his head, again getting that far-off look in his eyes. "What a waste."

I looked down at my watch. It was nearing 11:30. If we were going to ditch the blonde and the psychic before meeting Trace's agent, it was time to get this show on the road.

"Where were you the night she was killed?" I asked, cutting right to the chase.

I leaned in, watching closely for Carlyle's reaction.

Only he didn't seem surprised in the least at the question. "Yeah, the police suspected me at the time, too. Always the boyfriend, right?" He sighed. "I was at home. Alone. And before you ask, no, no one could verify my alibi then, and I'm pretty sure sixty years ain't helped that any. So go ahead and suspect me if you want, but I tell you I loved that girl with all my heart. I wouldn't have touched a hair on her head."

He clamped his mouth shut, his eyes going watery behind his thick frames.

We thanked him for his time, leaving him to his reruns and memories as we crammed ourselves back into my Jeep. Once we all got back to the *Informer* offices, we regrouped in the parking lot.

"So do we believe him?" Allie asked, consulting her notes.

I shrugged. "He seemed more pathetic than dangerous."

"But he was awful quick to point the finger at Johnny Rupert," Mrs. Rosenblatt pointed out. "Kinda suspicious, that."

I looked down at my cell display. It was a quarter to twelve.

"Listen, I'd love to stay and chat, but we have to get going."

"Where?" Allie pounced.

"Trace has an appointment."

"With who?" Allie persisted.

"Whom."

"What?"

"The proper grammatical use there is 'whom,'" I said, doing a bang-up job of avoiding the question, even if I did say so myself.

"Oh. Sure. I knew that. Well, if you need any help later…"

"Thanks!" I shouted, ditching her even before she could finish the sentence. Instead, I made a bee-line for my Jeep again, Trace a quick step behind. Once inside, I gunned the engine, making for Nico's.

Nico's was an ultra trendy restaurant in West Hollywood, sandwiched between a talent agency and an art gallery. I was well acquainted with the place not only because of their fabulous vegetarian Portobello burger, but also because it was a favorite lunch spot for celebrity new-moms to take their munchkins on a first public outing. I had a long-standing favorite spot to snap prime photos, just beyond the tall azalea bushes at the south end of the patio.

Unfortunately, the boys at *Entertainment Daily* had their own sweet spot as well. And, I noticed as we pulled up to the curb outside the patio, they were firmly camped out in it.

I did an inward groan.

The second Mike and Eddie caught a whiff of Trace, he'd be plastered all over the ED website in a matter of minutes. Along with his current location. Not good if you were running from two guys with one very big gun.

I reached into my trunk and pulled out a shiny, green windbreaker.

I shoved it at Trace.

"Here, put this on."

"It's ninety degrees out."

"There are two photographers hidden behind that azalea bush. Unless you want to be plastered all over the internet in five seconds flat, put on the jacket."

He held it up to his chest. Across the back was the logo of a plumbing company, a talking toilet saying, "Clean pipes are happy pipes."

He shook his head and muttered a, "Jesus," under his breath. "You better hope this works. Because if I get caught on camera wearing this…" He trailed off, the implications to his movie-star image understood.

But he put on the windbreaker.

Pulling the ball cap low on his head and turning the windbreaker's collar up high, Trace entered the trendy restaurant, me one step behind. I'd shoved on a matching ball cap as well, stuffing my long hair up under the hat. While Trace would cause Mike and Eddie instant celebrity stalker orgasms, the sight of me would at the very least arouse some interest in my companion. Definitely not something we wanted today. So, while the caps made Trace and me look like a couple of sixth-grade boys, at least no one would mistake us for movie stars.

After ascertaining that Bert Decker had not yet arrived, Trace slipped the hostess a benjamin to seat us near the front of the patio. Normally, a dark corner in the back would have been the preferred incognito spot. However, there were no dark corners on an open-air patio in California in the summer. And, even if there were, the paparazzi would already be hunkered there, waiting to take Trace's picture. (Trust me, I often did.) I pulled my hat lower over my forehead as I glanced over my shoulder at the *ED* brothers.

They were hunkered down just over the low fence that separated Nico's from the dry cleaner's next door. Carefully squatted on public property, but with a prime view of the Nico's clientele. Eddie had one hand in a bag of Fritos corn chips, the other down his pants. Mike was training his camera on a couple sipping Arnold Palmers at a table near the street. I squinted through the crowd, making out a head of dark hair on a mocha skinned woman, a familiar pair of dimples flashing in the guy's tanned cheeks. I sucked in a breath. J Lo and Mark Anthony. And they looked like they were arguing.

Hollywood Secrets | 101

Shit.

I resisted the urge to slip my camera from my bag and start firing away. What a primo shot. Felix would give his right arm for a shot like this. Or at least a small bonus.

"What?" Trace asked, sliding down in his chair. "What are you looking at?"

I elbowed him in the ribs. "That's J Lo and Mark Anthony!"

He leaned over, looking past me. Then shrugged. "I guess it is. So?"

"Sooooo... I can't believe I'm missing this shot!"

"You want a shot of J Lo?"

I nodded so hard that my cap bobbled on my head. "Uh, yeah!"

"Great. I'll invite you both over next weekend."

I blinked at him. "You can do that?"

Again he shrugged. "Why not? They were over twice in June. Mark likes my buffalo wings. You can come help me barbeque."

I had officially died and gone to paparazzi heaven.

A waitress/wannabe actress/model/spokeswoman approached our table and took our order. I did the talking, Trace looking inordinately interested in the sugar packets on the table to avoid eye contact. It seemed to work as the waitress didn't scream out his name at top volume. In fact, she barely gave us a glance at all, only sparing one slightly dirty look when we both ordered only coffee.

She brought us our cups and we slowly sipped in silence, both of us scanning the entrance for any sign of Decker. I'd seen enough photos of him at openings and after-parties that I was fairly certain I'd recognize the guy. Graying hair, paunchy belly, tanned skin though nary a wrinkle thanks to the likes of Dr. B and his cohorts. Unfortunately, as the minutes dragged on, no one fitting that description walked through the doors of Nico's.

"Cammy?"

I closed my eyes, instantly recognizing the male voice laced with a layer of fast-food grease. I thought a really dirty word, then spun around to find Eddie, mouth full of corn chips, waving at us from over the wall. "Fancy meeting you here, kid," he said.

I raised a feeble hand. "Hi."

"On a story?" Mike asked, his radar going up, eyes darting around the landscape like a meerkat sensing an approaching jackal.

"Just having lunch," I lied.

"Who's your friend?" Eddie asked, gesturing to Trace. Who had slunk so low in his seat, he'd shrunk at least a foot and a half.

"No one."

"Eddie Smets," Eddie said, extending a hand toward Trace.

Trace shook it, dipping his head to the right, wisely not making eye contact.

Eddie waited for Trace to introduce himself.

Trace waited for Eddie to go away.

"What do you want, Eddie?" I asked.

"Just being friendly," Mike answered for his twin.

Eddie was still staring at Trace. "Have we met before? You look familiar."

Trace shook his head.

"You don't say much, do you?'

Trace shook his head again.

"He's…got laryngitis." Wow, the lies were getting thinner and thinner. Any more and they'd be a post-Jenny Bertinelli.

"Huh."

And Eddie knew it.

"You get a load of that argument?" Mike asked, munching down hard on a chip as he gestured to the golden couple.

I nodded. "That was something, huh? You, uh, didn't happen to catch what it as about, did you?" I couldn't help asking.

Mike nodded. "Yep."

"Wanna share?"

"Nope."

"Jerk."

"Love ya, too, babe," he replied, doing a kissy-face at me.

"You sure I don't know you?" Eddie asked, ducking down and trying to see under the low brim of Trace's hat.

Trace slouched further and shook his head.

I looked down at my watch. It was a quarter past noon. If we waited around for Decker any longer I had a bad feeling that even a dull bulb like Eddie was going to connect the dots, and Trace would end up on the ED website plugging a plumbing company.

"Well, it's been fun," I said. A lie. "But we have to get going." Truth. "Hope you have a nice day." Total lie.

"See ya, Cammy," Mike said, shoving another handful into his mouth.

Eddie was a little cagier, watching as Trace and I stood, Trace unfolding to his full height. I could tell he was seconds away from recognizing the guy.

I quickly ushered my movie star out the door, across the street and back to my Jeep.

I heaved a sigh of relief as we peeled away from the curb without the telltale flash of Eddie's camera catching up with his pea brain.

"I can't believe Decker didn't show." Trace pulled off the windbreaker, sweat glistening on his cut arms as he shoved it into the back of the car.

On any other guy, it might have been "pooling," but I swear Trace actually glistened.

I tried not to drool.

Instead, I pulled out my camera and snapped a candid shot.

Trace blinked as my flash went off. "What was that? Did you just take my picture?"

"Hey, I gotta throw my editor a bone. If I don't turn something in by the end of the day, I'm toast."

Trace frowned. "You could have warned me first."

I could have. But the moment had been too good to pass up. If I was near drooling, our readers would be salivating like hungry Dobermans.

"Call Decker," I said. "Let's find out why he stood you up."

Trace did, putting his cell on speaker as we listened to it ring on the other end. And ring and ring. Finally it went to voicemail.

Not good.

"Maybe his flight was delayed?" I said.

But the way Trace's jaw was set in a grim line told me he didn't believe that any more than I did.

"Maybe we should be sure."

* * *

Fifteen minutes later we pulled up in front of a small, stucco one-story on the outskirts of Burbank. Like most houses in Southern California, this one had an impressive palm tree planted out front, shading the Spanish-style home from the grueling sunshine. Arched windows and clay-colored paint gave it an authentic feeling, mimicked by the hand-painted tiles flanking the walkway. I parked in the empty drive, and Trace and I made our way up the front path.

I stepped up to the door and rang the bell, listening to the chimes inside echo through the house. Only no footsteps approached. I did a repeat, this time cupping my hands over my eyes and peeking in the living room window to the left.

A pair of overstuffed sofas flanked a fireplace done in more blue Spanish tiles near the end of the room. A chic, distressed wooden coffee table sat between them, the latest copy of *Variety* spread open on its surface. Beside the paper sat a coffee mug with the slogan "World's Best Agent" emblazoned on its side.

But no sign of Decker.

"It doesn't look like he's home," I said, stating the obvious as our second attempt at the doorbell remained unanswered.

Trace crowded beside me to look in the windows for himself, a desperation creeping into his blue eyes.

"Maybe he's around back," Trace said, false hope lacing his voice.

Considering the temp was pushing the upper limits of the thermometer, I doubted he was sunbathing. However, no stone unturned…

"Sure. Maybe," I answered.

He led the way across Decker's browning lawn to a side gate, covered in vines and bright purple morning glories.

He tried the gate, pulling it toward us. It didn't budge. Locked.

With a quick look over his shoulder, Trace hoisted himself over the gate in one swift movement.

Show off.

I bit my lip, looking around for a way to get a foothold. Granted, I was only a few inches shorter than Trace, but I hadn't done all my own stunts in my last action flick, so I wasn't exactly as athletic as the guy. Okay, the truth was, I was all limbs. Gangly had been the adjective I'd heard most often throughout my adolescence. While I'd managed to pad my frame out a little in adulthood, I wasn't exactly what you'd call the graceful type.

Or the type who could leap garden gates in a single bound.

"You coming?" I heard Trace call from the other side of the gate.

"Yep. Sure. Be right there."

I spied a brick planter to the right of the fence and tested it. Solid. Moveable. It would do. I dragged it under the gate and gingerly stepped on top of the bricks, adding a full foot to my height. Just enough to get some leverage on the top of the gate. I did a little jump, pushing up with my hands and scrambling my feet up the side of the gate, sending a few innocent morning glories to their death in the process. Oops.

With a very unladylike grunt, I flipped my torso onto the top of the gate, then slid down the other side, managing to lodge a splinter in my palm in the process.

"Sonofa-" I put my palm to my lips, sucking on the sore spot.

"You okay?" Trace asked. Though I noticed his eyes were scanning the backyard for any signs of his agent, not flickering to the injured chick.

"Sure. Fine," I said, using my fingernails to dig out the offending splinter as I took in the backyard. It featured an uninspired square of lawn, a patio with a couple of chairs and a glass table with an umbrella sticking out, hedges butting up against the fence that separated him on three sides from his neighbors.

But, again, no Decker.

Trace moved to the sliding glass door at the back of the house, pressing his face against the surface so that his nose fogged up the glass. "I think I see him!"

I joined him. "Where?"

The back door led into a kitchen and family room combo.

Trace pointed to a La-Z-Boy chair in the corner of the room near the TV. With the back of the chair facing us, we couldn't see much of the occupant. But a pair of feet clad in black socks sticking out the front gave away his presence.

"There!" Trace pointed. He knocked on the glass. "Decker!"

No answer.

"Hey, Decker! Wake up, man!" Trace shouted, banging on the glass again.

Again, no answer.

But Trace was, as I was quickly coming to find out, a man not easily deterred. He jiggled the latch on the sliding glass door. It opened easily. What do you know – not locked.

I felt a flutter of concern in my gut. No one left their doors unlocked in L.A.

But apparently Trace didn't share my misgivings as he charged right into the room. "Hey, Decker," Trace called again.

I followed a step behind, feeling just the teensiest bit intrusive invading the man's home uninvited.

"Decker, wake up, man. I need to talk to you about-"

Trace stopped in his tracks, his gaze frozen on the man in the lounge chair. His eyes grew wide, pupils dilating, his jaw going slack as his color simultaneously drained from movie star tan to polar bear white.

"What?" I asked, coming around to stand beside him. I looked down at the chair.

And heard a piercing scream.

It took me a moment to realize it was coming from me.

The man in the chair was Decker, all right. I recognized his soft frame, salt-and-pepper hair, and tanning-bed complexion from the numerous photos I'd printed in the *Informer* throughout the years.

However one thing was different about the agent today.

A neat little round bullet hole in the center of his forehead, which led me to believe that Decker wouldn't be waking up anytime soon.

# Chapter Eleven

Living on a ranch, it wasn't totally uncommon to run across a dead animal. Coyotes would often pounce on smaller animals, sick livestock sometimes passed away in the night, and our cat, Tigger, was under the impression that anything lower on the food chain than he was would make a nice gift for his human owners.

But this was the first time I'd seen a dead human body. And, let me tell you, the fact we were the same species brought about a whole new host of sensations, none of them pleasant. They rolled around in my gut, threatening a repeat appearance of my morning Corn Flakes.

I doubled over in the middle, putting my head between my knees like I'd seen them do on TV, and took deep breaths. They smelled like the fabric softener I used on my clothes and a stale scent wafting from the body that I didn't want to examine too closely.

"Holy shit!" From the corner of my eye I saw Trace jump back a full two feet, his gaze shooting around the room as if looking for what might have made that neat little hole.

Me? I kinda didn't want to know.

I straightened up, finding my voice again. "He's dead, right? I mean, he kinda looks dead. Not that I've seen a dead guy before, but he looks like what a dead guy seems like it should look like." Yes, I was babbling. Again. Apparently both hot movie stars and dead bodies make me nervous. Go figure.

"He… he looks dead." Trace cocked his head to the side, his throat bobbing up and down. "Ah, geez, Bert."

"Maybe we should check for a pulse. They always check for a pulse on *CSI*," I offered. Yes, all of my experience with the dead came from prime time TV shows.

"Right. Yeah. A pulse. Good idea."

Neither of us moved.

"You first," he said.

I spun around. "Me? Nuh-uhn. You check. He's your agent."

"But you have all that first-aid knowledge," he said, pointing to his arm.

"I can put on a Band-Aid. That doesn't make me an EMT," I shot back.

We both stared at the dead guy. His eyes were open wide, staring at a point on the ceiling, unblinking. Which was a pretty big clue that a pulse would be nonexistent. Still...

I squinted one eye shut, bit my lip, and reached two trembling fingers toward Decker's neck. I cringed as they made contact, his skin cold and rubbery to the touch. It felt more like an uncooked chicken breast than human skin. My breakfast bubbled up into my throat again, but predictably nothing fluttered beneath my fingers.

I jerked my hand back like it was on fire, instinctively wiping it on the seat of my jeans as if I could wipe away the creepy sensation of his lifeless skin.

"Oh yeah. That sucker's 100% deceased."

"Holy shit." Trace ran a hand through his hair, his skin paling even further until it almost matched that of Decker. "How long do you think he's been..." He gulped, as if not able to actually say the word, "dead."

"Like that," he finally finished.

I shook my head. "I don't know. He's cold."

Trace just shook his head again, as if he couldn't believe we were staring at his dead agent.

"I'm sorry, Decker," he said quietly. "Jesus, this is all my fault." He gulped. "When I told those guys Decker had the flash drive I never thought they'd actually..." He trailed off, running his hand through his hair again.

"You think they did this?" I asked. "Your flash-drive guys?"

"It would be a hell of a coincidence if not, wouldn't it?"

Good point.

I stepped away from the body, as if putting a little distance between us would somehow mitigate the fact that I was standing in a room with a dead guy. I took a couple deep breaths, then pulled my cell from my pocket. My fingers trembled as I dialed. But I only got a nine and the first one typed in before Trace's hand shot out and grabbed the phone from me.

"What are you doing?" he asked, his eyes wide, his brows hunkering down tightly over them.

"I'm calling the police."

Trace shook his head violently from side to side. "No way. No cops. Remember?"

I stared at him. "You have got to be joking. I mean, last night was one thing. But this…" I trailed off, pointing at the lifeless agent. "Trace, it's a dead body."

"Yeah, and if I bring the cops into this, the next one could be mine."

"Tell the police what happened. Maybe they can help you."

"You're kidding, right?"

"They can protect you."

"How?" he asked, letting out a bark of laughter that held zero actual humor. "What are they gonna do, park a cruiser outside my house? These guys broke into my place last night, getting past security gates, alarms, and two full-time bodyguards. I have a feeling a black and white at the curb isn't going to deter them."

I refrained from pointing out that, by his own admission, his security team wasn't exactly the tops.

"Maybe they can put you into protective custody or something," I offered.

"That'll work real well. Trace Brody goes into witness protection. No one will notice me, I'm sure."

"You don't have to be sarcastic about it," I mumbled, crossing my arms over my chest.

"Look, these guys are serious," he said. "And they're not going to stop here," he gestured around himself at Decker's family room.

And that's when I really looked around the place for the first time. Along the back wall sat an antique roll-top desk, the top open, papers strewn every which way. Next to it a lamp lay on its side, the bulb broken. A small sofa sat in the corner, the cushions upended, the stuffing bulging out of their torn sides. The dead body in the center of the room had, until then, kind of stolen my focus (go figure), but it was clear now as I looked around that whoever had killed Decker had torn the place apart looking for something.

That damned flash drive.

I wrapped my arms around myself, suddenly feeling a chill despite the climbing temperatures outside.

Trace pulled his arm inside the sleeve of his shirt, then walked to the sliding glass door and began wiping the handle.

"What are you doing?" I asked.

"Getting rid of my fingerprints."

"You're contaminating the crime scene!"

He shot me a look. "Good!"

I bit my lip. Oh boy. I was in way over my head.

"We got to get out of here," Trace said, moving on to the outside of the door where his nose print was still clearly visible.

I looked back at Decker. He was kind of slumped in his chair, his head lolling to the side, his mouth hanging slack in a perpetual look of surprise.

"So what are we gonna do? Just leave him here?"

Trace paused, cocking his head to the side as he glanced at his former agent. For a moment genuine emotion shone there, and I wondered how close they'd been. But he only indulged in it for a second, shaking his head again. "There's nothing we can do for him now. Come on." He grabbed my hand, quickly pulling me back out the door, shutting the slider behind us, and wiping the handle again with his sleeve. Then we carefully backtracked through the yard, Trace covering our footprints as we went. Apparently he watched *CSI*, too. When we got to the gate, he hoisted me up first, giving me a boost up-and-over, before he climbed it himself, dropping with a quick thud on the other side.

Two minutes later we were racing down Verdugo, as if Decker's killers might somehow be hot on our trail. Which, of course, they weren't. If Decker was cold, that meant he had to have been dead for at least an hour. And considering the temp outside today it was likely closer to three or four. (Okay, I watch a *lot* of *CSI*.)

Four blocks down, I spied a Coffee Bean and pulled in. I needed some serious caffeine if I was going to approach this whole thing with a clear head.

"What are we doing here?" he asked, his gaze shooting to the rearview mirror as if he, too, were expecting a crazed gunman to appear behind us at any second.

"I need a coffee break." I held out my right hand. It was still shaking after having touched Decker's neck. "See?" I said.

Trace nodded. "Yeah. Coffee. That's a good idea." And as he got out of the car, I noticed his hands weren't all that steady either.

The Coffee Bean was L.A.'s answer to Starbucks – the uber trendy chain where people pretending they were too cool for Starbucks went to see and be seen. At any given time of day it is mandatory for all Southern California Coffee Beans to have at least two frustrated screenwriters pounding on their laptops in the corner, four wannabe actresses causally thumbing through scripts in hopes of being noticed, and one washed up sitcom star lurking near the entrance hoping someone will ask for his autograph if only he says his characters' catch phrase loudly enough.

We ordered our drinks from a barrista with long, red hair and a purple stud in her tongue. I asked for a black coffee and, to my surprise, so did Trace.

"What, no fashionable lattes for you?" I asked as we waited in line behind a blonde wannabe actress with a script sticking conspicuously out the top of her Juicy handbag. (See what I mean?)

He shook his head. "That sweet stuff gives me a headache. Sorry to disappoint you."

On the contrary. I was actually kinda impressed. Fleetingly I wondered what Jamie Lee drank. Probably something nonfat, nonsugar, nontaste. Not that I blamed her. I knew what it was like to have your ability to pay your rent tied directly to your looks. But that was a long time ago and not a lifetime I wanted to revisit anytime soon.

Our orders came up and we took them to a table near the back of the coffee shop to regroup. Only, no sooner had we sat down than the blonde wannabe noticed us.

"Oh wow. Oh wow." She immediately descended upon us, her heavily lipsticked mouth hanging open in a perk little, "O". "Trace Brody?" she asked.

Shit. We'd forgotten the windbreaker in the car.

"Ohmigod, it is you!" Pert Blonde said, rounding our table.

I saw Trace's "on" face slide reluctantly into place. "Hi there," he said, giving her his matinee-idol smile.

"Wow, it is so cool to meet you," she gushed, grabbing onto his hand and shaking like she wanted to detach it and take it with her. "I've seen all your films. You are such an inspiration."

"Thanks." I watched his eyes do a slow sweep of her frame and sucked down a wave of jealousy as he took in her micro-mini, long legs dedicated to countless hours of daily pilates.

"You know, you are like my idol," she gushed. "Did you know that we had the same acting coach? Well, okay, a different coach but at the same studio. I send my headshots in to your agent every time I get them updated. His assistant said he was definitely going to call me if a part came up that I'd fit. I'm expecting him to get back to me any day now."

"Don't hold your breath," I mumbled.

Trace kicked me under the table.

Luckily, Blondie was so engrossed in Trace I wasn't even on her radar.

"In fact, I heard that you're about to start production on that *Planet of the Apes* remake movie, and I really think I'd make a perfect ape."

I covered a snort, narrowly avoiding a nasal coffee spew.

She reached into her bag and pulled out a headshot.

I snuck a peek. Wow, someone had done a hell of a lot of retouching. In fact… I squinted up at the actress. I'd say her nose was at least an inch shorter in the photo.

"Here," she thrust the photo at Trace. "Maybe you could, you know, pass it along to the producers? I hear they're casting next week."

"Yeah. Sure. Glad to." He gave her another winning smile.

One she mirrored back in spades, her lips curling so far out I thought they might crack her face. "Ohmigod, that is so sweet of you. And, you know what, if you ever want to like get together and hone our craft sometime, I'd really love that."

I snorted. Hone our craft? If that wasn't code for something dirty, I didn't know what was.

"Uh… well…" Trace hedged.

"Here, give me your cell and I'll program my number in."
She held out one manicured hand.

Trace hesitated. But he must have decided that the fastest
way to get rid of her was just to hand it over, so he did.

If Blondie smiled any bigger, she was gonna break
something. She punched her number in, then handed the cell
back with a, "Call me," and flounced away, clearly on cloud
nine.

I leaned forward to see the number. She'd filed it under,
"Candi". I had a feeling that if she could have drawn a little
heart over the "i", she would have.

"What a bimbo."

Trace shrugged.

"You gonna call her?" I asked, taking a sip of my coffee.

He shook his head. "Are you kidding?" He picked up the
cell, quickly deleting the entry. "If Jamie Lee even saw this,
she'd go ballistic."

"The jealous type, huh?"

He grinned. "That French film I did? When Jamie Lee saw
the nude shower scene between me and my co-star she freaked.
Didn't speak to me for a full week. And we weren't even
together when I filmed that movie."

"Wow. She sounds like a bundle of fun."

He shrugged. "She's not so bad."

"'Not so bad?' Gee, if you're so madly in love with her,
why don't you marry her?" I teased.

"Ha. Ha. Very funny, tabloid girl." But he quickly picked
up his coffee cup, sipping to mask some emotion I wasn't fast
enough to read.

Instead, I mirrored him, sipping my coffee as well. We
were both silent a beat, but in the face of Blondie's shameless
flirting, I couldn't help the reporter in me from piping up.

"So, I gotta ask… what's it like to have beautiful women
throwing themselves at you all the time?"

"Please. She was not throwing herself at me."

"'Hone our craft'? If that wasn't code for playing the naked
mambo, I don't know what is."

"Naked mambo?" He grinned. "Cute."

"Don't change the subject. Did you ever give Jamie Lee reason to be so jealous?"

He shook his head. "Nice try. But, no, I haven't."

"Hm. You know, even if you had, that is exactly the answer you'd give."

He grinned. "Exactly."

The sound of the ELO trilling "Hold on tight to your dreams" from the phone in his hand broke in, saving him from further questioning.

"Saved by the bell," he said.

He looked down at the number. Not one he recognized if the frown between his brows meant anything. "If this is that blonde…" he trailed off, hitting the on button.

"Trace Brody." he answered.

But I could tell immediately from the look on his face that it was not some perky wannabe starlet. He went stark white, the levity we'd been trying to cultivate after seeing his agent disappearing faster than cellulite at Dr. B's office. His eyes went dark, his jaw clenching, and I knew that whoever was on the other line was no friend.

A fact that was confirmed as he mouthed the words, "It's them."

# Chapter Twelve

"The killers?" I mouthed back.

He nodded, his jaw tensing. Then he put the phone on speaker and set it on the table between us.

"What do you want?" Trace asked. I had to hand it to him. His voice was a lot steadier than mine would have been if I were talking to the guys that had just shot my agent.

"You know what we want," came the reply. The voice was male, deep, harboring just the slightest hint of an accent from back east somewhere. Jersey maybe? Or maybe I'd just seen too many *Sopranos* episodes and was reading into it.

"The flash drive," Trace answered. "Look, I told you I don't have it."

"Neither did your agent."

Even though I'd been 90% sure that these guys had killed Decker, hearing him refer to the agent in past tense confirmed it. A chill went up my spine as I gripped my coffee cup that much tighter.

"You killed him," Trace said, voicing my thoughts.

The man ignored the accusation, cutting right to the chase. "Where is it?" he asked.

"I swear I don't know. Jesus, if I did know, don't you think I'd tell you guys?"

This only got a grunt of response on the other end. Then, "Twenty-four hours."

"What?"

"You've got twenty-four hours to produce that flash drive."

Trace's eyebrows drew together in a frown. He shook his head at the phone. "Look, I gave it to Decker. I don't know where it is now-"

"Well then you better find it," the man cut in. "Otherwise you and your agent are gonna have a whole lot more in common."

Trace and I stared at each other, letting the implication sink in.

"Twenty-four hours," the man said again. Then he hung up.

Trace stared at the phone. Then looked up at me.

"I think he just threatened to kill me," he said, stating the obvious.

I looked down at the time readout on his phone. Two thirty-three.

"You sure you don't want to call the police?" I asked. "I mean, maybe they could trace the call or put a tap on your phone or…" I trailed off. Mostly because I couldn't think of any other ways the cops really could help. And even those had been thin.

But Trace shook his head. "No. The cops will just slow us down. What we need is to find that flash drive."

I set my coffee cup down. "Okay. Where do we start?"

He paused, glancing my way. "Look, I appreciate you keeping this whole thing under wraps, but I'm not sure it's such a good idea for you to be involved."

I blinked at him. "Are you serious? We just found a dead body together. I'm pretty involved at this point."

He shook his head. "Didn't you hear that guy?" he asked, gesturing to his phone. "He just threatened to kill me. I don't think I'm the safest person for you to be hanging out with."

I paused. His concern was touching. Even though I wasn't entirely convinced it was out of the goodness of his heart and not an attempt to stave off a front page story about himself.

"Are you really concerned about my safety or just trying to get rid of me?" I asked.

He paused. "Maybe a little of both."

I narrowed my eyes.

His mouth softened. "But mostly the former."

"Look, I can take care of myself. Besides, how far do you think you're going to get without my help? You can barely move two feet in this town without some fan accosting you."

"Well, maybe if I had a better disguise…"

I rolled my eyes. "Fine. I'll work on that. Now let's go find that flash drive." I stood, dropping my cup in the trash. "You coming?"

Despite his protestations that he wanted to play lone wolf on this one, he grinned, and I wasn't totally sure I didn't see a hint of relief in his face as he said, "Right behind you, Columbo."

\* \* \*

Since the drive clearly wasn't at Decker's home, the next most logical place to look was his office.

Bert Decker worked at *the* premier talent agency in Los Angeles, a place so big that simply uttering its initials usually got you entrance to any VIP event this side of the San Gabriel Valley. Originally taking up the penthouse floors of one of Wilshire's finest high rises, it had recently relocated to its own building in Beverly Hills. Or, more accurately, its own block. The place was so massive as to be able to house the housewives of both Orange County and New Jersey without anyone being in chair-throwing distance from one another. Affectionately, it was known to most industry folks as the Death Star. Though, whether that was because of the odd architectural feature of a giant hole in the middle of the building or because it housed the most powerful forces of evil in the galaxy, no one was quite sure. Either way, to say it was a *little* imposing was like saying Megan Fox was a *little* popular with teen boys.

I couldn't help being intimidated as we pulled up in front and let the valet take my Jeep. Trace reluctantly grabbed the windbreaker again and ducked his head as we quickly slipped inside, clearly not that excited about being out in the open. Though whether he was afraid of be shot by a paparazzo's camera or a thug's gun, I couldn't say.

I followed him through the two-story-high glass doors into the massive front lobby, filled with guys in suits with Bluetooths attached to their heads. While the exterior was all black glass and chrome (in true Death Star fashion), the interior was done in white marble floors, white marble walls, and white modern furniture. The Kool Aid man's nightmare. Mounted on the ceiling was an abstract light installation posing as artwork that threw multicolored beams of light across the room. As we crossed the pink and blue beams to the reception desk, it reminded me of my first middle school dance.

On the opposite side of the chic, underfurnished lobby was a huge marble desk manned by multiple receptionists wearing headsets and fake smiles.

Ones that got measurably bigger at the sight of Trace Brody approaching.

The only reason most people took low-level jobs at the Death Star was to be able to brag to their families back in Iowa about their fleeting contact with the big stars who frequently filtered in and out of the offices. And you didn't get much bigger than Trace.

"May I help you?" asked a Hispanic brunette with a smile that had seen one too many hours under her dentist's whitening lasers.

"I'm here to see Decker," he lied.

"Of course. One moment, please." She punched a couple buttons on her keyboard, quietly speaking into her headset as she called up to Decker's assistant. After mumbling discreetly into her mouthpiece, she turned back to us.

"I'm so sorry, but he's not in the office right now."

Which, of course, we both knew all too well. We also knew he wouldn't be coming back anytime soon. However, if we were going to gain access to his office, we couldn't tip our hand.

"When will he be back?" I asked, trying to play innocent.

"I'm sorry, I can't say."

"Well, shoot," I said, putting my hands on my hips. "We really need to see him. Trace left something in his office the last time he was here. You don't mind if we just go up and wait for him, do you?" I asked.

She turned her attention to me as if noticing me for the first time. She lowered her mouthpiece, looking up at me through a pair of fake eyelashes.

"And you are?"

"Cam."

She raised an eyebrow, clearly inviting more explanation.

"Trace's assistant," I said, pointing to the man in question.

He nodded in agreement.

The plastic receptionist gave me a once over, taking in my jeans and sneakers. Hardly a power ensemble.

"Did you have an appointment with Mr. Decker?" she finally asked.

I was tempted to say yes, but I knew she'd just hop on her headset and check with Decker's assistant. Instead, I slowly shook my head back and forth.

"Not really."

"I'd be happy to have you wait here for him to return," she said, indicating the white on white lobby.

Knowing just how long that wait would be, I shook my head again. "Maybe we could just go on up and look around for it ourselves?"

"What did you say you'd lost again?" she asked. Even though we both knew I hadn't said.

Fortunately, I'd been hanging out with Tina long enough that the lies rolled right off my tongue.

"Script pages. For a movie Decker wants him to do. The producers need a decision by tomorrow, so you can understand how Trace needs to get some alone time with the pages."

I could see her desire to please her bosses warring behind her big brown eyes with her desire to please the movie star client.

Trace sent her his million-dollar, 'sexy leading man' smile. "Please? I'd really appreciate it."

That did it. I watched as she melted like a grilled cheese.

"Well, I guess I can trust *you*," she said, batting her eyelashes at him. "I'll ring his assistant and tell her you're on your way up.

"Thanks!" I gave her a cheery wave. Which, needless to say, she never even noticed, her full attention on the movie star at my side as we walked into the elevator.

Once inside, Trace hit the button for the seventh floor.

"That was pretty slick, Miss *Assistant*," he said.

"What can I say? I'm a smooth talker."

"I guess you have to be to be a member of the paparazzi."

"Was that a dig at my profession?"

"I think it was a compliment."

"Liar."

He grinned. "Takes one to know one."

Once the elevator spit us out onto the seventh floor, we made our way down a short hallway filled with offices of junior agents. As we passed the open doors I could almost feel million-dollar deals being made as they shouted phrases like, "You're golden, baby," and, "This picture has you written all over it." I tried not to salivate. I could only imagine the amount of tabloid gold being traded behind these doors. To be a fly on the wall would mean front page headlines for a month.

I followed Trace to the last door on the left and entered to find ourselves in another lobby of sorts – the office of Decker's assistant. True to her word, the receptionist downstairs must have alerted her to our presence, as the older woman behind the desk simply smiled and said, "Go right in," indicating a doorway behind her.

We did. Passing through another set of doors into Decker's private office.

Unlike the rest of the building, this room was dark – almost cave-like. The walls were covered in dark wood paneling, the floor covered with two oriental rungs in deep burgundies and navy blues to match the fabric on the navy club chairs flanking a huge mahogany desk. Atop the desk sat a brass nameplate, two brass pen holders, and a brass paperweight shaped like the MGM lion. Along the south wall of the room sat two large bookcases and a file cabinet. Directly opposite was Decker's wall of fame, sporting dozens of framed photos of Decker with his arm around all manner of important people. Decker with Julia Roberts at the Oscars, with Ray Romano at the Emmys, and with Hugh Jackman at the Tonys. Smack in the middle was a framed picture of Decker with Trace at a film opening. They were standing next to a huge poster of Trace in action-hero mode advertising *Die Tough*, while the real deal smiled at the camera, the reflections of dozens of flashbulbs lighting up the sky behind him.

My gaze flickered from the photo to the live version, scanning items on Decker's desktop. It was funny, but the more I got to know him, the odder it seemed to think of Trace in terms of celebrity. Thing is, he didn't act like a movie star. I guess I expected him to act more… dramatic maybe? When I thought movie stars I thought of Brad Pitt and Paris Hilton-esque antics. Jet-setting off to exotic locales. Dressing in designer duds. Drinking frilly coffees with fifteen different flavors of syrups in them.

I glanced over at Trace, who had moved on to Decker's desk drawers. He didn't really fit any of those. Granted the plumbing ad and baseball cap were courtesy of yours truly, but his jeans and sneakers were all him. In fact, if it weren't for the fact his face was plastered fifty feet high on billboards up and down Ventura, you'd never know Trace was anything but your average Joe. With a killer smile and abs of steel.

Again I wondered just what sort of life he might have had before becoming the worldwide franchise of "Trace Brody."

He looked up and caught my eye.

I blushed, embarrassed at being caught staring at him.

But if he thought anything of it, he didn't say so. Maybe he was used to people staring at him. "You gonna help me here or what?" he asked instead.

"Right. Sure."

I shook my head, reminding myself we were on a mission. If we didn't find that flash drive, and fast, there would be no Trace Brody, movie star or otherwise.

I turned to the file cabinet on the opposite wall and began opening drawers. Most were files of headshots and resumes of the ever-hopeful who were dying to become one of Decker's clients. A few held scripts, printed emails from studio producers, multi-page contracts. All paperwork that was making my inner tabloid girl drool, but nothing that looked like a memory stick.

Reluctantly, I moved on to the bookcases.

Fifteen minutes later Trace and I had combed every surface of the room imaginable, and I was sure the brunette receptionist downstairs was beginning to wonder where we were. I plopped down into one of the blue club chairs.

"It's not here."

Trace straightened up from the floor where he'd been feeling under Decker's desk for some sort of *National Treasure*-like secret compartment. "It has to be." He surveyed the room again. "Maybe we missed it."

I looked around the room again. There were only so many places it could be. And we'd exhausted them all. "What if Decker gave it to someone else?"

Trace frowned. "Why would he do that?"

"Well," I said, my mental gears churning. "What if Decker got curious? Your call comes about guys with guns and Decker thinks maybe something important is on the drive. Maybe he should take a look before handing it over. Let's say he was a bit of an opportunist."

Trace shot me a look. "He was a Hollywood agent."

Right. Safe assumption. "So he looks at what's on the drive. And he finds something important. Maybe incriminating. Decker thinks maybe he can shake these guys down a bit. Make a fast buck. Instead of handing the drive over, he hides it so he can barter with it later." I paused. "That sound like something Decker would do?"

"Sadly, yeah, it does. Only, it looks like our guys would rather have Decker out of the picture than make a deal with him."

"Where would Decker hide the drive? If it isn't here and it isn't at his house, who would he trust with it?"

Trace fell into the chair beside me, staring at the ceiling. "I don't know."

I let my gaze wander around the room, finally resting on Decker's desk. An appointment book lay open.

"What's this?"

Trace glanced over. "Decker's schedule."

"I didn't think anyone kept them on paper anymore."

"Decker always kept a paper copy as well as a digital one on his Blackberry. Last year he lost all his phone data when a server at Verizon crashed, including his entire schedule for the month. He ended up missing three auditions before they could restore his data. After that he always kept a paper copy."

I walked over to the desk and glanced down at the schedule.

"Didn't Decker just come back from some meeting in Vegas?" I asked.

The schedule went back to the middle of last week. I saw Friday was the night of the awards show. Four days stood between then and now. And, since it was a weekend, the appointments were pretty light. Just one, in fact. His Vegas trip booking a gig for someone named "Carla".

"Who's Carla?" I asked.

Trace came to stand next to me.

Close next to me. I tried to ignore the instant heat radiating off his body. Or maybe that was me heating up all on my own.

"I don't know," Trace said, seemingly oblivious to the reaction his nearness was causing.

I cleared my throat. Yeah, his proximity wasn't affecting me either. Not one bit.

Trace flipped on Decker's computer address book and, after a little digging, uncovered that our Carla was a Carla Constantine, an actress who, according to Decker's files, he'd booked quite a few jobs for in the last month. He'd also made notes in his past schedules to "send Carla flowers" and "buy necklace for Carla", hinting at the fact his relationship with the actress might not have been solely professional.

"Think it's possible Decker gave the stick to his girlfriend?" I asked.

Trace shrugged. "I'm starting to think that anything's possible."

## Chapter Thirteen

According to his files on Carla, the latest job Decker had booked for her was a movie of the week currently filming at Sunset Studios. In fact, she'd been scheduled for a 6:00 am call time just that morning at studio 4G. Which was a good news/bad news situation.

The bad news: the Sunset Studios lot was closed up tight unless you were on the list.

The good news: Trace was on everyone's list.

Armed with a plan, we made our way back down the elevator and out through the ultra-white lobby, pausing only a few minutes as the valet grabbed my Jeep, before hopping in and heading toward Hollywood.

Sunset Studios was located on Hollywood Boulevard, taking up a full city block. A tall stuccoed wall ran the length of it, a throwback to the studio's early days when the studio mucky-mucks tried to hide sets from the public. And from prying journalists like myself. These days, however, it was mostly for show, as we journalist types relied on cell phone photos sent by extras and crew members out to earn an extra buck for our sneak peeks of the latest sets. And, thankfully for me, no wall could keep them out.

There were two entrances to the studios: a main gate on Hollywood and a second entrance off a side street. Trace elected the latter, pulling down a palm-lined street and stopping at the iron gate as an older gentleman exited the guardhouse with a clipboard in hand.

"Name?" he asked as I rolled down the window.

"Trace Brody," I replied. Then gestured to the actor sitting in my passenger seat.

The guard leaned in the window for a better look.

Trace waved.

The guard nodded, a smile wider than the Grand Canyon cracking his wrinkled face. "My word, it is Trace Brody. How you doin' today, Mr. Brody?"

"Great. Thanks," Trace responded. He was a good enough actor that it was almost believable.

"You know, my granddaughter is a huge fan of yours. She's got your poster up in her bedroom and everything. Any chance I could get an autograph for her?"

I rolled my eyes, but somehow Trace managed to keep that genuine-looking smile on his face.

"Sure," he said.

This caused the old guy to smile even wider. He flipped to a blank page on his clipboard and handed the thing through the window to Trace. "Her name's Maggie. That's with an I-E," he directed as Trace put pen to paper, signing his John Hancock. "Boy, this is real nice of you," the old guy went on. "Did I mention what fans we are of your work? We are, Mr. Brody. Big fans."

"Thanks." Trace scribbled a signature, then handed the clipboard back across me and through the window.

"Thank *you*, Mr. Brody."

"Mind of we, uh…" Trace trailed off, pointing at the gate in front of us.

"Right. Yes. Of course, Mr. Brody. Go on through," he said, waving him toward the open gates.

"Thanks," Trace repeated.

I glanced at him, shaking my head as we drove in.

"What?" he asked.

"Is there anyone who doesn't gush like an open wound at the sight of you?"

He turned and gave me a funny sidelong look. "You don't."

I shrugged. Now was probably not a good time to mention the butterfly convention in my stomach every time he got within a foot of me.

"I'm used to dealing with celebrities," I said instead. "All my subjects are famous."

"Subjects? Jesus, you make it sound like we're items for study or something. We are human, you know?"

Yeah. My traitorous body knew that fact only too well.

Luckily, he dropped it. "Park over there," he said, indicating a lot to our right.

I did as he asked, parking just beyond the gate and swapping my Jeep out for a shiny white golf cart, the studio's transportation mode of choice. Trace jumped behind the wheel and quickly drove us through the heart of the studio lot.

I'd been to the Sunset a couple of times as a tourist on their famed studio tour where they loaded up trams full of the star struck and drove around pointing out the various film sets from famous movies. If we were lucky, something was currently filming and we might sneak a peek at one of our favorite stars. Unfortunately, in my case, the highlight of the tour had been when a guy in a Hawaiian shirt two rows up from me had dropped his camera into the fake ocean the Jaws prop lived in and they'd had to fish it out with an oar prop from the set of *Titanic*. As exciting as the tourist tour was, this was my first real behind-the-scenes glimpse of the studio.

To the right were rows of squat warehouse-looking buildings, housing the sets of hit TV shows, movies, and the occasional music video. Some were permanently dressed as the living rooms of our favorite sitcom families, and others were rented out by the day for short-term projects such as Carla's movie of the week.

On the other side of the lot were the outdoor sets, a half dozen fake cities sectioned off into various neighborhoods. There was a Manhattan street, a row of Boston brownstones, and a New Orlean's café. A block over was the pristine suburban street where the prime-time soap *Magnolia Lane* filmed their hunky gardeners and gossipy housewives. And in the center of it all was the grassy square where the high school kids on the tween cable hit *Pippi Mississippi* ate their lunches between math class and cheerleading practice. In fact, I caught a glimpse of Pippi's blonde pigtails bouncing up and down next to the ginormous fountain as Trace whisked us by on his way to studio 4G.

Which, as it turned out, was near the back of the lot among the other leased sets. A couple of white trailers sat by the front of the warehouse doors, along with a rack of costumes and some rolling spotlights. Trace parked behind the trailers and we made our way up to the warehouse doors.

Movie sets are generally chaotic. Extras mixing with crew mixing with wardrobe mixing with the hundred other people needed behind the scenes to make everything work. While security at the gate was tougher than the president's, once you were on the lot, you could pretty much go anywhere and blend in to the crowd unnoticed.

That is, unless you were Trace Brody.

A tourists tram wound past the set just as we approached the warehouse doors, the helpful guide's voice booming over the loudspeaker.

"And just to our right is studio 4G where Katie Briggs is shooting her latest TV movie. And look who's out front? It's none other than Trace Brody!"

Three dozen heads turned his way, and we were suddenly assaulted by a cacophony of digital camera flashes.

"Trace is best known for his work in the action film *Die Tough*, last summer's blockbuster hit. Smile for the people, Trace!"

Trace did a feeble wave, as he also became the star of several vacationers' home movies. While wearing a plumbing ad.

Of course by the time the tram made its way past us and on to the next studio neighborhood, every extra, crew member, and production assistant on the movie-of-the-week set had turned our way, too, and were staring at Trace with open curiosity. Not surprising since they most likely knew he was not cast in this particular movie.

"Uh… hi," Trace said, waving to the crowd in general. "Anyone know where we can find Carla Constantine?" he asked.

A guy pushing a rolling camera looked up and pointed toward the first white trailer outside. "Cast trailer is over there."

"Thanks." He waved and ducked his head down, leading the way to the trailer.

I could feel a dozen pairs of eyes on our backs as we knocked on the white aluminum door. I had to admit, it was kind of unnerving being on the other end of this celebrity watching thing.

Luckily, a beat later our knock was answered by a voice from within. "It's open!"

Glad to escape the prying eyes, we opened the door and quickly slipped inside.

The interior of the trailer looked strikingly like my apartment. Though I wasn't entirely sure the trailer wasn't bigger. A sofa was one side, a small kitchenette in the corner and a pair of recliners off to the other. A metal table held bottles of water and script pages, all marked with highlighter and scribbled notes. A small woman with dark air sat on the sofa, her forehead screwed up in concentration as she memorized her lines from the script in her hand, her mouth moving as she silently read.

"Carla Constantine?" I asked.

She shook her head. "Nope. Sorry," she responded without looking up.

"Oh. Is she here?" I glanced around the trailer for any sign of another inhabitant.

"I dunno," came her response. Bored. Annoyed. Still not bothering to look up.

"We'd really like to speak to her," Trace added.

The brunette froze. Clearly she knew that voice.

She looked up from her script. "Trace Brody," she said on a breathless gasp.

"Hi." He stuck his hand out.

She shook it, then looked down at it with an "I'll never wash this hand again" expression on her face.

The only thing better than being famous in Hollywood was knowing someone famous. Or at least having met them so they could shamelessly name-drop at the next cocktail party in the hills.

A notion this girl clearly subscribed to.

"Wow, *really* nice to meet you too. Wow, I'm so… wow. I mean, I love your work. Wow, it's just so diverse."

I rolled my eyes. "Wow", did she have some vocabulary or what?

"My name's Cindi. With an 'I.'"

Of course.

"Wow, I am, like, your biggest fan. I mean, *biggest*," she breathed. She set down her script, showing off a pair of fake breasts that bobbed up and down beneath a too-tight T-shirt as she deeply breathed in the scent of true celebrity.

"Nice to meet you," Trace said, still trying to get his hand back from her.

"Listen, we were looking for Carla," I prompted again. "Is she here?"

Cindi with an "i" shook her head. "Sorry, they wrapped her already. She's gone for the day."

Shit.

"When did she leave?" I asked, still hoping maybe we could catch her.

"About an hour ago. Why?" she asked.

"We wanted to ask her a couple questions about Bert Decker."

"Her boyfriend?"

I perked up. "So they *were* dating?"

She nodded. "Sure. He even came to visit her on the set a couple times."

"Did she mention him ever giving her something?" I asked. Then off Cindi's confused expression added, "for safekeeping maybe?"

She shook her head. "No. What sort of something?"

I bit my lip. I wasn't sure how specific I wanted to get with Miss Co-star. She didn't exactly look like the type that could keep a secret.

"Oh, I don't know, like a bit of information. On a disc? Or flash drive maybe?"

Again she cocked her head at me. "Sorry. She didn't mention anything like that. But it's not like we are BFFs or anything, ya know? We kinda run in different circles."

"Did she mention when the last time she saw Decker was?" I asked, grasping.

"Sure. He was here today."

Trace and I both leaned forward.

"He was?" I asked. "When?"

She scrunched up her button nose. "Just before we broke for lunch? He said he'd just come from the airport. He was only here to see Carla for a couple minutes."

"Did Carla mention why he stopped by?"

"Not really. But you know, she did say that Decker had some big project going. And she was helping him with it."

I wondered if said project had anything to do with the flash drive.

"Do you know where we could find her now?" Trace asked. "Did she mention where she was going when she left?"

"Oh sure," Cindi replied. "Decker had booked her a stage role. In Vegas."

Mental forehead smack. "The gig's today?" This was turning into some great wild goose chase.

"Yeah. She was heading straight to the airport. Said she had a five o'clock flight."

I pulled out my cell and looked down at the readout. 4:20. There was a slim chance…

"She flying out of Burbank?" I asked.

Cindi nodded. "I think so."

"Thanks!" I called, grabbing Trace by the arm and making a bee-line for the door.

"So nice to meet you!" Cindi called after us. Though I was pretty sure it was directed at Trace and not me.

I made only one short stop at the unattended wardrobe rack before we navigated back out of the studio lot, then roared down Hollywood Boulevard toward the Burbank airport.

There are three major airports that service the L.A. area – LAX, Burbank, and Long Beach. While Sunset Studios was technically closer to LAX, the Los Angeles International airport was the major West Coast hub, which meant a nightmare when it came to parking, ticketing security, and getting through the place without being mugged or otherwise accosted. LAX was for international travelers and tourists. Burbank was the locals' secret, the alternate solution servicing almost as many domestic flights as LAX but with half the hassle.

Though, we realized as we pulled into the main thoroughfare, that still left the other half of the hassle to deal with.

After snaking through marginally moving traffic past the runways, through the arrivals terminal and baggage claim, we finally hit the short-term parking, where, after circling just three times, we found one empty space. Next to a yellow curb. Saying a silent prayer to the parking gods, I took it, beeping my Jeep locked as we ran for the elevator up to departures. After a quick look at the monitors, we found one flight leaving for Vegas that evening at 5:00. Unfortunately, the little status line next to it read "on time." I looked down at my cell readout. 4:40.

Which meant Carla was probably already at the gate.

Which meant there was no way we were getting to her without a ticket. The gates were past the security check-point where no one ventured without a boarding pass, photo ID, and a thorough inspection for shoe bombs. Not even Trace Brody.

"Great," I said, plopping down on a plastic chair beneath the monitors. "She's probably already boarding."

Trace squinted at the monitors, his eyes scrolling down the list of departing flights. "Most likely."

"Now what do we do?"

His eyes stopped at one entry. Another flight to Vegas. He grinned. Then turned to me.

"How's your blackjack?"

## Chapter Fourteen

I might have protested that this was a long shot. That we weren't even totally sure Decker had passed the flash drive off to Carla. That, even if he had passed it to his girlfriend, she might not have it on her now. But Trace must have seen one too many of his own movies, as he was all about the long shot.

"Got any other bright ideas?" he countered when I gave him a skeptical look.

Sadly, I did not.

So I backtracked to the car and grabbed my laptop and Nikon as Trace booked us two seats on the next flight to Vegas, leaving in an hour and a half. We then made our way through security (where they made me detach all the parts of my camera in case I had hidden weapons in the lenses), then hunkered down in a pair of seats at the terminal to wait for our flight. Luckily our gate was right across the fairway from a souvenir shop where I grabbed a bottle of Vitamin Water. Then I booted up my laptop ad settled in to get a little work done while we waited. I tapped into the airport's wireless system, and downloaded the photos Felix had sent for the next day's edition. Most were of stars going to the grocery store, out to eat, running errands, or caught in their pajamas as they picked up their morning papers. I pulled up my photo-editing program and began cropping, lightening, and sharpening the photos as Trace leaned back in the seat next to me, watching the news on the TV monitors mounted in the corner of the terminal's ceiling.

I was on the last photo (Jennifer Aniston pumping gas at a Chevron on Melrose) when I was interrupted by the sound of music playing from Trace's pocket. I cocked my head to the side, recognizing the tune. It was that song from the sixties by Jimmy Soul that went, "If you wanna be happy for the rest of your life, never make a pretty woman your wife..." I raised an eyebrow at him, wondering who that particular ringtone was reserved for.

Trace pulled his phone from his pocket and hit the on button, cutting the song short.

"Hey, Jamie" he said.

I raised the other eyebrow. Iiiiiiinteresting.

I leaned a little closer. This morning I'd been practically peeing my pants with paparazzi excitement at witnessing an honest-to-God phone conversation between the golden couple. And now, while I wasn't breaking out the Depends, I couldn't help the newshound in me doing a little squee that I could actually hear the other end of the conversation this time. If I leaned over. And tilted my head toward Trace's phone. And covered the other ear. Nope, I didn't look like I was eavesdropping at all.

"What's up, babe?" Trace asked, holding the phone to his ear.

"Ugh, you know I hate it when you call me, 'babe.' I'm not some truck-stop waitress."

Geez, picky, picky, I thought.

But Trace responded with an automatic, "Sorry. What's up?"

"What's up is that I just got back from my dress fitting."

"I knew she had a dress!" I said. Apparently out loud, as Trace turned to me raising a questioning eyebrow.

Yeah, totally not eavesdropping. I clamped one hand over my mouth.

Though, from the fact that he didn't move farther away, he apparently didn't mind.

"How did the fitting go?" he asked into the mouthpiece instead.

"It was a total disaster!"

"The dress didn't fit?"

"Well, of course it fit. It's a *designer* gown *tailored* to my measurements," she shot back.

I silently willed her to mention which designer by name.

"The problem is some paparazzi prick took my picture in it."

Trace glanced my way.

"Hey, don't look at me! I was here the whole time."

"Babe, there are going to be hundreds of pictures of you in that dress. What's the big deal?"

"What's the big deal? What's the big deal!" she screeched on the other end.

Trace pulled the phone away from his ear.

"The big deal, Trace, is that our wedding isn't for another two weeks. No one is supposed to see this dress for another two weeks!" Her tone had gone from distressed right up into whiney two-year-old threatening a full-blown tantrum. I could almost picture her stomping her foot in time to her complaints. "Do you know how the press has hyped up my dress, Trace?" she asked.

Again he shot a look at me, as if I was personally responsible for a world of hype.

I blinked back innocently.

"I may have read about it," he answered.

"If pictures of my dress leak before the wedding, I'll be yesterday's news before I even walk down the aisle. Imagine what that will do to my reputation! I cannot have my first pictures of my wedding dress leaked to the public by some slimeball with a telephoto lens."

"Did this particular slimeball happen to smell of pork rinds?" I couldn't help asking.

Trace repeated my question to Jamie lee.

"God, I don't know! He was fat, gross, and had a twin."

Mike and Eddie. Dammit! I cursed under my breath. Not only had they scooped me on the wedding dress, but the second it appeared in *Entertainment Daily*, Felix would know it, too.

"This is such a disaster," Jamie Lee whined again on the other end.

I had to agree. Though for entirely different reasons.

Trace closed his eyes and sighed out loud. "Okay. What do you want me to do about it?"

"I want you to buy me a new dress," I heard Jamie Lee say.

"Great. How much?"

"One hundred and fifty thousand."

I choked on my Vitamin Water. Holy tulle and lace, Batman! That was a hell of a price tag for one little dress. I made a mental note to call that amount in to Tina as soon as I had the chance.

"Fine. Get the dress, send me the bill," Trace said into the phone.

That was it. I was so dating the wrong guys. I thought back to my last boyfriend. The most expensive thing he'd ever bought me was a pair of flip-flops at Old Navy. And those had been on sale!

"Thanks, honey," Jamie Lee responded. Gone was the whiney toddler, in her place something dripping with enough honey to attract a whole colony of flies.

"So are we fine?"

"We are now."

"Great. Listen, I may be spending the night out of town," he said.

"Fine. Whatever. Listen, I gotta go."

And before he could comment further, silence on the other end said she'd already put in her last word.

"Boy, she's a peach," I said.

He shot me a look.

"I mean, not that I was eavesdropping or anything," I quickly covered.

He shook his head. "She's not that bad," he responded, shoving his phone back in his pocket.

"Again with that phrase. You better watch out, Trace, sounds like true love to me."

"Drop it," he said, pulling a stick of gum from his pocket. He unwrapped it, biting down hard.

"If you say so." I paused. Sipped my drink. Listened to the steady hum of travelers huffing to their gates.

Finally I couldn't take the silence anymore.

"Interesting ring tone you have for her."

He grinned. "Like I said, she's not *that* bad."

I couldn't help a little snort.

"A little drama comes with the territory," he said.

"Which reminds me…" I reached into my bag and pulled out the little item I'd liberated from the wardrobe rack back at the Sunset Studios. "This is for you."

I handed it to Trace. He took it, turned it over in his hand, held it up in front of him with two fingers.

"It looks like a dead squirrel. What is it?"

"A mustache."

He looked at it again. Then back at me. "You have got to be joking."

"Hey, you're the one who complained about the lame disguise. This is much better. There's sticky tape in the bag."

"I don't think so."

I put my hands on my hips. "You'd rather be mobbed for autographs wherever we go?"

He sighed. Deeply. "Fine. Point taken." He stood and made his way to the restrooms across the walkway. Two minutes later he re-emerged with the mustache artfully affixed to his upper lip.

"How do I look?"

I bit my lip to keep from laughing. "Kinda like a seventies porn star."

"Smartass," he hissed. Though, I could tell from the way the dead squirrel was twitching, he had half a smile brewing again.

I turned back to my photo assignments, finishing up the last Aniston pic, then emailed the lot of them back to Felix, along with the candid "glistening" photo I'd taken earlier of Trace.. I looked down at the time. We still had a good forty minutes before our flight left.

Remembering our interview that morning with Ben Carlyle, I decided to indulge my earlier curiosity about Tootsie's alleged admirer – Johnny Rupert.

I pulled up the Hollywood archives database and keyed in his name.

Johnny was the small-time actor who'd landed a few minor roles in a string of films put out by Sunset Studios in the forties and fifties. While I wasn't 100% ready to rely on Carlyle's assessment of the guy, I had to admit, as I pulled up the photo of Johnny, I could well imagine him the following-a-starlet-with-his-tongue-dragging-on-the ground type. He was slim, even for those days, and short. The less-than-masculine term "petite" came to mind. His features were all just a little too small for his face – a pinched mouth, a tiny, upturned nose, and a pair of close-set eyes rimmed in thick, black lashes. His black hair was slicked back from his forehead and, in the first photo I found, he was wearing the typical suit and tie of the time. He was standing on the Sunset Studios lot, in the same courtyard Pippi Mississippi inhabited today. His suit was just a little too big in the shoulders, a little too long in the wrists, belaying the fact that it was an ill-fitting wardrobe piece and not of his own personal collection. He was posed with two other actors, both similarly clothed.

I went back to the search results, coming up with only two more pictures of the guy, both clearly taken on the same day at the studios. Although the lack of photos wasn't terribly surprising considering his lack of big credits.

I opened a new window and pulled up a news search engine, keying in Rupert's name. After scrolling though a page of hits that had nothing to do with my Rupert, I finally came across a link to an old newspaper article detailing how he had, indeed, died in a car crash in the eighties. He'd been out with a Ralph Kingsly, another actor, on their way to Las Vegas for the weekend when they'd been struck by a semi truck whose driver had fallen asleep at the wheel and jumped the median. Johnny had been in the passenger seat and died instantly. His buddy, Ralph, had been airlifted to a nearby hospital and listed in critical condition at the time of the accident.

I wondered if Ralph had made it. I plugged his name into the internet movie database, searching for credits. A small list of roles came up under his name, indicating that he hadn't been mortally wounded in the crash. Though nothing was listed past 1970, when he'd apparently made his last film. I made a mental note to look for Mr. Kingsly when I got home.

Since I still had a few idle minutes, I decided to follow the one other we had as well: Becky Martin.

Here I came up with quite a few more hits, Becky apparently having appeared in quite a few films, many of them beside Tootsie. In fact, she'd taken over the lead role in the film Tootsie had been shooting at the time of her death. Hmmm… suspicious indeed. Carlyle hadn't mentioned this fact, though I had a feeling his sights were so set on Johnny, Becky's possible guilt hadn't even entered his mind.

I leaned in for a closer look at the girl. She was younger than Tootsie, probably early twenties if the fine layer of baby fat on her face was any indication. She was blonde, like Tootsie had been, though her hair had a platinum quality that appeared almost white in the black and white photos. Her nose was a little too big for her face – something that certainly would have been taken care of by Dr. B had she rose to stardom in modern times – but her eyes were big, blue, and rimmed in enough mascara to make her look like a china doll. Her hair was worn in a close-cropped bob, her bangs clipped just above her penciled in eyebrows. In several of the photos she wore a bow cocked off to the side.

But for all her attempts at a fresh, innocent look, her big blue eyes held the unmistakable glint of a calculating woman, a young lady who was on a mission to stardom no matter who got in her way.

I scrolled through the photos to see if I could come up with anything more recent, though she seemed to disappear after that last film.

Undaunted, I plugged her real name into my search engine. A few clicks later, I finally found what I was looking for. An obituary for a Rebecca Lubenschwartz. Or, as she was referred to in the article, Mrs. Schlomo Goldenfink nee Lubenschwartz. Talk about a mouthful.

She'd passed away in a nursing home outside Cleveland just last year after a long battle with Alzheimer's. The obit was short, sweet, and to the point, mentioning that she was survived by two children and a dozen grandchildren. Nothing alluding to her life as Becky Martin. I wondered if this was per her wishes. Had she taken off for Cleveland to outrun Becky Martin? Out of guilt perhaps?

Beside the obituary sat a photo of the late Ms. Lubenschwartz. I stared into the wrinkled face. Age had been kind to Becky, softening the hard look in her eyes, converting the baby fat to a strong jaw line that time had not touched. She wore a network of wrinkles next to her eyes, but they hung more like comfortable laugh lines than unsightly flaws. All in all, she looked like someone's jovial grandmother. Just as with Carlyle, I had a difficult time picturing her as a killer.

I downloaded the articles I could find and compacted them all into one file, saving the lot of it to my hard drive.

I was just sending the whole file off to Max when I looked up to find an older couple staring at Trace from across the terminal.

Great. More fans.

The guy wore a Hawaiian shirt and khaki trousers above topsiders, while the wife was dressed in capris and a blue hair scrunchie. Clearly out of towners.

The wife nudged her husband. "It's him," she whispered, pointing at Trace.

Here we go again.

Only the husband shook his head. "I don't think so, honey."

I glanced at Trace. Huh. What do you know, maybe the mustache was working.

"No, no, I'm certain. It's him. I mean, look at him. He looks just like the guy in that movie."

"What are the chances it's really him, darling?"

The wife shook her head. "No. I'm positive." She left her husband's side and in two quick steps was beside Trace.

"Excuse me," she said timidly.

Trace, thus far oblivious to the whole exchange between husband and wife, pulled his eyes from the TV news to face her. "Yes?" he asked.

"I don't mean to bother you, but I was wondering if I could ask…" her voice dropped to a whisper. "You're him aren't you? That actor?"

Trace pulled a forced smile. I could tell even he was getting weary of the fan-club routine. "Yes, I'm afraid I am."

The wife blushed. "Oh, my. See, I told you so, Harold."

The husband shrugged. "Well when the little lady's right, she's right."

"Oh, we just loved you in *You've Got Shemale*."

I choked on my Vitamin Water. "You've got what?"

The wife blinked. "The adult film. You know, the naughty spoof of that Trace Brody film, *You've Got Email?* I'd recognize that mustache anywhere. You were so good as the actor spoofing Brody." She glanced down at Trace's wee-willie-winkie region. "*So* good."

Trace opened his mouth to speak. But only a strangled sound in the back of his throat came out.

I swallowed a snicker. Okay, I tried to swallow it, but it came out anyway. "He was good, wasn't he?" I asked.

"Do you think we could get your autograph?" the wife asked.

Trace coughed into his hand, regaining control of himself, and mumbled, "Sure."

But not before shooting me a dirty look.

The husband thrust a napkin and Sharpie at the actor. Trace signed an indistinguishable scribble, , all the while turning three deep, lovely shades of red so that by the time they finally walked away he was nearing crimson.

As soon as they rounded the corner, he ripped the mustache off and tossed it a nearby garbage bin.

"That's it. You do *not* get to pick out my disguise anymore."

I nodded. Then snickered again.

I was about to make a wisecrack about his newfound fame, when a voice from the TV news in the corner caught my attention.

"...the body of a prominent Beverly Hills agent."

Uh oh.

Both Trace and I whipped our heads around to the TV as one.

A female newscaster droned on as a photo of the dead man in question appeared next to her.

"Bert Decker, a top agent in Hollywood, representing such talented actors as Trace Brody, was found dead in his Burbank home today by a neighbor. Sources have confirmed that police are looking at his death as a homicide."

Double uh oh. I turned to Trace to speak.

Only I didn't get that far, as the next words from the newscaster's mouth stopped me dead in my tracks.

"Police say they have a lead on the killer as DNA has been collected from hair fibers at the crime scene from an unknown source. While police have yet to put a name to the DNA profile, they can tell us that the hairs are from a blonde female."

I looked down at my hair.

Oh. Shit.

## Chapter Fifteen

"I'm an unknown assailant!" I yelled.

Trace clamped a hand over my mouth. "Jesus, you want the whole airport to know?" he mumbled.

I looked around. Two businessmen in the seats next to me were staring. Trace gave them his hundred-watt smile, nodding comfortingly, as he unclamped my mouth.

In deference to them, I pseudo-whispered this time. "You made me an unknown assailant! They have my DNA"

"Relax, they need a known sample to compare it to."

I shot him a look.

"What? I watch *CSI*, too."

"What are we going to do?" I asked.

As if to answer me, the reporter at the news desk piped up again. "Police say the hair fibers were found on the gate leading into Decker's backyard. They are currently looking into the identity of this unknown female."

"Fabulous!" I threw my hands up in the air.

"You're fine," Trace said, leaning back in his chair again, taking on that practiced casual pose he did so well. It was his "buddy film" look – smooth, slightly snarky, everyone's best friend but just a little on the mischievous side, too.

Only this audience wasn't buying it.

"Fine? Fine! I'm wanted!"

"They have a piece of hair, not a name. Look, if they actually suspected you, they would be marching through the airport to arrest you already."

I whipped my head right then left, wildly scanning the corridor for any sign of cops with guns drawn.

Thank God, I saw none.

Yet.

"Relax, Cam," he said.

I sat back in my seat and crossed my arms over my chest in an instinctively protective gesture. "Easy for you to say. It's not your hair fiber!"

"Look, let's just get that flash drive and everything will be fine."

He leaned his head back on the rest, closing his eyes, effectively ending the discussion.

Even though I wasn't so sure it would be that easy. Sure, if we turned the flash drive over to these guys, Trace's life expectancy would be going up significantly. But what about Decker's murder? And my DNA at the scene? I wasn't sure that just getting these guys off Trace's back was going to solve all my problems. Like it or not, the cops were involved now. And they weren't exactly on our side.

Exactly how I got myself into these situations, I wasn't sure. But I was so asking for a raise when this was all over.

\* \* \*

Twenty minutes later we boarded the plane, Trace pulling his ball cap down low over his eyes as we made our way through the connector tunnel. I saw him cast a longing glance at the first-class seats, but we'd both agreed that he'd be much more incognito traveling in coach. A decision I regretted the minute I sat down. I was wedged between a French guy who apparently didn't believe in American deodorant and a woman carrying a Chihuahua in a lap bag. The little dog yipped loudly as I sat down.

A mere hour and a thousand yips later, we landed at McCarren International where we grabbed a cab and made straight for the Victoria Club, which turned out to be a shiny mass of building done in art deco black and gold and trimmed with lots and lots of pink neon lighting. Unfortunately they didn't open until nine. I looked down at my watch. 7:35.

"Now what?" I asked.

Trace surveyed the street. It was in the older part of town, near the original downtown area. While the place had been cleaned up significantly in recent years, once again making the neon lit Fremont Street a tourist destination, the fringes of the neighborhood still spoke of the hard times the town had suffered. The Victoria Club was nestled between a pawn shop, a quickie wedding chapel that boasted "free buffet voucher with every marriage" and across the street from a hotel/casino sporting a flashing sign that read, "The Cowboy Cabana." I'd swear the exterior of the place hadn't been updated since Bugsy Siegel ran the place.

"Let's grab something to eat," Trace said, indicating the casino.

For lack of a better idea, I nodded in agreement. In all the commotion, I suddenly realized I hadn't eaten since breakfast. Mundane bodily functions like eating and sleeping had fallen to the wayside. But, faced with a little downtime, my stomach was rumbling something fierce.

We crossed the street and made our way through the smoky casino filled with slot machines and peeling blackjack tables. Unlike the rest of the country, Vegas maintained its status as a city of vice by being one of the only metropolises in the country to still allow smoking in public places. Even if those public places were restricted to casinos and brothels.

We made our way through the tobacco haze to the back of the casino to find the registration desk. An Asian guy in a cowboy hat sat behind the desk.

"May I help you?" he asked as we approached.

Trace gave him his hundred-watt smile.

"Great hat. We'd like to get a room, please?"

"Do you have a reservation?" he asked in heavily accented English.

I shook my head. "Do we need one?"

"Today special. No reservation required!" He clapped his hands to indicate just how "special" this was. Then he pulled a keyboard out from under the desk and turned to his monitor. "What size do you want?"

"A double, please," Trace answered.

"You in luck. We have one double available. Is very nice room."

"We'll take it," Trace said.

"We running special on this room today. You book two nights and get a free helicopter ride over Lake Mead."

"We'll just take the room, thanks," I said.

He shook his head. "Okay, I throw in free tickets to visit Hoover Dam. How about that, huh?"

Trace grinned. "I've never been to the Hoover Dam."

I elbowed him in the ribs. "Just the room for the one night, please."

"Okay, okay. You drive hard bargain. How about this? I give you honeymoon special – you book two nights and I throw in two tickets to see David Copperfield magic at the MGM and a bottle of our finest champagne?"

"I've never seen David Copperfield," Trace said.

I elbowed him again. Harder.

"Ouch!"

"Just the room, please."

The guy behind the desk put his hand up in a surrender motion. "Okay, okay. Just the room." He turned to Trace. "She no fun, huh?"

He grinned. "None at all."

I rolled my eyes.

"Name?" the guy asked.

"Smith."

He glanced up at the two of us under the brim of his hat. Then snorted. "Ah. Of course. Mr. *Smith.*" But he punched the name into the system anyway.

"Credit card?" he asked.

Trace bit his lip. Then turned to me with a whisper. "My name's on my credit card. It might be best if you…"He trailed off, doing a sheepish grin.

Seriously? Jamie Lee got a hundred-thousand-dollar dress and I got the room bill?

"Fine." I fished my wallet out of my bag and handed it to the man.

He glanced at the name on the card, raised one eyebrow, but, considering I wasn't a mega-movie star, he didn't mention the discrepancy. My guess was the place saw a number of "Mr. & Mrs. Smiths" filter through their doors each day.

After running my card and having me sign a slip saying I was liable for any extensive damages to the room, he handed Trace the room key.

"Four fifteen. Take the elevator on the right. You need help with your bags?" he asked, scanning behind us for nonexistent luggage.

"Nope. Got it. Thanks!" I said, steering Trace away from the desk.

"Enjoy your stay!" I heard him yell as we made our way to the elevator near the restrooms.

"What was that all about?" I asked once the elevator doors had closed.

"What?"

"'I've never seen the Hoover Dam.'"

He shrugged. "You don't exactly get to do touristy things when you're 'Trace Brody,'" he said, making air quotes with his fingers.

I shot him a look.

He grinned. "Relax. I wasn't actually going to take him up on it. If was just kinda nice to imagine for a minute."

Again, I felt like I was getting a small peek at the man behind the celebrity. I felt privileged… and unnerved all at the same time. Since me and my kind were the prime reason Trace didn't get to do touristy things. For the first time in my life, I felt kinda guilty. It wasn't a fun feeling. I swallowed it down as we exited the elevator, instead immediately pouncing on the room service menu as we hit the room. Unfortunately, this was not the billion-dollar a year Vegas Strip… and the menu reflected that. Cheeseburgers, ribs, and steak sandwiches dominated. I wrinkled my nose, finally settling on a side salad and a fruit plate.

"I thought you were hungry," Trace teased after putting in our order. (He, I noticed, went with the steak sandwich *and* the cheeseburger. How he kept his movie-star figure eating like that, I'd never know.)

"Hungry? Yes. Willing to put crap in my body just to fill my stomach? No."

He grinned. "Don't tell me you're one of those health nuts?"

"I prefer the term health conscious to health nut."

He rolled his eyes. "Jamie Lee's like that, too. Fat-free everything. If it has more than fifty calories in it, she can't have it in her refrigerator."

I shook my head. "No, I'm not a calorie counter."
Anymore. "I just… okay, take that burger you just ordered for
instance. Do you know where that comes from?"

"A cow?" He grinned again, clearly humoring me.

"Right. A cow. And where did the cow come from?"

"His mama cow?"

"Smartass."

He winked at me.

I ignored him with no small effort. God, he had a sexy
wink. "The cow likely came from some overcrowded farm
where he spent the bulk of his life in a pen not even big enough
turn around in to keep him from growing muscles. Muscles
produce less tender beef. Fatter cows give the good stuff. So
he's fed a steady diet of fattening foods and hormones designed
to make him grow faster, thus maximizing profits. Hormones
that are stored in his fat cells go into the meat you eat."

"Yuck."

"No kidding. But it doesn't stop there. Now, because he's
cooped up in the pen next to a bazillion other cows all cooped up
in their pens, diseases run rampant through these farms. So, Mr.
Future Cheeseburger is pumped full of antibiotics to keep him
from getting sick. All of which are stored in the fatty tissues
which then end up in your burger."

Trace cocked his head at me, seeming to take all this in.
Then he finally grinned. "But cheeseburgers are yummy."

My turn to roll my eyes. "Then chow down. But I think I'll
stick to my salad, thank you."

"Really? I mean, do you know where that lettuce comes
from?"

"Ha. Ha. Very funny."

"No, I'm serious," he said. Even though his eyes were still
laughing at me. "Unless that stuff's organic, which, considering
the venue here, I highly doubt, it comes from a farm that was
sprayed with pesticides to keep the bugs from eating crops.
Lettuce grows in layers. Each layer was sprayed with pesticides
before the next layer formed around the head, effectively sealing
the poison in. Not to mention the ground the roots are anchored
in is soaked in pesticides as well, meaning that not only is your

food coated in it, it's in the very cells of the plant. It's like one big poison ball by the time it gets to your plate."

I opened my mouth to protest, but he didn't let me finish.

"Oh, and it doesn't stop there," he went on, mocking me word for word. "Let's talk about the dressing for a minute, shall we? Hydrogenated vegetable oils, high-fructose corn syrup, preservatives, artificial flavors. That stuff is like injecting plastic right into your veins. Those oils will clog you faster than five cheeseburgers would. But if you want to go ahead and eat your poison-and-plastic salad, be my guest."

He finished with a self-satisfied smirk and plopped down onto the opposite bed, lacing his hands behind his head.

I waited a beat. Then couldn't help it. I broke out into laughter. Damned it if he hadn't beaten me at my own game. I grabbed a pillow and swatted him with it.

"You suck!"

"Hey, you started it," he said, putting his arms up to fend off my attack.

"Fine. We're even, health boy."

"Good. Now, if you don't mind, I'm going to go take a shower while I wait for my death on a plate to arrive."

I watched Trace cross the room into the little attached bathroom and listened as he turned the water on. I had to admit, I was impressed at his knowledge of food health. Even if he had used it against me. Not that it was news to me. I'd just read an article in *Vegetarian Today* on that very thing the other day. Apparently Trace had read it, too.

Interesting. I'd had him pegged as more of the *Maxim* reader.

I leaned back on the bed, clasping my hands behind my head the way I'd seen Trace do just a moment ago. As I listened to the sound of his shower, I found myself wondering just what other things I didn't know about Trace.

* * *

Once the food arrived and we both indulged in our poison of choice, I opted for a short nap while Trace said he wanted to do a little shopping downstairs. Considering he was still wearing my brother's tourist shirt, I didn't blame him. I was just stretching the sleep out of my limbs an hour later when Trace came back.

His tourist look was definitely history. Now he was dressed in a pair of pointy-toed, black cowboy boots, a chambray shirt, and a white Stetson hat that was an exact copy of the guy at the reception desk.

I stifled a laugh.

"Yeehaw, partner."

Trace grinned. "You like?"

"Like is a strong word," I hedged.

"My new disguise. I'm a cowboy."

"I can see that." I bit my lip as he did a little twirl for me to inspect the getup from all angles.

"Well, I'll say one thing for it. It's definitely not Hollywood."

"Perfect. Now let's go find Carla."

\* \* \*

Ten minutes later we were back across the street at the Victoria Club. After paying our cover charge, getting our hands stamped with symbols indicating we were over 21, and pushing through the crowd at the bar clogging the entrance, we were treated to our first look at the interior of the club.

A large dance floor to the right was bathed in strobe lights and packed wall to wall with gyrating bodies. Ahead of us was a scattering of tables and tiered booths angled down to a huge stage, currently vacant. And to the left was a glass and neon bar that spanned the length of the wall, again packed with tourists, local partiers, and the occasional working girl.

It took all of three seconds before a girl in the crowd (in a skirt short enough to be "working" but with an accent that clearly said she was from out of town) shouted, "Trace Brody?"

So much for cowboy incognito.

"My disguise was better," I whispered to him as he was quickly surrounded by club goers, all shoving Sharpies in his face. He pulled out his "on" face and obliged as I squeezed through the star-struck tourists toward the bar.

Behind it were two guys busy pouring pink, purple, and green drinks into fancy martini glasses. I hailed the larger of the two as he made his way to our end of the bar.

"Excuse me!'" I shouted, waving a hand his direction.

"Can I help you?" he asked, leaning over the bar towards me.

"We're looking for a Carla Constantine?" I shouted above the noise.

Though, apparently not quite above *enough* as the bartender shouted back, "What?"

"Carla Constantine!"

This time he nodded, then pointed to the stage set up in the back. "She's about to go on."

"Thanks!"

I threaded my way back through the crowd to Trace (still signing autographs – tough life, huh?) and, once he'd appeased the crowd of adoring fans, dragged him to a table near the stage.

"Our girl's about to go on," I told him.

No sooner had the words left my mouth than a booming voice cut through the canned music.

"Ladies and gentlemen, please put your hands together for the Go-Go-Girls!"

The crowd complied as one, clapping as instructed as the lights dimmed and shadowy figures took the stage. A rare moment of silence descended on the room before the first strains of the song "Walk Like an Egyptian" rang out through the room.

Cheers went up at the same time the lights did, illuminating the band.

I did a double take.

On the stage was the Go-Go's all-girl band circa the 1980s. The same Belinda Carlisle blonde hair, the same pixie-looking brunette on guitar, the same pop sound, tight leggings, and big hair. The only difference between the Victoria Club's version and the originals is that the real Go-Gos were all girls. These five performers were men. Badly disguised men, if Belinda's five o' clock shadow was any indication.

I felt Trace lean in next to me and whisper in my ear. "You've got to be kidding me."

Sadly, I didn't think they were.

I watched, wondering just which one of these "ladies" had been dating Decker as they walked like Egyptians all over the stage.

As the first number ended, and they transitioned into a rendition of "Vacation," I caught the eye of the bartender and mouthed the word, "Carla?"

He pointed to Belinda Carlisle.

Fabulous.

Three musical time warps to the eighties later, the band took a break and I made a beeline for Belinda as she teetered off stage in a pair of size-fifteen pumps.

I tapped him (her?) on the shoulder.

She (he?) spun around.

"Um… Carla Constantine?" I asked.

The person in question nodded, answering in a deep baritone. "In the flesh, honey. Who's asking?"

"Uh, my name is Cameron Dakota. I work for the *L.A. Informer*. And this is Trace." I gestured behind me to the actor.

Trace waved from his spot at our table.

Carla raised two drawn-in eyebrows. "Wow. I'm impressed. Mr. Big Shot himself coming to check out lil' old me in the show?"

"Uh, right." I said, nodding. "We were wondering if we could ask you a couple questions. Do you have a minute?"

"For Trace Brody? Are you kidding?"

Carla made straight for the table before I could even respond. She sat down opposite Trace and began shaking one of Trace's hands in both of her big paws.

"I am *so* happy to meet you. I am such a fan of your work. In fact, I almost died when Decker told me he represented you. I mean, that was like, what, one degree of separation between me and the Trace Brody, right?" Carla giggled. "Anyway, I am honored, thrilled, and tickled pink that you'd come see my show."

"Sure. You're welcome," Trace said. Though the hitch in his voice betrayed the fact that he was not entirely comfortable with the way she was caressing his hand.

"Uh, listen, Carla…" I paused looking down at his frilly mini-skirt. "Uh, it is Carla, isn't it?"

She nodded. Still not taking her eyes off Trace. Still not giving his hand back.

"Okay. Carla it is. Um, we had a question to ask you. About Decker. You two were dating?" I asked.

Again she nodded. "We've been seeing each other going on six months now."

"Right." Though, his use of the present tense meant he hadn't yet heard the news about Decker's demise. I bit my lip. I certainly didn't want to be the one to break it to him. My people skills where better behind a lens on a good day. I wasn't entirely sure how to deal with a six-foot-tall cross-dressing crier.

So I decided to keep with the present tense.

"I understand you met with him earlier today. At the Sunset Studios. Is that right?"

She nodded, her wig bobbing up and down. "That's right. We were discussing an audition I went on last week. It was for a Swiffer commercial. I was playing the messy dad, of all things."

I couldn't help raising an eyebrow.

Carla shrugged. "What can you do? It was a national commercial. They pay bank! There's not much we won't do for the almighty dollar, right? Decker said it just goes to show my range. I'm pretty sure I nailed it. I haven't heard back from Decker yet, but fingers crossed." She illustrated by letting of Trace's hand and crossing her digits.

Trace looked immeasurably relieved.

Me? I still didn't have the heart to tell Carla that I was pretty sure Decker wouldn't be calling him anytime soon.

"Did you and Decker discuss anything else today?"

She narrowed her heavily lined eyes. "Like what?"

"Well…" I looked at Trace for help.

"Did he give you anything for safekeeping?" he asked, clearly out of time for beating around the bush.

Carla looked from Trace to me and back again. I could see her eyes questioning just how much she should trust us. But I guess celebrity had its advantages, as she finally nodded.

"Yes. He did."

Trace sat up straighter in his seat.

"A flash drive?"

Again the nod.

"Do you still have it?" Trace asked, leaning forward.

"Why?" Carla asked.

Good question. Luckily, Trace was used to improvising.

"It has some information on it that I need."

"What kind of information?"

"A script."

"What kind of script?"

"A secret one."

"Huh."

"So can we have it?" Trace asked. I could feel him holding his breath as Carla sat back and crossed her arms (covered in pink jelly bracelets) over her well-padded chest, contemplating the two of us. I tried not to look as if Trace's life might depend on the answer.

Finally she smiled.

"Okay. Sure. For Trace Brody? Anything."

I let out a sigh of relief. I must be a better actress than I thought.

"Great," Trace breathed, mirroring my relief.

"Only I don't have it."

I rolled my eyes. Here we went again with the goose chase thing.

"I mean," she clarified, "not on me. It's at my place."

"Where is your place?" Trace asked, his posture rigid.

"Behind the strip.'

"Great. Let's go."

"Now?" Carla blinked big, wide eyes at us.

"If you don't mind?"

"Well, I guess I am done with my set…"

"Excellent. Let's go!" Trace stood.

"I'm parked out back," Carla said. Then she led the way through the crowd of people packed into the club.

Trace and I followed, threading our way through the crowd that was still dancing, this time to a male version of the material girl doing a solo up on the stage.

I struggled to keep up with Carla, amazed how agile he was in those high heels. He quickly jogged (yes, jogged. In four-inch heels!) through the crowd toward the back of the club. I saw Trace trying to elbow his way through by my side, all the while keeping his hat pulled low to avoid being mobbed by slightly inebriated tourists. Carla pulled ahead a few people, and I struggled to keep sight of his blonde wig through the masses. It was almost as if she was trying to lose us….

Oh shit.

A sinking feeling suddenly took hold in my gut.

I saw Carla hit the back of the club, then disappear through a door marked with a glowing green "exit" sign.

"I lost him," I heard Trace say in my ear, panting as he caught up.

"There. Out the back door," I indicated, rushing toward it.

We pushed our way through the crowd milling at the bar, finally plowing through the exit a mere few seconds after Carla.

We were in a parking lot off the back of the club. At current it was full of cars ranging from idling limos to beat-up Chevys. I quickly scanned the rows for any sign of Carla. And, considering I was looking for a six foot drag queen, it shouldn't have been hard to spot him.

Only I saw nothing.

I was just about to give up and go back inside when I heard the roar of a motor. Trace must have heard it too, as we both whipped our heads around in unison toward the left. An alley lined with green Dumpsters hugged the side of the building, its width filled with a tall woman in a mini skirt and a Belinda Carlisle wig on a motorcycle. She gunned the engine and race out of the back lot, down the neighboring street.

Sinking feeling realized.

"I have a bad feeling we may have been ditched," Trace said beside me.

Gee, ya think?

# Chapter Sixteen

We stared at the spot where the motorcycle had been, its exhaust still hanging in the air. Both of us were silent as it sunk in that our only lead had just taken off.

"I'm gonna kill him." Trace clenched his fists at his sides.

"Never trust a guy dressed as Belinda Carlisle," I said.

"I'm gonna tear him limb from pantyhose-clad limb." And from the way his "gangster movie tough guy face" had slid into place, I kinda believed him.

We went back into the club and spent the rest of the evening questioning the remaining Go-Go's. But apparently no one knew specifically where Carla was staying while she was in town for this gig. All we could gather was that she was staying with a friend – either Amy or Annie, depending on who you asked - off the strip.

In lieu of a better plan, we went back to our room at the Cowboy Cabana.

I booted up my laptop. If there was any way to find this Carla, the *Informer*'s databases were it. I typed the name "Amy" in the directory of phone numbers in Vegas. Of course about a million popped up, but I narrowed it down to those living within a mile radius of Las Vegas Boulevard.

Great. Only half a million left.

I leaned back on the bed, blowing out a big puff of air.

Trace, on the other hand, seemed to be wired, pacing back and forth across the hotel floor like he was going to wear a hole in the carpet.

"Don't worry. We'll find it," I said, amazed at how reassuring my voice sounded despite my lack of real conviction.

"Right. Sure." Though he didn't sound any more convinced than I was.

Okay, so we'd hit a little dead end. Maybe we needed to go at this whole thing a different way. Maybe instead of complying with the bad guys' demands, we should be trying to figure out just who these guys were.

I pulled up a Yahoo! search screen. "What was the name of the car company you said you used the night of the awards show?" I asked.

Trace rattled it off. "Arrive in Style. In West Hollywood."

I typed the name into the search engine box. Two seconds later I had a list of hits and clicked on the first one, taking me to the company's website. I highlighted the phone number and dialed, putting my phone on speaker so Trace could hear. Four rings in, someone picked up.

"Arrive in Style car service, how may I help you?" a nasally, female voice inquired on the other end.

"Hi, my name is Cameron Dakota. I'm Trace Brody's assistant," I said, going with my previous lie.

"How may I help you, Ms. Dakota?"

"Trace used your car service last Friday for an awards show arrival. I need some information about the car he was driven in."

"Okay, just one moment, please," she said, and I heard the sound of a keyboard clacking in the background. A minute later she came back on the line. "Yes I see that Mr. Brody ordered a car to drop him off in Hollywood outside the Palms Theater. The car was a Lincoln, black, wet bar in the back."

"That's it," Trace said.

"Can you tell me who the last person before Trace to use that particular car was?"

There was a pause on the other end. "I'm sorry, I can't give out our clients' names."

Right. Of course not. I bit my lip. "What about the driver of the vehicle? Can you tell me who that was?"

"Certainly."

A few more clicks, then she responded with, "Paul Haverston. He's been with us for years."

"Years, huh?" I felt my hopes fading. If he valued his job, the driver wouldn't be giving out personal client info any easier than the woman on the phone. Still, I had to ask. "Would it be possible for me to speak with Paul?"

"I'm sorry he's not available right now. He's driving another client." She paused. "Was there a problem with the car?" she asked.

"No, it was fine," I reassured her. "We just…" I paused, racking my brain for a good reason Trace might be so inquisitive. "He… could smell someone's cologne lingering in the car. And it was such a great scent that he wanted to know what it was so he could purchase a bottle for himself."

Trace raised one eyebrow, a grin spreading across his face.

"Oh," the woman on the other end of the phone said. "I see. Well, I wish I could help you, but again, company policy is to protect the privacy of our clients. I'm sure someone of Mr. Brody's status understands. I mean, for all we know, you could be a member of the paparazzi digging for a juicy story, right?"

I cleared my throat.

Trace bit back a grin.

"Right. Sure. You never know, huh?"

"Exactly," she agreed. "But I'll ask our driver about the scent when he gets back in. Maybe he can shed some light on it for you."

"Great. Thanks," I mumbled.

"Cologne, huh?" Trace said when I hung up. "Nice call."

I blushed, pretty sure it was wrong to be so pleased by his praise over my dishonesty.

"I hope that wasn't a comment on my scent," he said.

I felt my blush deepen. "No!" I said, a little too loudly. "I mean, no, it's fine."

"Fine? Hmm. Not exactly a rave review."

"I mean, it's nice. Really nice. You smell great."

He grinned. "You're blushing."

I ducked my head. "No I'm not."

"It's cute."

I crossed to the thermostat on the wall, partly to check if my scorching temperatures were internal or external and partly just to have something to do other than sit there and blush like a dweeb.

"Unfortunately," Trace said, apparently oblivious to the sudden heat wave in the room, "your excellent deceptive work doesn't get us a whole lot closer to the identity of our mystery men."

"You know," I said, thinking out loud as I sat back down on the edge of the bed, "if we couldn't get the name of the previous clients out of the company, chances are the bad guys couldn't get your name out of them either."

Trace grinned. "The 'bad guys'?"

"Well, what do you want to call them?"

His grin widened. "Let's go with bad guys. It's cute."

"That's twice in one night I've been cute. You better watch out or I'll give Jamie Lee a run for her money."

Trace raised an eyebrow. "I'd like to see that."

Oh God. There went that blush again.

I cleared my throat. "Anyway, it seems unlikely the company would give your name to the…"

"Bad guys," Trace finished with a smile. "Okay, so they can't get my name. And that means…?"

"It means – how did they know it was you who rode in the limo after them? That you were the one that picked up the flash drive?"

He raised both eyebrows. "Good point, tabloid girl."

"Thank you. So let's assume the ba-" I stopped myself.

Trace raised an expectant eyebrow.

"Our unknown assailants," I switched.

He grinned at me again.

I tried to ignore it. Not an easy task when he'd had years of practice making women the world over swoon with that same set of pearly whites.

Instead, I shifted a little farther away from him. "The unknown assailants get to wherever they've been driven, and they realize they've lost the drive. They call the car company looking for it. The company checks the car – no flash drive. Our bad guys have to assume that whoever was in the car after them must have taken it. So how do they find out it was you?"

"They must have seen me in the car. Easy enough thing considering the amount of cameras on me as I arrived that night."

I sat up straighter. As far as I knew, Trace's car had not been shown on the red carpet pre-shows. And I knew pretty well, having been glued to them all for any glimpse of Trace or Jamie Lee. While my tabloid status hadn't actually garnered me an invite to the red carpet, I still had my Wedding Watch duty to report on the event the next day (a.k.a. to speculate on the happy couple's status and couture).

I relayed this info to Trace. "So," I concluded, "these guys must have been at the event in person. Would that be possible? I mean, that the car would have had time to drop them off at the event, then double back to pick you up directly afterward?"

Trace nodded, the look in his eyes suggesting that the little hamster on his mental wheel was picking up speed. "It *is* possible. I drove down from Malibu to Decker's place earlier in the afternoon. The limo was just to make a showy entrance, so we really only rode in it for a total of ten minutes from his place to the awards."

"What time did the car pick you up?"

"Ten to six."

I raised an eyebrow. I knew the awards show had started at six on the dot.

"The bigger name you are the later you arrive," Trace explained. "At least that's what Decker says." He winced. "Said," he corrected himself.

Since I didn't really have any words of comfort, I glossed over the verb-tense gaffe and focused on the lead at hand.

"Let's say the car drops the bad guys off at the event, then takes ten minutes to swing by Decker's and pick both of you up. That sounds totally doable."

"So we've narrowed it down to the guest list at the awards show. That's what, only a thousand people?"

I slumped back down in my seat. "Two actually."

"Great."

I opened my mouth to attempt something reassuring when my cell rang out from my pocket. I pounced on it, hoping maybe the Arrive in Style lady had changed her mind.

"Cameron Dakota?" I answered.

"Hey, Cam. It's Allie."

The tension drained out of my shoulders. "Oh. Hi."

It must have drained out of my voice, too, as Allie answered back with a, "Well, gee, don't sound so enthused to hear from me."

"Sorry. I was just expecting a call from someone else."

"Who?" she asked, and I could fairly hear her jumping into journalist mode.

"No one important," I hedged. "What's up?"

"Okay. Um, well, some guy just called here looking for you. He left a message."

"Who was it?"

"That's the weird thing. It was clearly a guy's voice, but he said to say it was 'Carla.'"

The tension returned with a vengeance, and I hit the speaker button to let Trace in on the call.

"What did he say?" I demanded of Allie.

"Um, well, it was kind of a strange message."

"Hit me."

"He said that he has the item you're looking for. And, if Trace would like, he can purchase it for a hundred thousand."

"Dollars?" I asked, fairly choking at the amount.

"I guess."

"Sonofa-" Trace started.

"Who was that?" Allie piped up on the other end. "Was that Trace?"

I swatted Trace on the arm. "No. It was no one important."

"O-kay." Yeah, she believed that about as much as she believed the Loch Ness Monster was going to rise out of the water for a photo op with Big Foot. "What's this item? What is Trace selling to this guy?"

"Nothing important," I quickly shot back.

"Right. Nothing." She may be the queen of co-eds, but even she wasn't stupid enough to believe that. But luckily she was smart enough to know it was all she was getting out of me.

"Was that all he said?" I asked.

"'Carla' said he'd meet you at the lion enclosure at the MGM casino tomorrow at 1:00PM, and you could purchase the item then."

I motioned for Trace to hand me a pen, and I wrote the name of the casino on the back of a leftover room service napkin.

"Thanks, Allie."

"So... does this mean that you guys are in Vegas?" she asked.

"Uh, sort of."

"What are you doing there?"

"Nothing important."

"Right." She blew out a breath, and I could tell she was not entirely enjoying being my secretary with no chance of a story as payment.

Which reminded me...

"Hey, exactly how did you end up taking this call from Carla? Shouldn't it have gone to my desk?"

There was silence on the other end. Then, "Weeeeell...I figured that you'd want me to answer your phone in case any important calls came in that required your immediate attention."

Bullshit. What she really meant was any that required *her* immediate *thievery* of stories that came in for me while I was away.

"Stay away from my phone while I'm gone."

"What? I was just trying to help."

Help herself onto the front page.

"Just keep a healthy radius away from my desk until I get back."

"And when will that be?" she asked.

I bit my lip. "Soon."

"You need any help out there?"

"No!" I took relish in saying. Then quickly hit the end button.

Once I did, Trace immediately broke his silence.

"That wig-wearing sonofbitch! He's seriously trying to blackmail me?"

"It appears that way." I paused. "Do you think he knows about the bad guys after you?"

He shook his head. "It doesn't matter. We clearly were too eager to get at that drive. He saw an opportunity and took it. Sonofabitch!" he repeated.

"I hate to put it this way, but what's the big deal?" I asked. "I mean, a hundred thou isn't *that* much cash to you, is it?"

He shot me a look. "Contrary to what you may think of me, I don't actually walk around with rolls of hundreds in my pocket. Yeah, I can get the money, but unless our blackmailer takes plastic, it's gonna take a little time to get that amount liquidated. And time is one thing we don't have."

"Right." His twenty-four-hour deadline was quickly approaching. "What do we do now?"

Trace plopped back on the bed. "What can we do? Meet up with this creep tomorrow."

"And?"

"And bluff." He looked up at me. "How are your acting skills?"

I gulped. About to be tested to the fullest, I had a feeling.

*　*　*

Since there was little else we could do, we decided to call it a night. I slipped out of my jeans (under the cover of the hotel sheets – I wasn't quite ballsy enough to show off my Victoria's Secrets in front of a guy) and shut off my bedside light. Trace did the same (only he dropped trou in full view, stripping down to his boxers. Be still my beating heart!), then flipped on the TV. We watched a couple mindless sitcoms and one medical drama, before Leno appeared, his opening monologue punctuated by snarky comments about Jaime Lee's dress.

Trace immediately flipped it off. Apparently he'd heard enough about that for one day.

Instead, we lay in the darkness, listening to each other breathe. Even though we were each sequestered in our own double beds, I had the irrational thought that I was sleeping with Trace Brody. He was a good four feet away from me, but the thought sent tingles to places of my body that hadn't tingled in a very long time. I had to say, it wasn't altogether unpleasant.

"I'm sorry," Trace said.

I jumped a little at the sound of his voice, suddenly worrying that he might have female-tingling-parts radar or something.

"Sorry?"

"For dragging you into this. For not calling the cops."

"In case you didn't notice I kinda dragged myself."

I could hear him smile in the dark. "Yeah, you did."

"And, as for the cops, well, that wasn't an option. They said no police, remember."

"Yeah, they did, but..." He paused. Cleared his throat. "That wasn't the only reason I didn't want to call them."

I arched an eyebrow at him. "No?"

"No." Again with the throat clearing. "The truth is... I was afraid of the bad press."

"Oh for the love of..."

"I know, stupid, right? I mean, my life's at stake and I'm worried about looking bad in the papers. It's just... your thinking gets a little crazy sometimes living your life in the public eye. It's not an excuse, but there's no way you could possibly know what it's like to live your life in front of the camera."

I bit my lip. "Actually, I kinda do," I admitted.

Generally my past was not something I liked to think about, let alone talk about. But after the heartfelt admission, I felt I owed it to him to at least be honest.

"I used to do a little modeling," I said. "Granted I was no Trace Brody, but I'm not a total stranger to the fishbowl feeling."

I heard rustling on his side of the room as he propped himself up on one elbow. "A model? You?"

"I know. Shocking."

"No, I didn't mean it that way. I mean you're easily pretty enough to model. I just didn't... you just seem too... real."

"I'm going to take that as a compliment." Especially the pretty part. Damn if that tingling didn't just kick up a notch.

"Why'd you stop?"

"No reason," I hedged. "It just got old."

"Liar."

I grinned in the darkness. "When did you get to know me so well?"

"So what happened? You gain a pound? Blow a shoot? Get taken advantage of by some evil photographer?"

I rolled my eyes. "You watch too much TV. Nothing as cliché as any of that."

"So what was it?"

I sighed. "You want to know the truth? I just didn't recognize myself anymore."

Trace was silent a moment. Then, "I know the feeling."

"No, I doubt you do." I closed my eyes, transporting myself back in time. "I'd been modeling for a couple of years, and my career was really starting to pick up. I was going to all the right parties, meeting all the right people, living life fast and furious."

"Sounds cliché so far," Trace teased.

I ignored him, continuing before I lost my nerve. "I had just come off a runway show in New York, right after a swimsuit shoot in Malibu, and was in Paris for a magazine shoot. It had been weeks since I even knew what time zone I was in. Anyway, I was on set, waiting for the other girls in the shoot to get their hair done, and I picked up this fashion magazine to pass the time. It was all in French, so I couldn't read it, but the pictures were pretty. Especially this one picture of this woman in a long evening gown on a beach somewhere. Her hair was soft and glossy, flowing behind her, her neck dripping with jewels, her skin glowing perfectly in the warm sunset. She was glamour personified. And I was so jealous. I found myself wishing I could be like her. That if I could be that glamorous, that perfect, I'd have achieved something in life."

"Sounds like she did her job well, huh?"

I sighed out loud. "Too well. I looked closer at the woman's face and guess what? It was me. It was a picture I'd done on a shoot three months earlier in Cancun. I'd forgotten all about it. I *literally* didn't recognize myself."

Trace let out a loud bark of laughter. "Seriously? Oh, that's classic."

"That was when I realized just how fake my life had become. I was bouncing from glamorous locale to glamorous locale, playing part after part so well that I'd completely lost touch with reality. The glamorous woman in the picture had spent the better part of her youth mucking horse manure in rural Montana, making fun of everything that I now stood for. Everything about her was an illusion. Everything about me had become an illusion."

I took a deep breath, shaking off the unsettling feelings the memory had stirred. "Anyway, that's when I quit. Walked out right then, didn't even finish the shoot I was on."

"Wow. That must have taken some guts."

I shrugged. "Guts and foolishness are very closely related. I was making six figures as a model."

"I take it your tabloid doesn't pay that well?"

"You've seen my place."

"Point taken." He paused. "So, what drew you to it?"

"Even though I didn't want to model anymore, I still loved creating beautiful pictures. Stepping from the front of the camera to the back wasn't that hard – the principles of lighting, angles, composition are all the same. I know it's not exactly high art, but I can make a living doing what I love at the *Informer*." I paused. "Well, barely a living."

Having spilled my guts, silence fell over us. Again, the sound of his breath was the only thing I heard.

"So, you have any of those swimsuit shots saved?" he asked, laughter on the edge of his voice.

I tossed a pillow at him. "No!" Though the tingling was back.

"You're from Montana then, huh?"

I nodded in the darkness. "Yeah."

"You miss it?"

"Sometimes. But I go back to visit every year. Kinda keeps me grounded, you know?"

"No."

"No?"

"No. I have no idea about being kept grounded."

I rolled over to face his silhouette outlined against the bed sheets by the faint glow of neon lights through the window. "Don't tell me fame ain't all it's cracked up to be?"

"Oh, I'm not complaining. Hell, I know how many people would kill to be in my shoes."

I was glad to hear him say it. I'd never pegged Trace as the whiney celebrity type.

"It's just…" He paused. "Well, I guess they're awfully big shiny shoes to fill sometimes. Once in awhile I'd just really love

Gemma Halliday | 166

to put on an old pair of boots and… and go mucking around in manure. You know?"

I grinned. "Have you ever mucked in manure before?"

"No," he conceded. "But it sounds charming."

I threw another pillow at him. He tossed one back, hitting me in the middle.

"There's just such a thing as too perfect, you know? Like this whole wedding thing. It's the end of the world if the dress isn't perfect, the first photo of it taken at the perfect time, by the perfect photographer, leaked to just the perfect paper. Once in a while I'd really just like permission to be a total fuckup."

I grinned. "I'd say you've pretty much fucked up this whole flash drive thing."

He laughed. "I have, haven't I?"

I joined in for a second, then the laughs died down, bringing with them the silence again.

Maybe it was the anonymity of the darkness. Or maybe the revelation that he wasn't as deliriously happy as his airbrushed photos and multi-million dollar mansion would have you believe. But I found myself asking the question that had been plaguing me since I was first assigned to Wedding Watch.

"Why are you marrying Jamie Lee?"

There was a pause. Too long of a pause. Before he answered with, "What do you mean?"

"Do you love her?" I told myself it was the newshound in me asking, not the woman who'd just been sharing her deepest darkest secrets with him in bed in the dark.

"Jamie Lee is a great girl," he said.

"She is," I agreed. Though I noticed he didn't actually answer my question.

"I mean, what guy wouldn't want to be with her, right?"

"Right. You're the perfect couple." I should know. I'd used that exact phrase enough times in the *Informer* over the past few weeks.

"Yeah. Perfect."

I bit my lip. Nothing more to say, really. I closed my eyes, ignoring the odd letdown in my chest.

"Hey, Cam?"

"Yeah?" I asked.  A little too breathlessly, I realized in hindsight.

"Goodnight."

"Goodnight, Trace," I answered back.  Then I closed my eyes.

And tried to ignore that persistent tingling.

## Chapter Seventeen

I awoke early to the sound of Trace sawing logs in the bed next to me. I couldn't help smiling. The movie star snored. Awesome.

I quietly slipped into the bathroom, showered, turned my underwear inside out, and redressed in my clothes from the previous day. Trace was still snoring when I emerged, so I slipped out of the room in search of coffee.

Downstairs the casino was already buzzing with die-hard gamblers. Or maybe I should say *still* buzzing, as most of them looked like they were on the tail end of their evening rather than the bright side of a brand new day – hair disheveled, clothes wrinkled, eyes bloodshot and unblinking as they stared at cards, dice, and slot machine screens.

I navigated my way through the smoky haze to a little coffee shop nestled near the side door. I ordered two black coffees and a couple blueberry muffins to go, schlepping them back up to the room.

I arrived back at the room just in time. In time, that is, to see Trace emerging from the shower. Wrapped solely in a towel. And, considering this was not the Ritz Carlton, the towels were not of a generous size. I did a silent thank you to the gods of cheap management as my cheeks flushed at the amount of bare, tanned, toned-to-perfection skin facing me.

"'Morning," Trace said, grabbing a T-shirt from the chair by the window.

"You snore," I blurted out.

I mentally kicked myself. Very suave, Dakota. But as I stared at Trace au-natural (silently praying that the towel slipped off), there seemed to be a disconnect between my brain and my tongue.

Trace grinned. "I know. It's my one flaw," he said, throwing the T-shirt over his head. "I hope I didn't keep you up."

I cleared my throat, willing no more idiocies to spill forth. "No, it was fine. I tuned it out fine. I slept fine."

"Well, that's just fine." The grin widened.

Mental forehead smack.

I shoved a cup out in front of me. "Coffee," I said. "And a blueberry muffin."

Trace grabbed the cup, letting go of the towel at his waist. For a second I held my breath, mentally willing it to fall to the floor.

No such luck. He'd knotted the ends at his hip. Damn.

"Hey, thanks," he said, seemingly oblivious to my X-rated thoughts. He took a long sip.

I did the same, hoping the caffeine would clear the stupid out of my brain.

"God, this is good. Just what I needed," he said. He threw me a winning smile as he set his cup down, showing off a dimple in his left cheek. I hadn't noticed it before, but with a fine dusting of day-old stubble shadowing his face it was just visible.

And sexy as hell.

"You have a pimple."

He raised an eyebrow at me.

"I mean a dimple! Dimple. In your cheek. It's... dimply."

Jesus, I was like a walking fountain of stupid.

Luckily I was saved further moron spew by the sound of Trace's cell ringing from the nightstand. He glanced briefly at the readout before picking it up.

"Hey, babe."

Jamie Lee.

I shook off my momentary lapse into ridiculous adolescent drooling and tried to switch back into tabloid mode, listening to his side of the conversation for anything print worthy.

"Well, just order another one." Pause. "How expensive can a cake be?" Pause. "Christ! What, is it made of gold?" Pause. "Seriously? Gold leaf is edible? What do you know..." Pause. "Yeah. Fine. Just send me the bill." Pause. "Well, I'm not entirely sure when I'll be home. Soon." Pause. "What am I doing? Uh... I'm meeting a friend." Pause. "No, I'm pretty sure you don't know her." Pause. "Who? Uh... Carla Constantine." Pause. "One. But I'll be heading home right after that."

With any luck, I silently added.

"Okay. Love you, babe," he said, then hit the end button. Then he turned to me. "I hate lying to her," he said.

"Technically, you didn't lie," I pointed out. "You just left out a few key details."

"Yeah, well, the sooner this is all over, the better."

I couldn't agree more. The sooner I had this story wrapped up the sooner I could go back to viewing Trace through the lens of a camera. Much safer. Much tidier. Much less tingly.

Fifteen minutes later we were both clean, dressed, and so highly caffeinated we were buzzing in the tiny hotel room – anticipation and black coffee causing my leg to jiggle up and down uncontrollably on its own as Trace paced the room. And it was only nine.

Clearly we needed to get out.

I suggested we take a walk down Fremont, for lack of a better way of passing the time until our assignation with Carla. We were just crossing back through the casino, trying not to inhale the stale Marlboro lingering in the air, when I'd swear I heard a familiar voice.

Calling my name.

I looked up, squinting through the smoky air.

A blonde in a mini-skirt and a three-hundred pound psychic were bearing down on me.

No. Way.

I rubbed my eyes, hoping they were a smoke-induced mirage.

"Cam! Hey, Cameron, over here!"

No such luck.

I watched in horror as Allie and Mrs. Rosenblatt approached us.

"Hey, Cam," Allie said, skipping up to us. "Good morning."

That was debatable. "What are you doing here?"

"I thought you might need some help," Allie explained with a cheerful smile.

"Help with…?"

"Exactly." Allie gave me a hard stare. If I'd ever thought I'd outmaneuvered the new girl, I was sorely wrong. For a moment I glimpsed the news shark behind the co-ed façade and wondered just how much of the bimbo thing was real or an act.

"And you?" I asked, turning to Mrs. Rosenblatt. "Don't tell me you had some psychic vision of us."

She laughed. "Of course not. If I'd had a vision, you'd know about it."

Scary.

"No, when Allie said she was heading to Vegas, I hitched a ride. Max forwarded your email about Johnny Rupert's crash on the way to Vegas. I figured if we drove out here, maybe I'd get some vibes from traveling in his shoes, so to speak." She paused. "Plus, I always clean up at craps. Helps to be psychic." She gave me a wink.

"O-kay." I shook my head, turning to Allie again. "Look, I'm sorry to disappoint you, but there's no story here." At least none I was wiling to share.

"Bullshit," Allie said. Though it lost some of its rough edge when she punctuated the expletive by blowing a watermelon-scented bubble. "Something's going on here, and I wanna know what it is."

I changed my tactics. "No."

"Excuse me?"

"You heard me. No." Wow. That word was really fun to say. I made a mental note to use it more often. "This is my story."

Allie narrowed her eyes. "You are a photographer. You need someone to write copy."

"I'll get Tina."

"Too late."

My turn to narrow my eyes. "What do you mean?"

"Felix already gave the story to me."

"But you don't even know what the story is!"

She smirked, puffed out her oversized chest, twirled a lock of over-bleached hair. "What can I say? I'm very persuasive."

I'll just bet…

I said a silent curse under my breath, aimed at all beautifully buxom girls in general and one in specific.

"So, tell me. What are you doing, what does it have to do with Pacific Storage, and what really happened to Trace that night?"

I pursed my lips together. What I'd really like to tell Allie is exactly where to stick that perky little attitude of hers. But, considering she had me backed into a corner, I had little choice but to comply.

I turned to Trace. He just shrugged, seemingly convinced by Allie's bubble blowing. Or her boobs, I wasn't sure which.

"Fine. Under one condition. You cannot print anything until Trace gives the go-ahead," I said, glancing at the actor as I remembered our former deal.

He nodded.

"Deal." Allie stuck out one peachy-lotion scented hand.

I shook it.

And then I told. Everything. From the abduction to the shooting to the drag queen currently holding the mysterious flash drive hostage.

When I finished, Allie's perfectly shaped eyebrows were puckered in a look of concentration that looked almost comical in contrast to her Barbie appearance.

"Well, it seems obvious to me that the guys who lost the drive have something illegal on there. Otherwise, why not just call the cops to get it back?"

I nodded. "Yeah, plus they had guns. Definitely bad guys."

Allie lifted a brow at the term, but was wise enough not to comment. "What's our next move?"

I looked down at my cell readout. "We're meeting Carla at one and hope to convince her to hand over the drive."

"How do you plan to do that?"

"We hadn't exactly worked that out yet," I admitted, glancing at Trace.

"I was thinking we beat it out of him?" he suggested. I could tell by the way he was still clenching and unclenching his fists that he was only half kidding.

"Hmmm." Allie pursed her lips together, making little creases in the shiny pink lip gloss. "Well, then I guess it's a good thing we came along. Sounds like you're gonna need some backup."

I glanced from her slim frame to Mrs. Rosenblatt's bloated one. God help us if this was our backup.

"Wait," I said, something suddenly occurring to me. "I didn't tell you where we were staying. How did you even find us?"

Allie grinned. "Journalism 101. I traced your cell call."

I blinked at her, my jaw going slack. "You can do that?"

"Well, duh!" She rolled her eyes. "Amateur stuff. All you have to do is register the number with an online tracking service and they do the rest, triangulating your position based on cell towers."

"I thought only the police could do that?"

"Luckily, that's what most people think. That's why it works so well." She winked at me.

I was almost afraid to ask, but… "Where did you learn this stuff?"

Again with the annoyingly adorable grin. "Felix taught me."

Oh yeah, she was totally sleeping with him.

\* \* \*

After filtering out of the Cowboy Cabana, the four of us made our way to the parking lot where Allie said she'd give us all a ride to the MGM. We followed her to the far side of the lot where she stopped in front of a little green VW Bug. With a daisy planted in the dash.

I looked from Mrs. Rosenblatt to the car. Then back again.

"You've got to be kidding me?"

I shook my head as the four of us tried to pile into Allie's bug, likely looking like one of those overstuffed clown cars. Mrs. Rosenblatt took up the front seat, girth spilling over onto the gear shift as Allie squeezed in beside her. Trace and I shoved ourselves into the windowless backseat, his long legs twisting sideways to fit in the small space. Which left his right thigh sitting squarely against mine. It was warm, hard, and way too intimate. I tried not to have an orgasm on the spot as we rode toward The Strip.

"The Strip" is the common name for Las Vegas Boulevard from about Russell Road to Sahara Avenue. It's some of the priciest real estate in the country, housing one mega casino after another laid out side by side down the length of the street. As they all compete for land, they also compete for air, one towering higher than the other, and each one touting an over-the-top theme. There's the Paris casino with its huge Eiffel tower hovering over the sprawling casino (which you can visit the top of for only $15). There's the New York, New York, which is actually laid out inside like a New York neighborhood, complete with Irish pubs, Italian pizzerias, and souvenir shops on every corner. The outside is made to look like the New York skyline complete with New York harbor, a Statue of Liberty, and the Chrysler building. Circling the skyline is a thrilling roller coaster (that you can ride for only $14). Next to the New York, New York sits the Excalibur – a towering white castle where knights joust indoors at the Tournament of Kings dinner (and you can watch for only $54.95), and beside that the Luxor pyramid where you can walk through an exact replica of King Tut's tomb (for only $9.99).

And across the street from that sits the MGM Grand, one of the first themed casinos to hit the strip and turn Vegas from a mob-related rundown Sin City to a family friendly destination for all. The MGM is a huge building tinted green like the Emerald City and shaped like a giant T. Inside are theaters, bars, pools, and an animal enclosure to rival any zoo in the world, housing the distant cousins of the original MGM lion. Three of them. That were being fed big, red, bloody steaks as we approached. I watched the first one rip the meat apart, baring a set of teeth the size of steak knives. I shuddered, glad I wasn't a steak.

Considering we still had a couple hours before Carla was due to show, we wandered the casino, letting Trace do the tourist thing incognito as a cowboy. We ordered drinks by the pool, Allie bought a pair of fuzzy pink dice for her VW from a gift shop, and Mrs. Rosenblatt even won two hundred dollars at craps. (I was beginning to believe this whole psychic thing.)

Finally one o'clock rolled around and we made our way back to the lion enclosure, rimmed with tourists all taking video with their phones of the now sleeping lions. We claimed a piece of ledge on a nearby planter and hunkered down to wait for Trace's blackmailer.

And wait.

And wait.

After an hour I stood to stretch my legs.

"She's not coming, is she?" Trace asked. His fists were still clenched and unclenching again, the lines in his face taught.

I looked around the crowd. Families taking pictures, frat boys with tall drinks in their hands, a couple of girls in super short dresses.

"Doesn't look like it."

"Shit."

Clearly Trace was not a guy used to being stood up.

"You think she got cold feet?" Mrs. Rosenblatt asked.

I shook my head. "I don't know. Maybe." I paused. "Or maybe she had second thoughts about blackmailing a public figure."

Allie shook her head. "I doubt it. Her actions strike me as pure opportunist."

"Takes one to know one," I mumbled.

"What?"

"Nothing. Go on."

"Hmm." She eyed me, but continued anyway. "See, I don't think she'd just walk away from a payday like this. Hundred thousand would be a lot to someone like Carla. But," she said, turning to Trace, "maybe she realized it wasn't that much to guy like you. Maybe she decided to up the price."

"Sonofa-" Trace clenched his jaw with a click.

"I say we go talk to this Carla chick," Mrs. Rosenblatt piped up.

"Great plan," I said. "If we knew where she was."

Allie perked up in her seat. "I thought you might want to know that." She pulled a Post-it note from her pocket and slammed it down on the table top with triumph.

I leaned forward. An address was handwritten on the paper.

"You're kidding me, right?"

Allie's smirk covered her entire face. "Nope. Behold, the address that Carla called the *Informer* office from. I did a reverse number look-up after she hung up."

I stared at the blonde.

She grinned back.

"And you doubted my investigative skills." Then she blew another watermelon scented bubble, sucking it in with a loud pop.

I hated to admit it, but New Girl was actually coming in handy.

Trace grabbed the Post-it, staring at the address. "Gotcha, you bastard," he said to the piece of paper. "Man, when I get my hands on you…"

Only he didn't get to finish that threat, as his pocket began trilling the sounds of ELO. He pulled the phone out and hit the talk button.

"What?"

Immediately, I could tell who was on the other end by the way Trace's face drained of color. His eyes darted around our assembled group and, as confirmation, he mouthed the words, "bad guys."

I crowded in close to him to hear the conversation through the phone.

"Your twenty-four hours is up, Trace," the male voice on the other end said.

I looked down at my own cell readout. 2:33 on the dot. These guys were punctual, I'd give them that.

"Look, we just need a little more time," Trace shot back.

"More time?" the guy asked. "Or more incentive?"

I froze, the menacing tone behind his voice sending shivers down my spine at what sort of incentive he had in mind.

"What do you mean?" Trace asked, the wary line of his eyebrows mirroring my thoughts exactly.

"You have something that belongs to us."

"I told you I don't have-" he started.

But the guy on the other end didn't let him finish, instead cutting in with, "And now we have something that belongs to you."

Uh oh.

"What sort of something?" Trace asked, his voice tight.

Dread curled up in a little ball in my stomach, my breath in my throat as I listed to shuffling on the other end. Then a different voice altogether came on the line. One that, instead of laced with malice, was clearly laced with fear.

"Trace?" came the shaking voice. I could hear tears hovering behind the words. It was scared. Female. And recognizable by anyone who hadn't been living under a rock for the past two years.

Jamie Lee.

"Oh my God," Trace whispered, almost to himself. "Babe, are you okay?"

"Trace, they said they're going to kill me. They won't let me go unless you give them some flash drive. Ohmigod, Trace, they're going to kill me. Help!" she screamed as the voice faded into the background with more shuffling.

Trace's jaw clenched shut, his eyes going dark and unreadable, his skin a deathly pale now as the man came back on the phone.

"Midnight," he said. "The parking lot behind the New York New York. You show up there with the flash drive in hand and you get your girl back. Otherwise, America's sweetheart gets a bullet between her big blue eyes."

## Chapter Eighteen

The line went dead, but Trace still stood there, holding the phone to his ear, staring straight ahead, his jaw tensed, his expression the exact same "tortured hero" one he'd worn at the end of *Die Tough*.

"Trace?" I whispered, almost afraid to break into his silent rage.

Nothing.

I cleared my throat again. "Uh, Trace?" I put a hand on his arm.

He glanced down at my hand, then back up at my face, seemingly snapping back to reality. "Jesus, Cam, they have Jamie Lee."

Allie sucked in a breath at the other end of the table.

I immediately shot her a look. I swear, if she tried to print any of this…

"The bad guys?" Mrs. Rosenblatt interjected.

I nodded.

"This is all my fault," Trace said. "God, if anything happens to her…"

"It won't," I said. With measurably more conviction than I felt. "We're going to get that flash drive." I grabbed Allie's post it and shoved it into Trace's hand. "Let's go talk to Carla."

\* \* \*

By the time we all piled back into the clown car and traveled the four blocks to a street behind the Wynn casino that housed the address on the Post-it, Trace had almost regained a natural skin color.

Almost. I still worried that Carla might lose a limb or two when he found her.

The house was a small stucco-coated affair that had seen one too many Vegas summers to be a solid color. One side was a pale mauve, the other a sun-faded pink. An awning provided shade for the front porch, the green stripes threadbare and, I suspected, crusty to the touch, fried from the relentless sun.

I knocked once on the screen door. No answer. I hit it again, then waited. Nada.

"Maybe he's not home?"

"Maybe," Trace said. Then before I could stop him, he had the screen open, and his leg cocked back. Then he kicked in the door, the faded wood splintering around the lock, the door flying in.

I felt my jaw drop open. "You just kicked the door down! I thought they only did that in movies."

He sent me a wry smile.

"Wow." Allie's eyes were wide with a mix of emotions – surprise, awe, lust. Mostly lust. "That was awesome. Where did you learn to do that?"

"I do my own stunts," Trace said, stepping through the doorway.

I followed a step behind and found myself standing in a small living room, a sad avocado green sofa sagging in front of a TV with a fifteen-inch screen and a thirty-five-inch casing. It was showing a muted *Price Is Right* across the screen. The top half of Drew Carey's head was a green color that said this TV had seen better days. The place was trashed, clothes, shoes, newspapers and books covering every surface.

Beyond the living room was a kitchen, the white tiles cracked, the brown refrigerator covered in magnets and photos of people in various happy poses. A pile of dishes sat in the sink, a trio of aloe vera succulents sitting in the back window, wilting in the sunshine. Cupboards were opened, food all over the counter. To the right of the kitchen was a hallway, leading, I assumed, to the bedrooms.

"Carla?" I called out.

Nothing.

"Hello?"

"I don't think she's here," Allie surmised, genius that she was.

Trace walked to the kitchen, rummaging through the mess on the counters. "Someone's been here," he mused.

He was right. No one lived in this kind of mess. The place had been searched. One guess what the guys were looking for.

"What was that?" Mrs. Rosenblatt froze, looking off into space.

"What?" I didn't hear anything.

"That!"

At first I thought maybe she was having a psychic episode. Then, as I strained against the silence, I heard it too. A sound, faint, muffled. Coming from the hallway.

I dashed down the short hall to a single bedroom in the back of the bungalow.

Here the mess was even worse. A dresser was turned over, shoes covered the floor, clothes strewn across a double bed by the window. Cosmetics, wigs, and a couple empty pizza boxes littered the floor. A chair was upended in the corner, a mirror broken near the doorway.

I paused, stepping over the broken glass. "Hello?" I called.

The muffle piped up again in response, louder now. I followed the sound past the bed, to a closet on the wall beside it. I slid open the doors, shoving a pile of clothes out of the way.

Sitting on the floor, hands duct taped behind her, legs bound, a length of pantyhose tied around her mouth, sat Carla.

She mumbled and wiggled, looking like an oversized cocooned butterfly, her mini-skirt riding high on her thigh.

"Mmm, hmmmm, pmmm."

"What?" I asked, leaning closer.

"Mmm! Hmmm! Pmmm!"

I leaned in and removed the pantyhose.

"Untie me, you twit!" she shouted.

I was tempted to put the pantyhose back in.

But, considering she was our one lead to finding the drive and freeing Jamie Lee, I fought the instinct, instead tugging at the tape binding Carla's ankles.

"She's in here," I called over my shoulder to the rest of the gang.

"My hands. For the love of God, cut the tape. I've got a cramp in my legs so bad I may never dance again."

I complied, though I wasn't sure that loss would be altogether such a tragedy for the entertainment world.

Behind me, I could feel Trace burst into the room. Okay, I felt someone come in, but it wasn't until he opened his mouth that I knew unmistakably that it was Trace.

"You sonofa-" He lunged for Clara.

Clara made an "Eeep" sound, squealing as she ducked to the right behind a shoe rack. Trace tripped on a pair of heels, landing half on Carla and half on me.

"Uhn." I felt the air rush out of me.

"I'm gonna kill you," Trace said, undaunted. He wiggled off me (and I swear my body did not respond to the contact in any way shape or form. Not even a little. Nope. Not me.) and lunged again at the writhing form in the closet.

Carla scrambled onto her hands and knees (well, her knees anyway. Her hands were still taped behind her back.), crawling out of the closet just as Trace got hold of her right ankle.

"Help! Help," she pleaded, kicking wildly. "He's going to kill me!"

From the look on Trace's face, I'd say that was a proper assessment of the situation.

Trace scrambled to his feet, pouncing on Carla and pulling her up to a standing position by the scruff of the neck. He only had an inch or two on the woman (man? I wasn't sure what the PC pronoun was.), but his presence towered over hers as Carla whimpered like a dog about to be smacked on the nose for piddling on the carpet.

"You tried to blackmail me," Trace ground out through clenched teeth.

"Sorry?" she squeaked. Only it sounded more like a question.

"You will be," he threatened.

Clearly he was pulling out his "tough guy" face, the one he'd used in *The Deceased*, that gangster movie with Jack Nicholson. Eyes dark, jaw square, it was menacing, saying he'd had a hard life in a hard neighborhood and it would be easy for him to crack now. Violence oozed from his every pore, and I wondered just how much of this was an act and how much was genuine.

"What's going on?" Mrs. Rosenblatt asked, shoving her frame into the doorway. Allie's blonde head was visible behind her, jumping up and down to get a glimpse around the older woman's frame.

"Who are they?" Carla asked, her drawn in brows knitting together. (Okay, only one knitted. The other had smudged in the struggle and was hanging halfway down her cheek.)

"Hey, you, we'll ask the questions around here," I said. What can I say? I'd watched *The Deceased* five times. I could do tough guy, too.

Ten minutes later we had Carla extricated from her duct tape womb, and the five of us were sitting in the living room, Carla shoved between Mrs. Rosenblatt and Allie on the sofa, Trace and I perched on the chairs across from them.

"You stood me up," Trace said. I could tell it was taking all he had not to rip Carla limb from limb. Even though Carla was not the one holding Jamie Lee captive, she was the one in front of him, and was going to be the recipient of all of his frustration and anger.

And, in his defense, she had tried to blackmail him.

"I didn't mean to!" she protested. "I was just leaving to meet you when they attacked me."

"They?" I asked.

Carla swallowed hard. She looked from left to right. But, considering Trace was still growling at her through his tough-guy face, any thought of escape she might have been entertaining, she kept to herself. "These two guys. I was just leaving, locking the front door after myself, when these two guys came up and shoved a gun at me. They forced me back in the house."

"One with a crew cut and the other sort of ferrety?"

She nodded. "Yes! That was them. The big guy pointed his gun at me and told me that if I didn't give them the flash drive, he was gonna shoot me. Can you believe it?"

I had a feeling they weren't the first (or last) people who wanted to shoot Carla.

"What did you do?" I asked.

"I screamed my fool head off, is what I did. That's when the little guy shoved the pantyhose in my mouth and the big guy duct taped me all to hell and shoved me into the closet. I could hear them trashing the place, going through every room. Finally they just left. And left me in closet! I've been waiting in there for someone to find me ever since."

I sat back in my seat, disappointment weighing my shoulders into a slump. "The drive really is gone then." I wasn't sure how that boded for Trace and Jaime Lee. On one hand, they had what they wanted. On the other, they still had Jamie Lee. What were the chances they were just going to let her go with no hard feelings?

Only, Carla cut those thoughts short, a sly smile spreading across her features. "Actually, it's not."

I raised an eyebrow.

"They searched for it, but they didn't find it."

"Where is it?" Trace asked. (translation: growled.)

We collectively leaned forward in our seats to get the answer.

"In a locker."

"Where?" I asked.

"Somewhere safe."

"I swear to God, I'm gonna pop you in the mouth…" Trace lifted off his seat.

"You wouldn't."

He growled.

Carla squealed.

"Okay, it's at the bus station," Carla confessed. "Just don't hit me! My face is my livelihood."

I rolled my eyes. Oh, brother.

"Let's go get it." Trace stood up and grabbed Carla by the arm. Hard.

She winced, but wisely kept her mouth shut.

The five of us made for the door. I thought about locking it, but, honestly, the place was so trashed I had a feeling burglars would take one look and move on. It was a lost cause.

We traipsed out to the VW, only when we got there, I paused. To say it was going to be a tight fit was the understatement of the year. After two different attempts, we finally threw Trace and Carla in the back, Mrs. Rosenblatt again shoved into the front seat where half of her hung out the window frame. I ended up shoved half on Trace's lap, half on the floor. Not that I totally minded. Then again, it was a little like asking a nine-year-old if he minded eating all of his Halloween candy before dinner.

The bus station turned out to be a stop on the outskirts of Vegas along the old route 66. While public transit was the green mode of choice, most people still loved their cars enough to prefer traveling through the desert in an air-conditioned SUV. Not to mention that a car trip along the fifteen from Vegas to L.A. took four hours. The bus took six. For most travelers, it was a no brainer.

So it was no surprise that the station was sparsely filled, a smattering of the elderly (too tired to drive long distances) and the twenty-something crowd (who preferred to drink and ride rather than abstain the whole way in a car) the only occupants.

Inside the floors were made of linoleum, the ticket desk a rusted metal thing near the door and two vending machines in the corners selling peanut-butter crackers and Coke the only concessions to the new decade. Two rows of plastic orange chairs, held together by a rusted metal bar, served as the waiting area.

Along the far wall sat a row of orange metal lockers, eerily reminiscent of the ones I'd used in junior high. Each held a lock, half of them with keys hanging out, and a pay slot for coins beside it.

We traipsed to the lockers, drawing stares from the station's occupants. Though I could hardly blame them. A three-hundred pound psychic in a muumuu, a blonde with a pair of breasts so big they could be used as flotation devices, a movie-star cowboy, and a six-foot-tall drag queen didn't exactly make for an inconspicuous group.

After some minor prompting (Trace promised to make Carla a 'true' woman if she didn't comply.), Carla led us to locker number 315.

"Where's the key?" I asked.

Carla reached in to her shirt, extricating the tiny key from her bra. "I figured no one would look there."

Not if they could help it.

She shoved the key into the slot and pulled the rusted, metal door open with a creak.

There, sitting all by its lonesome in the middle of the locker, was a small black flash drive.

I suddenly felt as though I'd found the holy grail, angels singing a chorus, a flooding light from heaven falling upon me.

"That's it?" Allie asked. I could tell she was hoping for something lined in gold and flashing a neon sign that read, "Caution: scandal within!"

Trace reached into the locker to grab it.

But Carla was quicker.

Her manicured fingers jumped in and snatched the drive right out from under him. Just as quickly it disappeared into her bra where the key had come from.

"Not so fast, big boy," Carla said, the sly smile reappearing. "This here drive is worth a cool hundred thou."

Trace's jaw clenched so tight I swear he could produce diamonds between his molars. "Give. Me. The. Drive."

"When I get my money."

"You really think you're in a position to haggle?" I asked, putting a hand on my hip.

"Yes, I am. I have the drive," Carla said, shaking her tatas.

Only, there was at least one person among us who didn't mind grabbing a man's breasts. In fact, I was beginning to get the feeling that nothing would stand in the way of Allie getting her story. She shoved a hand down Carla's shirt before the drag queen could do more than let out another "Eeep" in protest. A second later she emerged with the flash drive. And a rolled-up sweat sock, leaving Carla noticeably flatter on one side.

"I got it!" Allie said, triumphantly holding it above her head.

Mrs. Rosenblatt immediately snatched it from her hands. "I'm getting a vibe!" she said. Her eyes rolled back in her head, doing a zombie impression as she clutched the drive tight both hands. "It holds… an embarrassing video. Involving a donkey. And a midget."

I rolled my eyes.

"Give it to me," Trace said, prying the drive from Mrs. Rosenblatt's hands.

"No, it's mine!" Carla shouted. She stomped one pump-clad heel down on Trace's foot.

"Sonofa-" he yelled, catching himself just in time to keep from tainting his good guy image for the public group assembled in the station. Only his surprise gave Carla just the edge she needed to pry the drive from Trace's hands. She took off at a dead run toward the back entrance to the station, toward the platform.

Without thinking, I took off after her, feeling Trace at my back, Allie and Mrs. Rosenblatt bringing up the rear.

"A hundred thou, if you want the drive!" Carla shouted behind her as she pushed through the glass doors onto the loading platform, running the length of it.

If we'd made a funny group coming in, the five of us running down the platform at a full sprint must have been downright laughable. I, for one, would have been in hysterics, had the life of one kidnapped starlet not hung in the balance.

The platform was hardly what you'd call crowded, a group of frat boys wearing UCLA sweatshirts hovering near the end of the platform the only ones waiting on the next bus. Which, I noticed, I could hear rumbling in the distance.

"Thief! Stop thief!" I heard Mrs. Rosenblatt calling from behind me.

The frat boys, clearly coming off a night-long bender of spending their monthly allowance looked up to see us approaching.

"He's trying to attack me!" Carla shouted, pointing behind her at Trace. "Help!"

"Hey, buddy," one of the frat boys with bloodshot eyes said, stepping between him and Carla. "What's the problem here?"

Trace plowed through him like a linebacker making for the end zone.

"Hey!" Frat Boy yelled, his drunk ass bouncing off the platform.

"Hey!" his friends yelled. I saw one of them throw a rude hand gesture Trace's way out of the corner of my eye. But I didn't stop running.

I saw the bus coming closer, more people filtering out onto the platform from the waiting area, getting ready to jostle each other for window seats. The headlights of the bus were visible in the not too far distance.

And Carla was running out of platform.

Maybe it was her heels that slowed her down. Maybe it was the thickening crowd of people in her way. Or maybe she was just out of shape and cramping from having been taped up in the closet for an hour.

But I closed in on her. Three feet. Two. I closed the gap to just a few inches, so close I could almost reach out and touch her sequin clad back. I went for it, taking a flying leap forward. My feet left the ground, all one hundred and ten pounds of me slamming into Carla from behind.

"Uhn."

All the air went out of her in a whooshing sound as I body-slammed the drag queen.

It's true that the bigger they are the harder they fall. And Carla was a big girl. She slammed onto the concrete platform knees first, skidding a full six inches forward, ripping her pantyhose in the process, before she slid to a halt. I held on for dear life, one arm wrapped around her neck, the other fisted in hair that I prayed it was not an easily detached wig.

Instinctively, she threw her hands out in front of her to break her fall. Which might have been a great way to save her livelihood-making face from smacking into the concrete and leaving nasty road rash on her cheeks.

But it was a horrible way to hold on to a hundred thousand dollar flash drive.

I watched as, as if in slow motion, the flash drive flew out of right hand, sliding across the platform, twisting end over end as it neared the edge, then disappeared into the road.

"No!" Carla yelled.

"No!" I screamed.

"No!" Mrs. Rosenblatt and Allie shouted.

"Oh, God, no!" I heard Trace yell behind me.

But it was useless.

The five of us watched in horror as the approaching bus made its way into the station, the wheels rolling over the asphalt, obliterating the drive beneath them with a slow grind as it came to a halt in front of the platform.

**Chapter Nineteen**

"You clumsy sonofabitch!" Trace yelled, catching up to us. He hauled Carla up off the ground by the scruff of her neck again.

"Eep!" Carla squirmed like a child.

"Hey, that's no way to talk to a lady!" Frat Boy shouted.

Geez, how drunk was he?

"It's not my fault!" Carla protested. "She tackled me!" She pointed an accusing finger at me.

Trace shook her so hard her teeth rattled. "You're going to pay for this."

"Let go of the lady, man!" Frat Boy said, advancing on us. Behind him four of his pals formed a solid wall of drunk post-teens.

Trace eyed them, clearly calculating his odds. But, as much as I could tell he wanted to pummel Carla into a pulp, it wasn't going to get the drive back. And he knew it.

Finally he let go, shoving Carla toward her group of would-be rescuers. Instead, he ran a hand through his hair, making it stand up on end as he stared at the spot where the drive had met its demise.

"Shit," he breathed.

"Aw, geez, I'm sorry, kid," Mrs. Rosenblatt said, huffing as she caught up to us. She put a motherly hand on Trace's shoulder.

Since there was clearly nothing more we could do there, we left Carla in the care of the drunk frat boys. I couldn't wait until they sobered up and realized just what kind of damsel in distress they had jumped to the aid of. I had a feeling this was one weekend where they would strictly be adhering to the "what happens in Vegas, stays in Vegas" credo.

"So, now what?" Allie asked as we crammed back into her VW.

"Now we do what I do best," Trace said. He had a faraway look in his eyes, his jaw set in a grim line.

"What's that?" Mrs. Rosenblatt asked.

"Fake it."

I raised an eyebrow.

"These guys are expecting me to give them a flash drive tonight. So I will. I know what it looked like. We can duplicate it. As long as it looks the same, they won't know that it isn't the real deal until after we get Jamie Lee back."

I had to admit, it was worth a try.

I pulled up my GPS, typing in "Wal-Mart" until the nearest one popped up on the screen. We followed the highlighted route to the super center, then trudged inside and surveyed the selection of flash drives. They had five different options, the plain, black, 2-gigabyte variety the closest looking to the one we'd lost. For $29.95, we had a reasonable decoy. I only hoped it worked.

For Jamie Lee's sake.

While I'd never been that huge of a fan Jamie Lee personally, I had to admit, she played well on screen. And she sold copies of the *Informer* like hotcakes. Her classic girl-next-door face coupled with her *Playboy* bunny–next-door body made her the perfect celebrity. Her appeal to both middle-aged men and tween girls was universally high. It didn't get better than Jamie Lee when it came to Hollywood personalities. And I couldn't imagine Hollywood without her.

I glanced at Trace. I had a feeling he couldn't either, though his reasons were distinctly more personal.

A thought that stirred mixed emotions in me. Clearly Jamie Lee was the kind of girl Trace belonged with. Clearly a tabloid photographer was not. Clearly I was nothing more to him than a means to an end, a way to get that drive, Jamie Lee, and his life back. Okay, maybe we'd forged a sort of tentative friendship in the meantime, but I had no delusions about it continuing once things went back to normal.

I shook the thought off as I used my credit card to buy the drive, then we all squished back in the VW, ready to implement our brilliant plan.

But it was only 5:00 pm.

We hit a drive-thru, grabbing a round of burgers (and a side salad for me), but that only killed about half an hour. We were antsy. Trace was jiggling his knee, Allie twirling her hair, Mrs.

Rosenblatt whistling the *Mission Impossible* theme song
nonstop.

And we had seven hours left.

I pulled a Google screen and located a yellow pages
directory for Las Vegas. For lack of another way to kill the time,
I typed in the name Ralph Kingsly, the friend Johnny Rupert had
been traveling with the day he'd died. I remembered that the
article I'd found earlier had said that Kingsly was a Vegas
resident at the time of the accident. I knew it was a while ago,
but I though it was worth a shot to see if he was still around Sin
City. I hit pay dirt two pages into the Kingslys. One Ralph P.
Kingsly lived on Palm Terrace Boulevard in the nearby suburb
of Henderson. What were the chances it was a different guy?

"Feel like taking a side trip?" I asked the collective carload.

"What are you thinking?" Ms. Rosenbaltt asked.

"Ralph Kingsly. Traveling companion of Johnny Rupert's
when he died. He lives about ten minutes from here."

Allie shrugged. "Sure."

Trace looked lost in thought. Not surprisingly he didn't
answer. But he didn't protest either, so Allie headed toward the
215.

* * *

Henderson is a small suburban town nestled to the south
east of Las Vegas. A mere ten-minute ride down the freeway
from Las Vegas Boulevard, it's a light year away from the flash
and decadence Vegas is known for. Henderson was one new,
dusty beige housing development after another, punctuated by
the occasional strip mall and Home Depot center. The road was
dotted with minivans and SUVs full of car seats, and flanked by
Little League fields that were an unnatural green for the desert.

Kingsly's address was in the Sand Hill development, on
Desert Sands Drive just off Warm Sands Road.

The front of the house was a nondescript beige (dare I say,
sand color?), the yard a rock garden dotted with cacti and
succulents. Identical to every other house on the street,
distinguishable as Kingsly's only by the wooden numbers

affixed above the garage. We followed the paved pathway up to the front door and knocked.

A beat later, the door was opened by a small man in a bright red track suit, zippered clear to his throat despite the temperature. His skin was a pale gray color and a tracheostomy tube in his neck indicated this was not a well man. A blast of cool air accompanied him, a welcomed respite from within.

"Ralph Kingsly?" Allie asked.

He nodded. "Yes," he wheezed, covering the hole in his neck with one hand. "May I help you?" he asked, politely raising only one eyebrow at the odd assemblage on his doorstep.

"We work for the *L.A. Informer*. We were wondering if we could ask you a few questions about a story we're working on."

He cocked his head to the side. "Sure. But I'm not certain how I would be of any interest to a tabloid."

"We wanted to ask you about Johnny Rupert and Jennifer Tootsie Wilson's death."

He nodded. "Ah. In that case, you better come in."

He stepped back to allow us entry, the lot of us filing in behind him as he led the way through the foyer to an equally beige living room. He motioned for us to sit on his beige sofa, settling himself in a straight-backed beige chair opposite.

"Can I get you something to drink?" he asked once we were all seated, his breath wheezing oddly through his throat as he spoke.

I tried not to stare.

Kingsly gave me a smile. "Throat cancer."

Apparently I was staring anyway. I felt myself blush at my breach of manners. "I'm sorry," I said, for lack of a better response.

He shrugged. "Me too. But that's what comes of a lifetime of being such a chic smoker." He gave me a wink. "They were almost worth it."

I smiled back, taking an immediate liking to him.

"Now, what can I tell you about Johnny?" he asked, clasping his hands in front of him.

"We understand he knew Tootsie?" Mrs. Rosenblatt started.

He nodded. "Yes. They were close."

"How close?" Allie pounced.

He raise an eyebrow. "They were very good friends. Johnny was quite distraught when she passed away."

"From what we hear, Johnny and Tootsie were more than friends, if you get my drift," Mrs. Rosenblatt pressed.

Kingsly laughed, the sound rasping out through the hole in his throat. I tried not to grimace.

"You've got it all wrong," he informed us. "Johnny wasn't into Tootsie."

"No?" I raised an eyebrow. "He bought her flowers, candy, took her to the theater. Sounds like he was into her to me."

"Let's just say that Tootsie wasn't Johnny's type."

"She was young, beautiful, a movie star. Whose type wouldn't she be?"

Kingsly did a patient, fatherly smile. "Someone who wasn't into beautiful *women*."

Suddenly the pieces clicked into place. "Wait, are you saying…"

"Johnny was gay," Kingsly said.

Mrs. Rosenblatt smacked her palm to her forehead loudly. "No wonder Alfred was getting mixed signals from Johnny."

Kingsly screwed up his wrinkled forehead. "Alfred?"

"My spirit guide."

His forehead screwed further, making him look like a Shar Pei.

"Not important," I said waving Mrs. Rosenblatt off. "What is important is why Johnny paid so much attention to Tootsie if he wasn't into her."

Kingsly sighed and leaned back into his chair. "Johnny needed a cover. In those days people weren't nearly as tolerant as they are now, even in Hollywood. Sure we suspected certain people of having certain tendencies, but if they ever came right out and said it, they would be ostracized faster than you could say, 'studio system.' If he wanted to have a prayer of ever landing a leading role, Johnny had to keep his preferences under wraps."

"Did Tootsie know?" I asked.

Kingsly nodded. "She got a kick out of it. Said it made her boyfriend crazy jealous."

I raised an eyebrow. Crazy enough to kill? I wondered.

"How jealous?" I probed.

He shrugged. "Jealous enough to buy her a mint in jewels, or so Johnny said." He leaned in closer. "One night they went to an opening at the Mann together. The next day Ben shows up with a diamond bracelet. Johnny had a good laugh out of it. Poor guy as going crazy trying to compete with a gay man." Kingsly laughed again.

"Did Johnny ever mention who he thought might be responsible for Tootsie's death?" I asked.

He shrugged. "He didn't talk about it much. Honestly, he was crushed when Tootsie passed. She was like a sister to him. He took a few small roles after her death, but his heart just wasn't in it anymore. He moved on to teach theater to kids instead. Johnny always had a way with children."

"Did he ever talk about a Becky Martin?" Mrs. Rosenblatt asked.

Kingsly stared at a spot just over my head, squinting his eyes as if trying to clearly read an old memory.

"She was one of Tootsie's friends, right? Blonde girl, big blue eyes?"

I nodded. "That's her."

He shrugged. "I honestly didn't take much notice of her at the time. I'm not sure Johnny did either. She was more like Tootsie's shadow than a personality of her own. I know she used to tag along now and then when Tootsie and Johnny went out, but he rarely saw her after Tootsie passed."

A knock sounded at the door and a woman in nursing scrubs pushed in. "Hello? Mr. Kingsly?"

"Come in, Donna." He turned to us. "Donna's my physical therapist. I hate to cut this short, but…" he trailed off, gesturing to his nurse.

We all made our polite goodbyes and left Mr. Kingsly to his attendant.

"Well that was a bust," Mrs. Rosenblatt said as we got back into the car.

"Not entirely," I pointed out. "I think we can cross Johnny off our list. If Tootsie was his beard, he had a lot more reason to keep her alive than want her dead."

"What time is it?" Trace asked.

I could see his jaw tense, the lines in his face pronounced. He could care less who had done Tootsie in fifty years ago. What he cared about was making sure Jamie Lee didn't get done in now.

And I couldn't blame him.

"Seven fifteen," Allie supplied, looking at her purple and silver watch bracelet. Little pink hearts served as numbers. Way too adorable to be worn by a grown woman.

It was hours until our rendezvous with the bad guys, but I could tell Trace was antsy to do something.

"Let's go to the MGM."

\* \* \*

Our plan was simple. I would be watching the drop point, and the second Trace had Jamie Lee safe, I was calling Allie and Mrs. R, who were waiting by the security office. The bad guys would be surrounded faster than you could say "card counter." And everyone would live happily ever after.

Trace's role in all this was handing over our blank flash, and hoping like hell he got Jamie Lee to safety before they realized their real data was smashed to smithereens by the 3:15 to Barstow.

In theory, it was simple. In reality, butterflies were doing the jitterbug in my stomach as I drove Trace to the meet point in Allie's VW.

I pulled into the back parking lot and cut the engine.

He reached for the door handle, then paused, turning back to me. "I owe you an apology," he said.

I raised an eyebrow at him. "For what?"

He grinned. "For calling you 'tabloid girl.'"

I blushed. "No prob," I said.

"Look, I feel…" He trailed off.

I held my breath while I waited for him to finish that sentence.

"… really guilty."

"Oh." I don't know what I had hoped he might say, but guilt wasn't the emotion I aspired to invoke.

"For everything," he continued. "This whole situation is my fault. I should have just called the cops in the beginning. I should have called them the second these guys showed up."

"Trust me, they wouldn't have believed you. Been there, done that."

Trace shook his head. "If anything were to happen to…" Again he trailed off, as if not able to finish that thought, let alone voice it out loud.

"Don't worry. It won't," I said with false confidence. "Our plan is great."

That was crap. Our plan sucked. Our plan was kindergartener simple. Our plan depended solely on faking out the guys with guns. Not exactly a certainty. However, if Trace could fake it, so could I.

"Jamie Lee will be fine," I repeated.

Trace lifted his eyes to meet mine, something unidentifiable burning in their very blue depths.

"I meant if something were to happen to you."

"Uh… oh." I think I swallowed my tongue. "To me?"

He nodded. Slowly. "Look, I know we didn't start out on the right foot, but I've sort of become fond of you."

"Fond." Like one is fond of their designer Cockadoodle?

"Yeah." He paused. "No. No, fond isn't really the word. I've… what I mean to say is… I mean…"

I raised an eyebrow. Could it be that the movie star was actually flustered?

He stopped. Took a breath. Opened his mouth to speak again. "Cam, I-"

But the sound of my cell screaming from my pocket interrupted him.

I ignored it, instead focusing on his face. "What? You what?"

"I… I think you should get that."

Damn!

Okay, not that I knew what I expected him to say. He was probably going to just say he wanted me to be careful. So I wouldn't get hurt so he wouldn't have to feel guilty. No biggie. Nothing meaningful. He was engaged to one of *Cosmo*'s "bikini bodies to die for." There was nothing so important that he might have to say to the likes of me.

I grabbed my cell and hit the send button.

"Cameron Dakota?"

"We're all set," came Allie's voice. "You guys in place yet?"

"Just about," I answered.

"K. I'll be waiting for your call. Break a leg!" she said. I wasn't entirely sure she was aware we weren't trying out for the high school glee club here.

I disconnected.

"They're in place."

Trace nodded. "Right." He tightened his jaw, squared his shoulders in a show of confidence I wasn't convinced he was feeling. "Let's do this then."

"Good luck," I said as he hopped out the door.

"You too."

I watched as Trace crossed the lot to the drop point specified by the bad guys. Then I pulled out, driving around the lot to a position at the far west side, across the street. I parked under a concrete overhang, keeping to the shadows, and cut the engine. I grabbed my telephoto from the trunk and sat on the back bumper. Across the lot I could see Trace's silhouette outlined in the moonlight. I crouched low and trained my lens on him. After adjusting the focus I got a clear shot of him at this distance. He was pacing. Hands in his pockets, eyebrows drawn low, lips drawn taught. I zoomed in on his face, unable to keep myself from snapping a few shots. The emotion there was raw, real. This was beyond playing "worried boyfriend" face. This was real. For a moment, I envied Jaime Lee.

I know, ridiculous. Who is jealous of a chick that's likely bound, gagged, and being held at gunpoint?

But I was. No one had ever cared about me as much as I could see Trace caring right now. I hoped Jamie Lee knew how lucky she was. I hoped she didn't take him for granted. Because the last few days had confirmed my belief that he deserved better. He deserved someone who would pace over his well being, too.

I widened my shot again, taking in the surrounding area and hunkered down to wait for our bad guys.

For the first few minutes I resisted the urge to check my cell readout for the time every second. But ten minutes into it, the urge won out. 11:38. 11:41. 11:47. At 11:54 the butterflies in my stomach started to ramp into a full fledged frenzy, and I regretted the two gallons of caffeine that I'd consumed over the last two days.

At 11:58 my fingertips started tapping nervously on the lens.

12:00 my left foot started tapping on the pavement.

12:03 I was going into full body convulsions.

12:05 I almost wet my pants when a Dumpster lid slammed shut on the other side of the parking lot.

But at 12:11, I froze.

A large, black SUV pulled up three spaces down from Trace. And parked.

I held my breath, popping off a rapid series of shots as the driver's side door opened and our crew cut friend got out. His buddy stepped out of the passenger side, and in the moonlight I could see the unmistakable glint of a black gun in his hand.

I shifted my vision to Trace. His jaw clenched. He'd seen the weapon, too.

"Be careful, handsome," I whispered.

I watched as Trace drew himself up to his full height, throwing his shoulders back, pulling bravado out from where, I didn't know. Quite likely he was drawing on every acting class he'd ever taken to pull this one off. It was the role of a lifetime. And if he didn't nail it, it could well be his last.

I gulped down that thought, instead focusing on my part in this, popping off more shots of the pair of kidnappers as they approached Trace.

The ferrety guy held the gun straight on him as the crew cut guy said something.

Trace shook his head, pointing at the SUV. Crew Cut answered. Trace shook his head again.

Crew Cut had his back to me, so I had no chance to read his lips, but I could well imagine how the exchange was playing out. We'd agreed ahead of time that Trace didn't show them the flash drive until we knew Jamie Lee was with them. If they realized the drive was empty before handing over the girl, we knew she was toast.

Reluctantly, Crew Cut finally nodded in Trace's direction. He steered Trace around the SUV to the back, then opened the back door.

Trace lurched forward, his entire body shifting, the expression on his face betraying the fact that his beloved was, indeed, in the car, despite my view of nothing from this vantage point.

Again, I felt a pang of jealousy, but swallowed it down. No time for silly indulgences now.

Instead I watched as the doors closed and Ferret held out his hand. Clearly he wanted the drive now.

Trace made a gesture at the back of the SUV.

Ferret shook his head.

I saw Trace's mouth form the word, "Fine." Then he reached into his pocket and pulled out something small and black. The fake drive. I mentally crossed my fingers the bad guys were dumb enough to fall for this.

Luckily bad guys are almost always dumb… otherwise they'd have been able to make it as good guys.

Ferret grabbed the drive, turned it over in his hands once, then smiled, seemingly satisfied. He shoved it in his pocket.

"Excuse me?"

I yelped like a terrier and jumped a foot in the air, spinning around to find a parking cop standing next to the VW.

"Jesus, don't do that to me!" I said, laying a hand on my heart. It was beating so hard I'd swear it was visible under my shirt.

"This your vehicle, ma'am?" he asked.

"Uh… " This felt like a loaded question. "Kinda?"

"May I see your driver's license, please?" he asked.

I pursed my lips together, my gaze pinging back to Trace and the SUV. "Now?"

The cop narrowed his eyes. And nodded. "Yeah. Now would be good."

"Uh… sure. Is there a problem, officer?" I asked.

He put his hands on his hips. "You're parked in a red zone."

I looked down at the curb. Yep. Bright red.

Shit.

"Uh... okay... sure." With a fleeting glance at Trace, I quickly fumbled in my bag for my ID, quickly handing it over to the guy before putting the camera lens to my eyes again. I could see Trace talking with the Crew Cut guy, pointing at the back of the truck. Clearly he was angling for them to release Jamie Lee.

"I'm going to have to call this in," Parking Cop said, rounding to his white golf cart.

"Sure. You do that," I said, only half listening as I watched the scene through the lens unfolding.

Trace gestured to the back of the SUV. He'd kept his side of the bargain, now it was time to let Jaime Lee go.

I had my hand hovering over the phone to call our cohorts. As soon as Jamie Lee was safe in Trace's arms, I'd hit send and Allie and Mrs. Rosenblatt would have the place crawling with security.

Only, I realized as Ferret stepped forward, still training the gun on Trace, that we'd been naïve to think it was ever going to be that easy.

Ferret shook his head, his big white teeth gleaming in the moonlight. Nope. He had no intention of handing over his hostage yet.

Trace took a step forward.

The gun moved into his ribs.

Trace froze.

I froze.

"Ma'am, do you realize you have seven outstanding parking tickets?"

"Uh, huh. Great. Thanks," I said automatically, my entire being focused on the scene playing out fifty yards from me.

"I'm sorry, but I'm going to have to impound your vehicle and bring you in on an outstanding ticket warrant."

"Wait – what? Now!?'" I watched as Crew Cut then opened the back of the SUV, but instead of producing one obscenely famous brunette, he shoved Trace into the van and shut the door after him.

I had a sick sense of déjà vu as I watched Ferret step around the car and get back into the driver's side, the lights turning on as the engine roared to life.

No, no, no, no no!

I pulled up Allie's number on my cell and hit send. I listened to it ring.

"Ma'am, did you hear me? You're going to have to come with me."

Only Allie didn't pick up.

And the SUV started pulling away.

Shit, shit, shit!

I looked at the cop, his pen hovering over his ticket pad.

I looked at my phone.

I looked at the truck pulling away,

And I made a split decision.

"Sorry, I'll pay them, I swear!" I said. Then jumped into the VW and revved the engine.

"Ma'am, I'm going to have to ask you to exit the vehicle," the parking cop yelled. "Ma'am!"

But I ignored him, instead pulling out of the parking lot as he hopped into his golf cart, radio at his ear, no doubt calling in an APB on the VW, and gave chase. At about twenty miles per hour.

Me? I was flying out of the parking lot, sailing down the ramp, one eye on the road in front of me and one on the taillights of the SUV as they whisked Trace away for the second time in as many days.

I flew onto the parking ramp, narrowly missing a limo carrying an entire bridal party sticking out of its sunroof, and just managed to catch sight of the tail end of the delivery van flying out onto LV boulevard as it pulled into traffic. Thankfully they were stopped a block ahead of me at the pedestrian crossing in front of the Excalibur, but their light turned before mine, making me do a little dance in my seat and chant, "Come on, come on, come on."

Finally my light turned, and my tires made a screeching sound on the asphalt as I surged forward, cutting over two lanes, trying not to lose Trace.

Again.

I watched as the SUV got on the freeway, pulling onto the 15 and heading west. I followed suit and two minutes later again caught up to them as I furiously surged forward, then fell back so as not to be noticed.

We played this cat-and-mouse game for a full five minutes before the truck exited the freeway, pulling off onto Jackson Street.

I did the same, searching the road ahead of me for my quarry. They turned right at the light ahead, and so did I, trying to stay a respectable two car lengths behind. Not that it mattered much. We were in an industrial part of town, one largely deserted at this time of night and without streetlights. My headlights in their rearview screamed out, whether I was five feet behind or fifty. Invisibility wasn't an option. The best I could hope for was that I didn't lose sight of the van.

Finally the black SUV pulled off the road, into the drive of one of the many warehouses lining the dark street. I drove past, noting the sign: Pacific Chocolates. What did you want to bet this was Buckner Boogeheim's failed chocolate venture? I didn't know how he figured with the flash drive, but it was clear that this was no coincidence.

I drove to the next block and flipped a U-turn, then cut my lights and doubled back to the warehouse.

I passed it again, pulling into the parking lot of the building across the street and tucked the VW behind a deserted guardhouse.

I got out and grabbed my camera, quickly jogging across the street in the dark. I rounded the front of the massive metal Pacific Chocolate's warehouse, keeping to the shadows. I spied the SUV parked in the back. The lights were off and I could see the diver's seats were unoccupied. My eyes cut to the building. A door led into the back, light shining through a crack underneath. Beside it was a small window. I crouched low and crab walked along the perimeter of the building, making my way to the window. I stood on tiptoe, gingerly peeking over the sill.

Inside I could see what had once been some sort of office. Now it was an abandoned desk and pair of chairs that looked like rats had been gnawing on them.

And sitting in said chairs were Trace and Jamie Lee.

Jamie Lee's mascara was streaked down her face like she'd been crying. Trace's back was to me so I couldn't see his face. Ferret stood over them both, a gun in his hand as he spoke to Trace. I wished I could hear what he was saying, but it was just a faint murmur from here.

I grabbed my cell from my pocket and dialed Allie's number again. I hit send and listened to it ring once on the other end before Allie's voice came on.

"Cam? Is that you?"

But just as I was about to answer her, I heard a sound behind me.

Uh oh.

I spun around…

Too late.

Pain exploded behind my right ear, and I was suddenly staring at the ground.

The last thing I heard before everything went black was Allie's far away voice shouting, "Cam? Speak up, Cam, I can't hear you!"

## Chapter Twenty

I have no idea how much time passed, but when I finally opened my eyes, I felt as if I'd been asleep for days, my eyes heavy, my limbs stiff, and my head throbbing like a salsa band was practicing in there.

Slowly, I pried one eye open, then the other, making a quick assessment of the rest of me. Arms, intact. Legs, working. Mouth… felt a little like a lint trap, but all the teeth were there. Other than the goose egg I could feel blooming on my forehead, I felt pretty much okay. Though, as I tried to wiggle my fingers and toes, it became alarmingly apparent that my hands and feet were bound. Never a good sign.

I blinked back pain and disorientation, trying to get a handle on my surroundings. It was dark, but I could tell I was inside the warehouse now. Cavernous metal walls surrounded me, small windows near the ceiling affording minimal light to filter into the large room. Squinting through the dark, I saw crates piled to the left and right of me, and the floor was a cold concrete beneath the butt of my jeans. I could make out the mingling scents of must, mold, and chocolate lingering in the air.

I wiggled on the ground, testing the bonds at my hands and came up against sticky plastic. If I had to guess, I'd say I'd been duct taped.

As I wriggled, I heard a sound to my right and strained through the darkness to identify it. A large form moved in the shadows to my left. I prayed to God it wasn't a rat.

"Hello?" I tentatively called out.

"Cam?" came the reply.

I could have cried with relief.

"Trace! Are you okay?"

"Fine. Mostly. You?"

"The same," I said, ignoring the dull ache still throbbing in my head. "My hands and feet are bound."

"Mine too. Hang on. I'm coming over to you," Trace said.

I heard rustling, and a minute later the large form took the shape of Trace's body, inch-worming along the concrete toward me on his butt. As I'd guessed, lengths of gray duct tape had been used to secure his feet together, his hands behind his back.

"Ouch," he said as he approached, his eyes going to my forehead. "You sure you're okay?"

I nodded.

"Liar."

"It's that bad, huh?"

He didn't answer. Which didn't do a whole lot to reassure me.

"Is Jamie Lee with you?" I asked, my eyes sweeping the area behind him as they began to adjust to the darkness.

He shook his head. "She was in the car with me, but they separated us when we got here."

"They have the flash drive?" I asked.

He nodded solemnly.

What were the chances they weren't checking its contents right now?

"They're not going to be happy when they find out there's nothing it," I said.

"Which is why we need to find Jamie Lee and get the hell out of here before that happens."

I nodded. "Turn around. Maybe I can get the tape off of you."

He complied, the two of us sitting back to back, our fingers fumbling at the other's wrists. After what felt like an eternity of grunting and twisting, I finally managed to slip my fingers under a corner of the tape at his wrists and pulled, a ripping sound causing me to do a silent "woohoo!" Five minutes later his hands were completely free, and he was undoing my bonds. We made short work of the tape at out feet, then stood, stamping feeling back into our limbs.

"Any idea where they took Jamie Lee?" I asked.

Trace looked down the rows of empty crates piled to our right and left. "I don't know. They knocked me out. She was gone when I came to."

I did a mental eenie-meenie-minie-mo. "Let's go left," I decided.

Trace nodded, leading the way through one row after another, slowly scanning the shadows for either of our gun-toting friends as we slunk around the empty crates.

I cringed as my stomach involuntarily groaned at the scent of chocolate lingering in the air.

"Shhh," Trace said.

"Sorry," I whispered back. I would have pointed out that it wasn't like I could control my stomach's response to chocolate, but I could tell Trace was too on edge to care. His posture was tense, his jaw clenched shut, his eyes unreadable black, his mind clearly with Jaime Lee. Trying not to wonder what the guys with guns had in store for her. Hoping we got to her before they could follow through.

As we rounded the last row to the left, the empty crates gave way to a series of offices along the far wall. Four doors stood open. One was closed. And light filtered out under the door.

Trace gave me a silent knowing look in the dark, then, keeping to the shadows, approached the closed door.

I followed a quick step behind, my heart beating double time.

To the right of the office door was a window, dirty horizontal blinds closing off our view. Trace and I crouched down and duck-walked underneath it. He peeked up, narrowing his eyes as he tried to see between the bottom of the blinds and the top of the sill.

"Can you see anything?" I whispered.

He nodded. "She's here." His voice was flat, void of all emotion. Or maybe so heavy with it that I couldn't read one from the other, I wasn't sure.

I moved in closer, gingerly lifting my eyes over the sill. If I closed one eye and tilted my head all the way to the left, I could just see through the slats of the blinds.

The abandoned office only held a few items of furniture – a small metal desk with a rusty stapler and empty pen cup on top, a couple of crates in the corner, and a straight-backed wooden chair – holding our starlet. Jamie Lee was no longer bound, but the fact that Ferret and Crew Cut were standing over her with a gun pretty much assured that she wasn't going anywhere without force.

"What are we going to do?" I whispered in the dark.

But I quickly realized I was talking to myself.

Trace had already left the window and was at the door to the office.

"Wait! Don't you think we should make a plan or-"

Too late.

Trace used his I-do-my-own-stunts skills once again, and before I could stop him he had his cowboy-boot-clad foot cocked back and was slamming it forward into the door. The wood around the lock splintered and the flimsy door flew inward in one swift movement.

I took half a second to be duly impressed, then jumped up and ran after him.

I hit the doorway just in time to see Trace lunge for Ferret, surprising the guy enough that he knocked the gun from his hand, the weapon sliding across the floor until it came to a rest under a metal desk.

"What the-" Ferret went down with a hard crunch as Trace tackled him to the ground. Trace cocked Ferret square in the jaw, knocking his head back so fast I feared he'd have whiplash. He was momentarily stunned, but quickly regained his composure, sending a punch to Trace's gut that made the air whoosh out of him in a sickening sound.

"Ohmigod, ohmigod, Trace! Do something!" Jamie Lee shouted, waving her hands in front of her in a flapping motion.

Which didn't help Trace any, but served to spur Crew Cut into action, the hulk of a guy jumping to his pal's aid. He grabbed Trace by the arm. Trace shook him off, but it gave Ferret just enough respite to clock Trace in the nose, rocking his head backward. I cringed. Trace was good, but two on one was hardly a fair fight.

"Ohmigod, ohmigod! Trace!" Jamie Lee screeched.

"Get her out of here!" Trace shouted to me as Crew Cut pinned the actor's arms.

Frantically I grabbed the first thing I could lay hands on – a wooden crate of stale chocolate bars - and swung it in Crew Cut's direction. The corner of it hit him in the back of the head with a thud hard enough to shatter the wood, sending a rain of candy bars down on the struggling trio. While it wasn't exactly a death blow, fortunately it stunned him long enough for his grip to loosen on Trace and for me to grab Jamie Lee and haul her toward the door.

"Ohmigod, who are you?" she squealed. "Ohmigod! Trace, help!" She flapped her hands in front of her in classic girl-fight fashion, smacking me in the face.

I swear to God if I lived through this, I was going to kill her.

I held tight to the back of her shirt, propelling her forward.

"The gun! Get the gun!" she screeched.

Good thinking. Still gripping the back of her shirt, I spun toward the metal desk.

Too late.

I found myself nose to nose with the barrel of said gun. In the hands of Ferret.

"Freeze," he growled.

Like I had a choice.

I froze, my eyes cutting to the right, finding Trace, his nose bleeding and quickly swelling, pinned up against the wall by Crew Cut's bulk.

Not good.

I bit my lip.

Ferret's beady eyes were shooting daggers at us as a thin trickle of blood trailed down his chin. Crew Cut was shifting menacingly from foot to foot. Jamie Lee was alternating between screeching, "Ohmigod" and sobbing in my arms.

But it was Trace's eyes that held me. Dark, defiant, no long playing a role but a real guy in real trouble. He stared at Jamie Lee with a look of devotion that I would have killed for.

Then his eyes cut to me.

Back to the semi-hysterical actress.

To me again.

The meaning was clear. He was counting on me to get his girl out of this mess alive.

I shot a look to the door. It was a good three feet away. No way could we make it there before Ferret got off a shot.

I looked around the room for anything I could use as a weapon. Chair? Out of reach. Crate? Shattered. Desk? Too heavy for me to lift.

"Ohmigod, I am too young to die!" Jamie Lee sobbed, waving her hands in front of her face again.

I looked at her - flapping, sobbing, throwing a fit a two year old would find over-the-top. And I did the only thing I could think of.

I shoved the spastic actress square into Ferret.

"OHMIGOD!" She screamed, tipped over on her spiky heels, her flailing hands flapping at Ferret as she crashed into him.

On instinct his finger squeezed the trigger, a loud crack ripping through the air as his shot went wild, Jamie Lee knocking into his arm. At that instant, Trace kicked Crew Cut in the shins and lunged forward, propelling himself toward Ferret and the gun.

Ferret went down, Trace went down on top of him, Crew Cut went down on top of *him,* and Jamie Lee found herself at the bottom of the dog pile.

"Uhn. Help! I can't breathe!" she wheezed.

I dove for the desk and grabbed the stapler. Hardly a deadly weapon, but…

I aimed it at Ferret. Which was kind of hard considering he, Trace, Crew Cut and Jamie were all grappling together on the ground so fast they were a blur.

I squeezed the stapler, a small metal staple flying out…

… and hitting Jamie Lee in the temple.

"Ouch! Trace, help!" she screamed.

Oops. My bad.

I squinted one eye shut and tried again, aiming for Ferret.

I squeezed.

"What the hell!"

Five small, metal staples hit him square in the face. Not enough to damage, for sure, but definitely enough to distract him long enough for Trace to smack his head against the floor. I heard a sickening crunch and blood spurted out from Ferret's nose. I think I even heard a couple teeth tinkle along the concrete floor. I swallowed down the sick feeling in the pit of my stomach, as I watched Trace palm the gun. He stood up, panting, but pointing the gun with a straight arm down at Crew Cut and Ferret.

"You move, and you're a dead man."

I grinned. It was exactly the same line he'd uttered at the end of *Die Tough*.

But I figured that the bad guys had seen the movie, too, because they didn't, in fact, move. The look in the actor's eyes was enough to tell them that even if the line was a fake, the intention behind it was real. Trace looked only too eager to put a hole or two in the guys.

The five of us sat frozen as the sound of sirens in the distance moved closer.

"You okay?" Trace asked, not taking his eyes off his pinned prey.

"Ohmigod, Trace, they were going to kill me!" Jamie Lee sobbed.

"No, I meant you." His eyes cut to me for a quick second. "Your arm."

I looked down.

And for the first time registered a dull ache in my left bicep as I saw a red stain spread along the sleeve of my T-shirt. I blinked. Apparently Ferret's shot hadn't gone *completely* wild.

"I've been shot," I said dully. And then for the second time that day crumpled to the ground as I watched the world fade to black.

\* \* \*

I came to in a haze of blue and red flashing lights, police radios crackling, and my battered self laid out on a white stretcher surrounded by paramedics in blue uniforms with stethoscopes hanging off their necks, shouting a bunch of words I didn't know, let alone could pronounce. I was pronounced "stable" (one of the few words I understood) and whisked away to the nearest hospital for surgery. Three hours later I had a semi-private recovery room, a hell of an anesthesia hangover, and the bullet they'd dug out of my bicep as a souvenir of the evening. It was somewhere around dawn, and I was just about to close my eyes for a well-earned rest, when my two partners in crime came bustling through my hospital room door.

"Cam!" Mrs. Rosenblatt immediately rushed toward me, enveloping me in a boa-constrictor worthy hug. I could hardly breathe, but, to be honest, after the night I'd had it was nice to be breathing at all.

"Oh, honey, are you okay?" Allie asked.

I nodded. "Mostly."

"You look like hell," Mrs. Rosenblatt observed.

"Thanks," I mumbled.

"Let me do a healing chant for you," she offered, then put a beefy palm on my forehead and started to hum low in her throat.

Frankly, I didn't have the energy to protest at that point.

"What happened?" Allie asked.

I went over the entire evening's events from the time we parted ways until I saw stars and a bloody hole in my own arm.

"Holy cow, you reporters live the dangerous life," Mrs. Rosenblatt said when I was done. "I can just imagine the look on that guy's face when you used Jamie Lee as a weapon against him."

I grinned. Painfully. "Yeah, he did look a little surprised."

"I wish I'd been there," Allie said wistfully, no doubt thinking of the lost opportunity to report a firsthand account.

Which reminded me…

"Yeah, why weren't you there? What happened to you guys? Why didn't you pick up your cell?"

Allie rolled her eyes. "The parking garage blocked cell reception. We didn't realize we were in a dead zone until it was too late, and you were already gone."

"It wasn't until you called us again from the warehouse that we honed in on your exact location and called the police."

"And they believed you?" I asked, remembering my own attempts to get the authorities on my side.

"Well, not exactly…" Allie hedged. "We kinda told them that we'd found that car the parking cop was looking for. After he put out the APB on you at the MGM, the police were more than happy to drive out and pick you up on the outstanding tickets warrant."

I laughed out loud, even though it caused another round of throbbing in my head. Who would have thought that my parking violations would be my saving grace?

"Wait, how did you guys even know about the parking cop's APB and the warrant?" I asked.

Allie grinned. "Police radio of course."

I blinked. "You have a police radio?"

"I can tap into one. On my iPhone."

"They have an app for that?"

She rolled her perfectly made-up eyes at me. "No, silly! But I can pretty easily break into their scanner frequencies."

"How on earth did you learn to do that?" I asked, staring at the bubbly blonde.

"Felix taught me."

Oh, yeah, she was totally sleeping with him.

# Chapter Twenty-One

**AMERICA'S FAVORITE COUPLE SURVIVES HARROWING ORDEAL**

TRACE BRODY AND JAMIE LEE LANCASTER ARE ONCE AGAIN SAFE AND SOUND IN MALIBU, BUT THEIR HAPPY ENDING WASN'T QUITE SUCH A GUARANTEE JUST A FEW SHORT DAYS AGO. JAMIE LEE WAS KIDNAPPED – YES, KIDNAPPED! – BY TWO ARMED MEN, BUT TRACE, IN HOLLYWOOD LEADING-MAN FASHION, SINGLE-HANDEDLY RESCUED HIS BELOVED IN A FILM-WORTHY SHOWDOWN.

WE CAUGHT UP WITH TRACE AND JAMIE LEE AT THEIR COZY LITTLE LOVE NEST JUST YESTERDAY, WHERE THESE EXCLUSIVE PHOTOS SHOW AN AFFECTIONATE JAMIE LEE PLANNING HER HONEYMOON IN PARIS WITH HER OWN PERSONAL HERO-

I minimized the browser window, not able to stomach the photo spread that went with the online article. So far I'd already seen Jamie Lee with her arms around Trace outside their Malibu "love nest," Jaime Lee with her arms around Trace at the local Starbucks, Jamie Lee with her arm around Trace as they visited the travel agent… you get the picture. The two were joined like Siamese twins. It was sweeter than a barrel of cotton candy and making me just as sick to my stomach.

It had been a full week since I'd been back from Vegas, but *Entertainment Daily* was still milking the story for all it was worth. Of course the *Informer* had been the first to run with the story, Allie typing it up in the backseat of her VW as she, Mrs. Rosenblatt and I had driven home. Trace and Jamie Lee had flown home first class.

In fact, the last I'd seen of Trace had been from a prone position on a stretcher as the police took his statement in triplicate and the paramedics whisked me away to the hospital. I'd spent two days in recovery answering a slew of police questions (Yes, I was the "unknown assailant" whose DNA was all over Decker's place. No, I didn't kill him. Yes, I cross my heart and hope to die promise to pay those parking tickets.), halfway hoping to see him visit my hospital room, halfway telling myself it was stupid to even halfway hope. He had his life back, he had Jamie Lee back, and I had the story of the century to turn in to Felix complete with a photo spread that would beat anything *ED* could print for the next ten years. Whatever tentative partnership Trace and I had forged had ended, and we'd all gotten our happy endings, right?

Well, everyone except Ferret and Crew Cut who, according to Allie's digging, had yet to do any talking to the police. Whatever was on that flash drive remained a mystery. But, considering the two had not only been caught red-handed kidnapping two Hollywood celebrities, but also were in possession of the gun that exactly matched Decker's murder weapon, I didn't think either of them would be seeing the outside of a jail cell for a very long time.

The bad guys were in prison, I was back at the *Informer,* and Trace was apparently back at his love nest with Jamie Lee, if Mike and Eddie's article was any indication. All was right in the world.

Only for some reason all that was right left a slightly hollow feeling in the pit of my stomach.

"Hey, Cam."

I looked up to find Tina approaching my desk, her hair propped up in two pigtails held in place with a pair of pink skull holders that perfectly matched her pink skull jumper above her black boots.

"Hey, Tina."

"You read today's *ED* article?"

I nodded. "Single-handedly my ass." I looked down to where my arm was still in sling. Though, luckily, my goose egg had faded to a lovely baby poo brown splotch on my forehead that my hair mostly covered if I tilted my head forward enough.

"Well, they never really do get a story right, do they?"

"Mike and Eddie? Never."

"Though…" Tina grinned. "Tell me that it's really true. You really used an Oscar-nominated actress as a weapon?"

I couldn't help an answering grin as I remembered the flailing actress. Without the threat of imminent death, I had to admit the scene had been kind of funny.

"I'm sorry Allie got headline. I swear I was going to hand the story to you, but she kinda jumped in before I had the chance."

Tina shrugged. "Not your fault. Allie would eat her own young for a story. Speedial me first next time you catch a hot movie star skinny-dipping and we're cool."

"You have my word." "Anyway," Tina went on. "I saw the *ED* article and just had to come by and offer my condolences."

"For what?"

"The photos. Of Jamie Lee and Trace. Must be hard to look at."

I shrugged. "They aren't that good. I could have got better."

"That wasn't what I meant and you know it."

I bit my lip. Was I that obvious?

As if to answer me, Tina bluntly said, "Face it. You dig him."

"I do not!" I protested. Probably a little more loudly than a person telling the truth should have.

Tina put her hands on her hips. She cocked her pigtails to the side. She stared hard at me. "Don't bullshit me, Cam. Allie told me how you guys were looking at each other the whole time you were in Vegas. She totally thought you'd end up together."

"Since when do you and Allie speak?"

"Don't change the subject."

I sighed, studiously avoiding looking at my minimized window. "Fine. I guess after getting to know Trace, he isn't all that bad."

Tina smirked. "That's a start."

"But it doesn't matter in the least what I think of Trace. He's… obviously happy where he is."

Tina placed a hand on my shoulder. "Sorry. I guess you win some, you lose some."

Easy for her to say. She was on the winning side of a relationship.

Not that I wanted a relationship. Not that I'd ever even contemplated a relationship with Trace. I mean, Trace was in Malibu, I was on the wrong side of Hollywood, stuck between a dry cleaner and the Happy Time Go souvenir shop. He was planning a honeymoon in Paris. I was planning Chinese for one. Again. Our lives were worlds apart. Sure, we'd forged some sort of friendship while we had been working together. And, likely if I waved to him on the street, he'd wave back. But that was about as far as my imagination had taken it.

I swear.

I slumped down in my seat as Tina walked back to her cube, pulling up the *ED* window again, masochist that I was, and stared at the first photo of Trace.

He was sipping a cup of coffee – black, I now knew – outside Starbucks after his morning run. His hair was a disheveled mess, the morning sun shining off his sandy highlights. Sweat glistened on his exposed biceps, making his warm, honey tan seem even darker than normal. His eyes were bright and happy with the kind of satisfaction that I knew could only come after putting a good five miles on your Nikes. He looked… perfect.

"Cam!"

I quickly closed the window as if I'd been caught looking at porn and spun around. "Yeah? What?"

Mrs. Rosenblatt ambled up to my cube. "You busy?"

I glanced at my dark monitor. "Nope. Not at all. Not doing a thing."

Geez, when did I get to be such a crummy liar?

"Great," she said, thankfully seemingly oblivious. "I need a favor. Max needs a couple pictures of Ben Carlyle to run in tomorrow's edition."

"With the Tootsie article?"

She shook her head. "Nope. This time it's an actual obit. Carlyle passed away last night."

"Oh no. Please don't tell me we gave the man a heart attack?"

Mrs. Rosenblatt shook her head. "Died peacefully in his sleep. But get this – he left a note. Apparently it was filed away with his lawyer for reading only after his death."

"What did it say?"

"It was a confession."

"Get out!"

She nodded, her fleshy cheeks wobbling. "Yep. Turns out he was not only dating Tootsie, but he was also seeing Becky Martin on the side."

I had a hard time imagining one woman, let alone two, falling for the aged anti-Romeo.

"But he seemed to have such contempt for her."

"That was because she dumped him as soon as he offed Tootsie," Mrs. Rosenblatt explained. "According to his note, Tootsie found out about the affair and threatened to ruin both Carlyle and Becky's careers. And she had the clout in those days to do it, too. Carlyle freaked out and shot her, using Johnny as a scapegoat."

"Poor Tootsie," I said.

"No kidding."

"So what happened to Becky Martin?"

"She couldn't stand the guilt. Even though Carlyle pulled the trigger, she felt responsible. She moved back to the Midwest shortly after the death."

"And Ben Carlyle kept his secret all these years," I mused.

She nodded again. "But at least people will know the truth now. Max's story is running in the weekend edition."

I whistled low. "Weekend edition? Jackpot. Good for Max," I said. "Felix must be happy."

"Boy howdy, is he!" She grinned so wide I could see the lipstick stains on her molars. "Not only did he give Max a three-page spread, but he gave yours truly a little something, too."

I raised a questioning eyebrow.

"I'm coming onboard as the *Informer*'s resident psychic and astrologer."

I grinned. "Congratulations." I had to admit, it might be fun having Mrs. Rosenblatt around. "Give me ten minutes and I'll email you a couple pics of Carlyle."

"Thanks, doll!" she said, giving me a wave as she waddled away.

I pulled up the archives database, running Ben Carlyle's name through the system. And swallowed a shock as a picture of a very debonair guy, handsome enough to give Clark Gable a run for his money, popped up. Wow. I guess the years could be cruel to a guy harboring a lonely secret like his.

I Photoshopped, cropped, and bundled a few choice photos of the late Mr. Carlyle, then emailed the entire thing off to Mrs. Rosenblatt.

Just as Felix came by my cube.

"Hey, did you see the article in *ED* about Jamie Lee?"

God, could no one let this go?

I nodded. "I saw it."

"Did you read it?"

I bit my lip. "Most of it."

"Most?" Felix swore under his breath. "Jesus, does no one actually read anymore? No wonder our paper is going down the tubes."

"Sorry," I mumbled.

He waved it off. "Well read it, then tell me why, after my photographer has been on two full months of Wedding Watch, I have to read about Jamie Lee's real name in someone else's paper."

I paused. "Her real name?"

"Yeah. Apparently *ED* scared up some picture of her driver's license pre-stardom with an incredibly unflattering photo and her real name."

He leaned over me and typed the url for *ED*'s website into my browser. The happy couple's smiling faces grinned at me front and center again. I shoved down that hollow feeling again. They belonged together. They were the perfect couple. Even I had to admit they looked perfect staring up at me in all their airbrushed glory from my screen.

Felix scrolled down past the honeymoon plans to the second part of the article. A photo of the driver's license photos came up on the second page.

"There," he said. Then shook his head. "Though in the girl's defense, if I were stuck with that name, I'd change it, too."

I leaned forward, squinting at the fine print on my screen.

Then froze.

Suddenly I felt everything becoming clear, like a fog being slowly lifted off the ocean to reveal the water in sparkling lucidity as I read the name.

Jamie Lee Boogenheim.

## Chapter Twenty-Two

"No way," I whispered.

Even though I knew with sudden certainty that it was the *only* way things made sense. I thought back to the awards show where the whole mess had started. I'd watched on TV as Jamie Lee had arrived…almost twenty minutes before Trace. Just long enough for her limo to double back to Burbank and pick up Trace and his agent.

I quickly pulled up a search engine. While I'd limited my previous searches to Buckner Boogenheim, I now broadened it to anyone with that distinctive surname. Three minutes later I hit pay dirt with a Clive Boogenheim in a criminal database. He'd done three years for assault in New York. I looked at his mug shot pictures. I'd be damned if it wasn't Ferret.

I grabbed my keys, dashing for the elevator.

"Cam?" Tina called as I dashed past her cubicle.

But I barely heard her. My brain was on hyper speed, too may unanswered questions burning in it.

But there was one thing I knew for certain.

I was getting the straight story out of one whining, overpaid and overhyped actress if it was the last thing I did.

As I well knew from the *ED* article, Jamie Lee was in the final stages of moving out of her Hollywood Hills home and into Trace's place in Malibu. I made for the hills, hoping she was still packing today. Or, more likely, supervising the packing. Either way, I mentally crossed my fingers as I sped down the freeway.

I made the twenty-minute drive in ten (I was still wanted for unpaid parking tickets, what was a small speeding warrant on top of that?), pulling up to a screeching halt outside Jamie Lee's cliff-side retreat. A moving van was parked to the right of her drive, guys in jeans and muscle shirts hauling expensive furniture into the back. I grabbed my trusty ball cap from my backseat and shoved it on my head, tucking my hair underneath. I jumped out of the Jeep, quickly blending in with the workers and slipped in the side door of Jamie Lee's place.

White marble tiles greeted me in the entryway, bubblegum colored walls and crystal chandeliers screaming of a decorating style just this side of Barbie's Dream House. Poor Trace. I followed the sounds of voices through the entry to a large room across the hall.

"God, how many times do I have to tell you? Lift carefully. These are not flea-market items. They cost more than your house, *comprende*?" Jamie Lee yelled at one of the movers.

The Hispanic guy nodded at her, then rolled his eyes as soon as he turned his back to her, hauling a vanity table out of the room.

Which left Jamie Lee alone in the room. If I was going to corner her, I'd never have a better opportunity than this.

I took a deep breath.

"Jamie Lee?" I asked, taking a step into the room.

She spun around, one hand on the pink Prada bag at her side, her long locks flying over one shoulder in an artful move.

"What?"

"Uh, could I have a word with you?" I asked.

She sighed. "I told you people which items go and which stay. Can't you remember a damned thing?"

I shook my head. "I'm not with the movers."

She narrowed her eyes at me. "Okay. So what the hell are you doing in my house then?"

"I'm Cam. Cameron Dakota. From the *Informer?*"

She still drew a blank look.

"From the warehouse? I saved your life?"

"Oh." She threw her hair over her shoulder again. "Right. Sure."

Such gratitude.

Then again, it was obvious to me now that whole damsel in distress thing had been a sham. Apparently, I hadn't given her acting skills enough credit.

"What do you want, Shannon?"

"Cameron," I corrected. "And I wanted to ask you a few questions…" I paused. "… about Buckner Boogenheim."

Her perfect smile faltered for just a second before quickly reapplying itself to her face. "Who?"

"Your…" I took a guess, calculating her age. "Father?"

"I don't know what you're talking about."

"The game's up, Jamie Lee. *Entertainment Daily* printed your real name this morning."

She waved me off. "I never read the tabloids."

One more reason for me to hate her.

"Well, plenty of people do. In fact, everyone west of the Sierra Nevadas knows you're really Jamie Lee Boogenheim."

She narrowed her eyes at me, calculating her next move carefully. "Okay. Fine. So Buckner Boogenheim is my father. So what?"

"And Clive?"

She paused again, answering more slowly this time. "My brother."

"Which leads me to ask… exactly why would your brother kidnap you and tie you up?"

This time the smile didn't so much falter as disappear completely, leaving her face a smooth, Botoxed blank slate. "I have no idea what you're talking about."

"Nice try." I took a step closer to her. "You were the one who lost the flash drive," I said. "You realized Trace must have picked it up and concocted this entire elaborate scheme to get it back from him."

This time she said nothing, just stared at me with her big, brown eyes.

Which I took as a sign I was wearing her down.

"It's true, isn't it? But what I don't understand is why you didn't just ask Trace for the drive? Why go through this whole charade?"

She took a step backward, toward a pair of French doors leading to a perfectly landscaped garden. I moved to the right, blocking it, effectively cutting off any escape route.

"Maybe," I said, working my theory out loud as I advanced on her. "Maybe you couldn't be sure Trace hadn't seen what was on the drive. Maybe it was so terrible that you couldn't let him know the drive was yours. Maybe it contained…" I paused, taking a shot in the dark. "… a sex scandal?"

"Puh-lease!" She rolled her eyes toward the ceiling. "I know better than to tape my own indiscretions."

Though, I noticed she didn't deny having indiscretions. I filed that info away for later.

"Okay, what was it then? What was on the drive?" I asked.

Again she narrowed her eyes at me. But she must have realized she was as metaphorically cornered as she was physically, because she finally answered, "Money."

I raised an eyebrow. "Money?"

"Bank account numbers. To accounts in the Cayman Islands."

I pursed my eyebrows together. "I don't get it. What's the big deal about that?" While it wasn't exactly kosher with the IRS, I didn't think she was the first star to put a little cash away offshore.

"It was from my father's business."

"The storage place?"

She laughed. "You really are naive. The storage place is just a front. He's involved in several other *activities*," she said, enunciating the word.

"Illegal activities"?" I asked.

"Mob."

Wow. And here I thought *I* watched too much TV.

"So…" I said, the wheels turning. "What a better way to launder the money than through his daughter, right? No one would ever suspect America's Sweetheart of filtering mob money."

"Exactly. Unless they found that drive in my possession. I was supposed to take it with me that night to hand it off to one of my father's business associates before the show. But as soon as I got there, I realized I didn't have it. I must have dropped it in the car."

"The same car you saw Trace arrive in."

She nodded. "I didn't think anything of it until I realized the drive was gone. I had my assistant call the car company, but they didn't find it in the car. So I figured Trace must have picked it up."

"But you couldn't ask him, because if Trace knew about these *activities*, he wouldn't have kept it quiet."

"Are you kidding? Mr. Boy Scout?" She scoffed. "Never."

"So, you had your brother go after it instead."

She nodded. "Clive had a friend from prison. It was simple; they would corner Trace, get the drive, and everyone would be happy. Only Trace couldn't seem to hold on to it, the stupid ass."

I felt my back go up on his account. "If you think he's such an ass, why are you marrying him?"

"Are you kidding? You can't buy publicity like this wedding. It's the best thing to happen to my career since *Die Tough*. I figure I enjoy his millions for a couple years, then milk a little more publicity out of a very public divorce where yours truly gives exclusives to every paper in town." She paused. Then gave me a dirty look. "Well, *almost* every paper in town."

Gee. I was crushed.

"So… why are you telling me this?" I asked, suddenly getting a bad feeling.

She grinned. "Because I have a feeling you won't be telling anyone else anytime soon."

"Why is that-"

But I didn't get to finish as Jamie Lee answered the question by reaching into her Prada and emerging with a shiny black gun.

"Oh."

I was really beginning to hate guns.

She grinned. "Yeah. Oh." She took a step toward me, her heels echoing in the empty room. "Now, let's take a little walk, shall we?" She gestured toward the French doors.

Since I wasn't the one holding the gun, I didn't think I was in any position to argue. I pulled open the door, leading the way outside as I felt the barrel of the gun poke into my ribs. It was cold, hard, and caused an instant sweat to break out along the back of my neck as she nudged me outside into the sunshine.

The French doors gave way to a flagstone patio flanked by expertly sculpted hedges, tall grasses, and native flowers. Beside the patio was a sprawling swimming pool, almost as large as Trace's, though this one was minus the rock waterfall.

"To the pool, blondie," Jamie Lee instructed, the gun barrel nudging me forward.

"What are you going to do?" I asked. Not that I really wanted to know. A play-by-play preview of my death wasn't really all that enticing. But the longer I could keep her talking – and not shooting - the better my chances of one of the movers discovering us back here.

"*I'm* not going to do anything. *I'm* an innocent victim here," she said. She did her trademark big, doe eyes at me. I'd always hated that look on her. "I simply walked into my backyard to find a member of the paparazzi trespassing on my property. When I confronted her, she pulled a gun on me. We struggled, and the gun went off."

"While conveniently pointed at me?" I finished for her. "You really think anyone will believe that?"

She grinned. "You've been essentially stalking me for weeks. What's not to believe?"

Shit. She was right.

"Look, maybe we should just talk about this. What if I offered you a deal? Maybe a little free publicity? I could airbrush a couple great bikini shots for you. Or maybe-"

"Ohmigod, shut up!" she shouted.

I shut up.

She took a step toward me.

I took a step back, feeling the heels of my feet come up against the side of the pool. Talk about cornered.

She narrowed her eyes. She clenched her jaw. Gone was America's Sweetheart, and in her place was a glimpse of the tough New York mafia-connected girl she'd grown up. Personally, at the moment I much preferred the former.

"Say good-bye, Shannon."

"Cameron," I automatically corrected her.

"Shut up!" she screamed, punctuating the sentiment by pointing the gun straight at my face.

I bit my lip, feeling my insides go numb. The sun beat down on me, but my skin was suddenly ice cold, my mind frozen, my eyes seeing only the barrel of the gun. Time seemed to stand still as images flashed in my mind – the paper, Tina, Felix, Ben Carlyle's Clark Gable face hiding a shriveled old murderer, and Jamie Lee's perky socialite persona hiding a criminal secret of her own.

I closed my eyes, chicken that I was. If my brains were about to be splattered all over Jamie Lee's perfect swimming pool, I didn't want to see it.

I felt Jamie Lee take a step forward, and felt myself cringing involuntarily in anticipation of what was next.

And then I heard it.

A loud crack shouting through the air, echoing off the hills.

I waited for the pain to follow. Oddly enough, it didn't.

I slowly pried one eye open, searching my person for bullet holes.

What I found instead was Jamie Lee laying on the ground, clutching her left thigh as bright red blood seeped onto her designer jeans.

"Ohmigod, ohmigod! You shot me, you bitch!"

I looked down at my hands, confused. "I don't even have a gun."

"Not you, you twit! Her!" Jaime Lee pointed behind me.

I whipped my head around…

… to find Tina, standing with her boots planted shoulder width apart, her pigtails flying in the breeze, arms straight out in front of her holding a tiny pink gun with little yellow flames along the side. The barrel still smoking.

I sagged to the ground in relief. "My hero," I breathed.

She grinned. "Don't mess with the paparazzi."

\* \* \*

Two hours later the police were swarming the place. Jamie Lee was taken into custody, the shot in her leg deemed a flesh wound. The movers were happy to take the rest of the day off, having already been paid a hefty deposit by Jamie Lee. Tina started typing up her exclusive story on her Palm even before the police arrived, grinning from ear to ear at the thought of finally scooping Allie. And I told my story to a uniformed cop, a plainclothes policeman, a special crimes unit detective, and an assistant DA so many times that I almost had it memorized by the time they finally told me I could go home. I was just trudging back to my Jeep, watching the last rays of daylight disappear over the hills when I saw a familiar face through the growing number of newshounds crowding the drive.

Trace.

I bit my lip, watching as he spoke to an officer who let him through the yellow crime scene barricade.

He made quick strides toward me. "Are you okay?" he asked.

I nodded. "Yeah."

He glanced down at my arm. "Nice sling."

Thanks. I nodded to his bandage. "We match."

He grinned. Then fell silent.

I shuffled my feet nervously, not sure what to say next.

"I take it you heard about Jamie Lee?" I finally settled on.

He nodded. "I did."

"I'm sorry."

"Thanks." Trace shoved his hands in his pockets. "But..."

"But?" I asked. Maybe a little too expectantly. I mean, what was I expecting? He was Trace Brody. I was Tabloid Girl. The divide there was so large the Grand Canyon didn't hold a candle to it. We lived in two completely different worlds, the only overlap between the two coming in the form of a telephoto lens.

I staunchly reminded myself of this fact as I waited for Trace to finish.

"Well..." He looked down at the ground. "You should know something. I mean, when you print it I want to make sure you get the story straight."

"Oh." Right. It was about the story. Duh. What did you expect, Tabloid Girl? This was not *You've Got Email*, or *Die Tough*, or even *Held for Ransom*. Happy endings did not happen like that in real life.

And not to members of the paparazzi.

"So what should I know?" I asked. Not that it mattered. Not that I cared. Not that I was just trying to stall and prolong the short time we might have together before we went back to being reporter and subject.

"I decided to cancel the wedding."

I froze.

"Cancel?"

He nodded. "Yeah. This morning. I was actually on my way over here to break things off with her when I heard about the shooting on the radio."

Oh, reeeeeeeally. Now this was getting interesting.

An interesting *story* I reminded myself. Just a story.

"That's… well, I guess that's good. I mean, if you were breaking it off anyway, I guess it was less of a blow to find out who Jamie Lee really was, right?" I reasoned.

He nodded. "I guess so. Yeah."

He paused. Took step closer to me. "Do you want to know why I was breaking it off with her?"

I swallowed hard.

A story. It's just about the story.

"Sure," I said.

"I was breaking things off with Jamie Lee because I realized I didn't love her."

"Oh?" Why my voice cracked on that word, I had no idea. I cleared my throat loudly.

He nodded. "In fact…" He took another step. Closer. So close he could almost reach out and touch me. "I realized I'm in love with someone else."

"Oh?" I squeaked out again. The throat clearing hadn't helped at all. My voice was total Minnie Mouse.

Again he nodded. Slowly. Not taking his eyes off my face.

I bit my lip. Swallowed hard. "With anyone I know?" I asked.

I held my breath, waiting an excruciating two seconds before he nodded again.

"Yeah."

"Who?" I heard myself asking. Though I was amazed I could speak at all, my body feeling totally paralyzed by his eyes.

He took another step toward me, standing so close now that I could feel the heat from his body warming me in places I couldn't speak of in polite company.

My entire body waited as he slowly answered on a whisper…

"You."

I felt myself exhale, my head floating above me, my entire being unsure if he'd really said the word or if I'd wanted him to so badly I was hallucinating.

"Me?" Minnie Mouse squeaked out again.

He smiled, his eyes assessing me.

It wasn't his romantic comedy face, or his hot action hero face, or his tortured hero redeemed by just the right woman face. It was just his. Trace's. The guy behind the actor. The real man. Staring down at me, his eyes sincere, his lips close to mine. So close I could taste the peppermint gum on his breath. So close, all it would take was the merest of movements before our lips were touching. All he'd have to do was lean down the slightest bit more and he'd be kissing me.

And that's what he did.

I sighed, my whole body going slack as his warm lips fell on mine.

At the end of *You've Got Email*, the romantic lead, Trace, and the cute, plucky, we're-all-rooting-for-you lead actress finally, after weeks of near misses, kiss. When I saw it in the theater, the entire audience did a simultaneous "Awwwwwww" and there wasn't a dry eye in the house.

This was better. By a mile.

It was soft, sweet, warm and demanding all at the same time. I totally melted, my knees buckling so that his arms sliding around my middle was the only thing holding me up.

I have no idea how long we stood like that, but his lips were red and raw when we both finally came up for air, panting, eyes glazed over, lust an almost tangible thing hanging in the air between us.

"Wow," I whispered.

"Ditto," he said.

"You do know this is totally ending up on the pages of the *Informer* right?" I teased.

He rolled his eyes. "Of course. Why do you think I'm into you? It's purely for the publicity." He gave me a wink.

I punched him in the arm

"Ouch," he said, rubbing his bandaged bicep. Then he gave me that lopsided grin that melted hearts daily on the big screen. "So, what's your big headline to go with this story?"

"'Big shot movie star sleeps with member of the paparazzi?'"

He raised one eyebrow. "Oh does he?"

I nodded. Slowly. Unable to help the grin from spreading across my face. "Oh, yeah, he does." And I kissed him again.

\* \* \*

"What the hell is this?"

Felix came bellowing toward me, waving a copy of *ED* in his hand as he approached.

"Um. What's what?" I asked.

"This." He shoved the paper on my desk, pointing to a picture on the third page. Trace Brody and his new girlfriend caught kissing on the patio of Nico's yesterday at lunch.

I bit my lip.

"Ummm…"

"Is this the late lunch you took yesterday?"

I nodded.

"The one you told me was a working lunch?"

More nodding.

"That was charged to my expense account?"

"Well, I can't expect Trace to pay every time."

He narrowed his eyes at me. "Fine. But just explain to me why I have to see photos of *my* staff showing up in someone else's paper?"

I shrugged. "Hey, it's hard to outrun the paparazzi."

He ran a hand through his hair, making it stand up on end, looking even more slept in than usual.

"When did I lose control so badly?" he muttered.

"Sorry, boss. I'll try harder to ditch Mike and Eddie next time."

"Great. Fine. Dandy," he said, spinning on heel. "And next time you'll let Trace pay!"

I grinned. Then saluted him. "Aye, aye, chief."

He grumbled to himself as he stalked off to his office, depositing the *ED*'s paper firmly in the trash bin on his way.

"Ouch. Boss isn't in a good mood today, huh?" Tina appeared at my cubicle, her hair streaked a bright violet today.

I shrugged. I had a feeling after the photos I turned in tonight, he'd forgive me.

"So, up for Chinese tonight?" Tina asked. "I'm solo for dinner."

I raised an eyebrow. "No Cal?"

"He's working. Body guarding some visiting dignitary. I'm all yours for egg rolls."

I shook my head. "You know I'd love to but I can't. I already have plans."

She leaned her chin into her elbow on the top of my cube wall. "Do tell. These plans involve any celebrities I might know?"

I grinned. "A barbeque at Trace's. With J Lo and Marc Anthony."

I could see Tina mentally drooling. "Seriously? Jesus, you're going all movie star on me, Cam."

"You're just jealous."

"Dammed straight I am! Just promise me one thing?"

I raised an eyebrow. "What?"

"When you invite me to the wedding, be sure to seat me next to Paris Hilton, okay? I've been dying to get the goods on her for years."

I grinned. "You got it, girl."

She straightened up and dusted lint off her checkered mini-skirt. "All right. Well, as much as I'd love to sit around and hear every little detail of Trace's new love life…" She trailed off, raising an eyebrow my way.

I shook my head. "My lips are sealed. What happens in the bedroom, stays in the bedroom."

Tina stuck her tongue out at me. "Figures. Well, I've gotta go. Allie's trying to scoop me again with this Barker story."

"Chester Barker?"

Chester Barker was a producer who was famous for his train-wreck reality shows. If there was any way to exploit the human condition, Chester had found it, done it, and televised it. So, it hadn't come as a total surprise when he'd been found dead in his multi-million dollar mansion just a week after wrapping his latest assault on the American people – *Stayin' Alive,* a survival show where sixteen strangers are dropped off in the middle of nowhere and have to outsmart, out strategize, and outlast the rest, not only surviving the elements, but also a dance off for a panel of celebrity judges each week at the jungle tribunal. It was trash TV at its worst. And the ratings had been through the roof.

"Yep. That Barker," Tina confirmed. "Allie's like a dog with a bone on this one. If I don't dig up some fresh dirt soon, Felix is liable to give away my front page status."

"Good luck!" I called after her.

I looked down at my clock. 4:35. I grabbed my Nikon and bag and was just about to shut off my computer when the elevator doors slid open and Trace walked out. To say every head in the place turned his way would not be an exaggeration.

He spotted me and waved.

I grinned so big I feared I'd crack my face.

"Hey," he said, leaning down and depositing a quick kiss on my cheek. "Our guests are on their way. You ready, babe?"

I risked cracking, my smile growing. I loved it when he called me babe.

I grabbed his hand.

"Am I ever."

## About the Author

Gemma Halliday is the author of the *High Heels Mysteries*, as well as the *Hollywood Headlines Mysteries* series. Gemma's books have received numerous awards, including a Golden Heart, a National Reader's Choice award and three RITA nominations. She currently lives in the San Francisco Bay Area where she is hard at work on several new projects.

To learn more about Gemma, visit her online at
www.GemmaHalliday.com

SNEAK PEEK
of the next
*Hollywood Headlines Mystery*
by Gemma Halliday:

# HOLLYWOOD CONFESSIONS

"Well, we were all very impressed with your *body* of work, Miss Quick."

Was he talking about my tits?

I wasn't sure, but I nodded at the man sitting across from me anyway. Balding, paunchy, non-descript gray suit. Your typical managing editor.

"Thank you, Mr. Callahan," I said, keeping my voice as even as possible, despite the anxiety that had been building throughout our interview. He and I both knew that my portfolio contained a very small body of work. So small that I almost hadn't even bothered submitting it when I heard that the *L.A. Times* was looking to fill a desk. I'd only been a working reporter for just under a year, not long compared to most veteran newshounds. Then again, it was the *L.A. Times*. I'd have to be a moron not to at least apply for the job. And, moron was one thing I was not.

"I've shown your clippings to my colleagues, and they all agreed that your *assets* would be a wonderful addition to the paper." He glanced down at my chest.

Yeah, he was totally talking about my tits.

I shifted in my seat, adjusting my neckline. I knew I should have gone for a higher-cut blouse, but this one matched the pink pin-stripes in my skirt so perfectly.

"Wonderful," I said, stopping myself from glancing at my watch just in time. I'd already been sitting in his office for over an hour – way longer than my lunch break allowed.

"After consulting with my assistant editor, we've decided we'd like to offer you a freelance opportunity here at the *L.A. Times*."

"Really?" As much as I was trying to play it cool, my voice rose an octave, sounding instead of a professional business woman more like a kid who'd just been told she could have ice cream for dinner. "Ohmigod, that would be... wow. Really?"

He nodded, a grin spreading across his paunchy cheeks. "Really. Now, I know you were hoping for a staff position, but if this opportunity goes well, there's a chance to transition from freelance to something more permanent."

Freelance, staff, one-shot-deal, I didn't care. It was the *L.A. Times*! The holy grail of any reporter's career. And they wanted me! I had died and gone to heaven.

"That sounds great! Amazing. Wow, thanks."

"Wonderful! We think you'll be perfect to write a weekly women's interest column."

I felt my face freeze mid-goofy grin. "Women's interest... you mean like relationship stuff?"

"No, no," he said, shaking his head. "Nothing so limiting."

"Oh, good."

"Not just relationships. We'd love for you to write about *anything* important to women. Lipstick, shoes, cleaning product reviews."

I felt that ice cream for dinner melting into a soft, mushy puddle. "Cleaning product reviews?"

He nodded, his jowls wobbling with aftershocks. "And lipstick and shoes. You know, women's subjects."

I felt my eyes narrowing. "Mr. Callahan, I graduated at the top of my class from UCLA. Didn't you read my resume? I'm an investigative journalist. I write stories, hard hitting news stories. Did you see the one I wrote about the misappropriation of campaign funds last fall?"

"I did."

"And the Catholic Church scandal?"

"Sure."

"And the way I busted that story about middle school drug dealers in the heights wide open?"

He nodded again. "Yes, they were all very good," he said.

"But?"

"But, Miss Quick. We are a serious paper here."

"And I'm a serious journalist!"

He looked down at my skirt, the tiny frown between his bushy eyebrows clearly not convinced that serious reporters wore pink.

"Mr. Callahan," I tried again the desperation in my voice clear even to my ears, "I know I may not have the experience that many of your reporters do, but I am a hard worker, I love long hours, overtime, and I will do anything to get the story."

"I'm sorry, Miss Quick. But my assistant and I have reviewed your file and we both agree that someone with your..." He paused. "...*assets* would best serve us writing a woman's column." His eyes flickered to my chest again, then looked away so fast I could tell his mandatory corporate sensitivity training had been a success.

But not so fast that I didn't catch the double entendre.

I narrowed my eyes. "Thirty-four D."

Mr. Callahen blinked. "Excuse me?"

"The pair of tits you've been staring at for the last hour? They're a thirty-four D."

"I... I..." Mr. Callahan stammered, his cheeks tingeing red.

"And if you like that number, I have a few more for you," I said, gaining steam. "One-thirty-four: my I.Q. 2300: my SAT score. Four-point-O: my grade point average at UCLA. And finally," I said, standing and hiking my purse onto my shoulder, "Zero: the chances that I will degrade not only myself but my entire gender by writing a column that supposes having ovaries somehow limits our level of intelligence to complexities of eye shadow and sponge mops."

Mr. Callahan stared at me, blinking his eyes beneath his bush brows, his mouth stuck open, his jowls slack on his jaw.

But I didn't give him a chance to respond, instead, I forced one foot in front of the other as I marched back through the busy newsroom that I would not be a part of, down the hallways of my dream paper, and out into the deceptively optimistic sunshine.

I made it all the way to my VW Bug before I let my indignation and anger morph into big, fat tears. Goddamnit, I was not just a pair of headlights and a short skirt! I had a brain, a pretty damned functional one, even if I did say so myself. I was a smart, diligent reporter.

But all anyone at any of the major newspapers that I'd interviewed with since graduation had seen was Allie Quick: 36, 26, 36.

Seriously, you'd think boobs wouldn't be such a novelty in L.A.

I wiped my cheeks with the back of my hand, sliding into my car and slamming my door shut, taking my aggression out on Daisy. (Yes, I named my car. But don't worry, I had stopped myself just short of putting big daisy decals on the side doors. I just had one small daisy decal on the trunk. A pink one. To match the silk pink Gerbera daisy stuck in my dash.) I immediately slipped my polyester skirt off and threw it in the backseat. Hey, it was California. It was summer. And my air conditioning had broken three paychecks ago. Don't worry, I had a pair of bikini bottoms on underneath.

I pulled out of the parking lot and pointed my car toward the 101 freeway.

Twenty minutes later I exited, traveling through the Hollywood streets until I pulled up to the squat stuccoed building on Hollywood Boulevard stuck between two souvenir shops. At one time the building might have been white, but years of smog and rainless winters had turned it a dingy gray. The windows were covered in cheap vertical blinds, and the distinct odor of stale take-out emanated from the place.

I looked up at the slightly askew sign above the door. The *L.A. Informer*, my current place of employment. A tabloid. The lowest form of journalism in the known universe. I felt familiar shame curl in my belly at the fact that I actually worked here.

At least it was a step above sponge mops.

Maybe.

A very small one.

I pulled Daisy into a space near the back of the lot with a sigh, slipping my skirt back over my hips before trudging up the one flight of stairs to the offices.

The interior was buzzing as usual, dozens of reporters hammering out the latest celebrity gossip on their keyboards to the tune of ringing telephones and beeping IM's. My cube was in the center of the room, just outside the door to my editor's glass-walled office. Luckily at the moment his back was turned to me, a hand to his Bluetooth, shouting at someone on the other side just loud enough that I could hear the occasional muffled expletive.

I ducked my head down, slipping into my chair before he could notice just what a long lunch I'd taken. I quickly pulled up the story I'd been working on before I left that morning: Megan Fox's boobs – real or fake.

Yeah, CNN we were not.

Swallowing down every dream I ever had of following in Diane Sawyer's footsteps, I hammered out a 2 by 3 inch column on the size, shape, and possible plasticity of the actress's chest. I was just about finished (concluding that – duh – there was no way these puppies were organic), when an IM popped up on my screen. My editor.

*Where have you been?*

I peeked up over the top of my cube. He was still shouting into his earpiece, but he was now seated at his computer, eyes on the 32 inch flat screen mounted on his desk.

I ducked back down.

*At lunch.*

*Pretty long lunch.*

I bit my lip.

*I was hungry.*

There was a pause. Then: *Come into my office in three minutes.*

Great. Busted.

I glanced at the time on my computer. 1:42. I finished up my article, hit save, and two minutes and forty three seconds later got up from my chair, smoothed my skirt, puckered to redistribute my lipgloss, and pushed through the glass doors of his office to face the music.

He was still on the phone, nodding at what the guy on the other end was saying. "Yes. Fine. Great." He motioned for me to sit in one of the two folding chairs in front of his desk. I did, tugging at my hem again as I watched him pace the office.

Felix Dunn was somewhere between late-thirty and early forty, which put him at least a good ten years my senior. Old enough that fine laugh lines creased the corners of his mouth, but young enough that his sandy blonde hair was cut in the same shaggy style I'd seen high school skateboarders wear. He was tall, with the lean lines of a runner, though I'd never actually seen him jog. He was dressed today in his usual uniform of a pair of khaki pants and a white button down shirt paired with tan Sketchers. His clothes were wrinkled, looking like he'd slept in them, his hair sticking up just a little on top. I would have said he was pulling a causal chic thing, but I knew Felix well enough to know that it was more laziness than a practiced look.

Not that Felix couldn't afford to look every bit the metro-sexual fashionator, but Felix had his own priorities. He was what you'd call a cheap rich guy. He lived in a multi-million dollar home in the Hollywood Hills, thanks to old family money, but he still opted to buy his socks on sale at Walmart. I'd heard a rumor going around the office that he was actually a British lord, some distant relation to the queen, but he always seemed to have left his wallet at home when the check came at lunch.

"Listen, I've got a meeting now," Felix said into his earpiece, his British accent creating a lilting rhythm. "I've got to go, but I'll call you tomorrow."

He hit the end button on his Bluetooth, then turned to me without skipping a beat.

"The Megan Fox bit, where are we?"

"Done. Just need to proof it, and it'll be on your desk."

"Conclusion?"

"They're fake."

"You're sure?"

I gave him a look. "Seriously? I had more faith in your boob connoisseur status."

He shook his head as if disappointed. "Can't trust anything to be authentic these days."

"If it makes you feel any better, her ass is real."

He grinned. "I'm ecstatic. Listen, I have a new story I want you to work on."

Even though I knew it likely involved the man vs. natural made status of a celebrity's body parts, I still got a little surge of adrenalin in my belly. I couldn't help it. I loved the thrill of ferreting out the truth, making sense of a chaotic series of facts.

I hadn't been lying when I told Mr. Callahan at the *Times* that I lived for the story.

"Shoot," I told Felix. "I'm all ears."

"It involves-"

But he didn't get to finish as the door to his office flew open again, one of the other reporters bursting through. She had violet hair and wore a hot pink baby-T with a picture of Oscar the Grouch on it and black jeans with little skulls on the back pockets above a pair of shit-kicker black boots. Tina Bender.

"I got it!" she said, triumphantly, holding a photo high above her head.

Felix raised an eyebrow her way. "And what might 'it' be?"

"The frickin' story of the century." She slammed the photo down on Felix's desk.

Felix leaned forward to get a good look. I did the same.

The photo was of the outside of a gated home, if I had to guess, I'd say a mansion somewhere nearby. Beverley Hills or Malibu if the palms lining the impressive driveway were any indication.

"Chester Barker's estate," Tina said, confirming my suspicions. "In Beverley Hills."

Felix leaned in. "The dead producer?"

Tina nodded. "Murdered to be precise. This was taken just before his body was found by the maid."

I remembered the story. Chester Barker was a reality TV show producer who had been found dead in his Beverley Hills estate two weeks ago, face down on his bathroom floor, foaming at the mouth. At first the consensus had been accidental drug overdose, but on further inspection, the police had found evidence that Barker had been drugged on purpose. The verdict of murder had sent the media - both tabloid and legit - into a virtual feeding frenzy, the *Informer* staff included. Personally, I'd been searching high and low for any angle on Barker for days.

Unfortunately, it appeared Tina had found it first.

"Where did you get this photo?" Felix asked.

"One of my informants."

Tina had informants all over Hollywood, her network farther reaching than Verizon's. Something I sorely envied. The first thing they'd taught us in journalism class was that a reporter was only as good as her informants. And, unfortunately, Tina's outnumbered mine ten to one.

"Check out the right corner," Tina said, pointing to the picture.

Felix and I did, both leaning in. In the corner of the picture, near the iron gates, was a figure, his back to the camera, a baseball cap with a squiggly red snake on the brim of it pulled low on his head.

"Who's that?" I asked.

Though Tina ignored me. As always. For some reason, Tina and I had gotten off on the wrong foot when I'd first come on board here. Probably because Felix had given me her biggest story right off the bat. While I'd felt kinda bad for her, my bank account had been hovering low enough that my Visa was rejected at the dollar store. I needed the job, and I'd needed that story to prove to Felix I deserved a paycheck despite my minuscule portfolio. So, despite feeling sorry for Tina's loss, I'd taken the story and ran with it. Luckily, I'd delivered, Felix had kept me on, and my bank account now afforded me the luxury of shopping at Walmart's clearance bin.

I know, decadent.

But Tina had never forgiven me, and a hard and fast rivalry between the two of us had been born.

"Who's that?" Felix asked, repeating my query.

Predictably, Tina did *not* ignore him.

"That, my dear editor, is Chester Barker's killer."

Felix raised an eyebrow.

She shrugged. "Or at least it could be. A shadowy figure seen outside the mansion at the time of the death. Pretty suspicious, huh?"

Felix nodded, eyes still on the photo. "Any idea who our suspicious character is?"

She shook her head. "But I am *so* on this story. Give me twenty-four hours, and I'll have his name, address and credit score."

Felix bit the inside of his cheek for a moment, thinking over the proposition. Finally he said, "Okay. Run with it. The Barker story is all yours, Tina."

Her grin was twice the size of her face. "Ay, ay, chief!" She gave him a mock salute before fairly skipping out the door.

Felix pulled out a magnifying glass, training it on the photo. I waited while he silently scrutinized the shadowy figure, trying to make out any identifying marks.

Finally I couldn't take it anymore. I cleared my throat.

Felix's eyes jolted upward, as if surprised to still find me there.

"Uh, you said you had a story for me?"

"Oh. Right. Allie. Yeah." He cleared his throat, setting the photo of the would-be killer aside. "I got a tip this morning that Pippi Mississippi has changed her hair color. I want you to go talk to her hairdresser and either confirm or deny."

Tina got a murder, and I got a dye job. Figures. Even at a tabloid no one took my journalism skills seriously.

## HOLLYWOOD CONFESSIONS
Available June 2011

CPSIA information can be obtained at www.ICGtesting.com
Printed in the USA
LVOW091530180712

290619LV00012B/106/P